1.02

D0629506

Mary of Magdala

MARY
OF
MAGDALA

A NOVEL

ANNE WILLIMAN

BROADMAN PRESS
NASHVILLE, TENNESSEE

ISBN: 0-8054-6008-X
Dewey Decimal Classification: F
Subject Heading: MARY MAGDALENE—FICTION
Library of Congress Catalog Card Number: 90-31943

Printed in the United States of America

Library of Congress Cataloging-in-Publication Data

Williman, Anne C.
    Mary Magdalene / Anne Williman.
        p.   cm.
    ISBN 0-8054-6008-X
    1. Mary Magdalene—Fiction.   2. Bible. N.T.—History of
Biblical events—Fiction.   I. Title.
PS3573.I4564M37   1990
813'.54—dc20   90-31943
                                                              CIP

To
Marcia and Dick Childs
My parents, who are always there

1

The last time Mary saw her husband, he promised her another servant. "Yes, you'll have what you want," he said as he pulled on his cloak. "Don't mention it to me again!"

"Thank you, my lord," she murmured, ignoring the edge in his voice. She had known that, because he loved her, he would give in eventually.

Nevertheless, they had argued for months over the issue, Mary pointing out again and again that Tabitha was old now and no longer much assistance. Merab, the younger servant, could not take care of everything herself. The obvious solution was to hire a third girl.

Ara had not agreed. "We already have more servants than almost anyone else in Magdala. If you must have more help, let Tabitha leave and find a new employer who will give her work she can handle—perhaps a household without children. Then we can afford to find a young servant for you."

Mary was too loyal to Tabitha to send her away, but she felt that was not the real issue anyway. "You always think of money!" Mary had told her husband irritably more than once. "Your father's business is doing better than it has ever done before, and he hires so many men that you yourself almost never go out in the boats anymore."

"Ah, yes, but how did I get to that place?" he would say, drawing her close. "It was by being cautious with finances, spending as little as possible in just the right places, that my father's enterprise has prospered. Why, fish from Eli are known even in the Holy City now, thanks to me."

Ara sounded arrogant, but Mary knew he was right. He had been shrewd and worked hard to expand his father's small-time fishing operation into what looked like it could become a source of fish even for Jerusalem. That was Ara's dream, and it had been from the first day he went into the business.

Mary had to admit that she enjoyed the benefits of her husband's efforts. It was satisfying to have two servants (and to be getting a third!), when nearly everyone else in their small town had one or none at all. Dressing in her finest meant jewelry from Egypt and expensive silk robes directly from Persia. Years had passed since her hands had scrubbed clothing clean in the stream or ground grain for bread. She did not even participate in the expert weaving and dyeing of fabrics for which the village was known.

Of course, there were disadvantages too. Ara was often away, and in spite of his feelings for her, when he was home, he had little time for his wife. He was always studying new trade routes or looking into different methods of improving the number of fish caught by the men.

In addition, Mary had no real friends. Perhaps because of her higher standard of living that had developed in the past five years, she came across as haughty. Well, if that meant being satisfied with her life-style, so be it. And when it hurt too much to see the other women stop chattering when she arrived, Mary told herself to be thankful for all she did have.

Mary was thankful for her children. Kezia, just having passed her fifth summer, already promised to be a beauty. Her long hair was the color of ripe dates and shone by sunlight or by torch light. She had rosy cheeks and a smile that dripped honey until she was forbidden something she wanted. Her son, Joshua, at seven, was nearly as tall as his mother's shoulder. He was Ara's joy in life, but seemed to have little interest in the fishing business or in the synagogue school he attended. His dark eyes reflected mischief, often acted upon, as the rabbi had told Ara several times now. His hair, the same color as his sister's, was untamable, and his body was lean, unlike his father's stockier form.

Mary loved both the children with complete devotion, and her love was made more intense by her lack of companionship among the village women and Ara's frequent absences. But now that Kezia and Joshua were no longer babies, they made it clear they did not need her to the extent that she would like. Lately, Mary had been hoping for another pregnancy.

"With a new baby in the household, we would really need the services of another girl," she had told Ara one day, feeling a bit guilty mentioning it when she had not yet conceived. However, sometimes she felt she had no recourse but to try anything within her power to make him see her side.

Of course, he had asked right away if she meant a child was coming, and she answered vaguely, neither denying it or confirming it. It was possible she was pregnant though unaware of it yet, and if not, surely it would happen soon.

Mary was never sure if Ara's change of heart was due to her newest tactic or simply weariness at hearing her ask him so often. After granting her request, he walked out the courtyard gate with his robe flapping in the breeze and his gait determined.

For the rest of her life, Mary would hold in her heart that glimpse she had of Ara—his heavy cloak of sheepskin across his broad back to keep him warm during the long, and for him, unusual night of fishing. His gray robe was hanging out below it and would be girded up to his knees when he reached the boat.

This evening, he would work as hard on the nets as any man there. His head covering was hiding his shoulder-length hair which was a lighter color than his children's. It was still thick, even though he was nearing thirty. His shoulders were thrown back in the pose of authority, which befitted the employer of many of the fishermen in Magdala, because his father Eli was giving more and more of the responsibility of the business to his only son.

Though she could not see his face, Mary knew each line of it well—the large nose, flashing eyes, and tiny scar from a fishhook that marked his cheek above the heavy beard. Each feature was familiar and dear to her. At night, Mary often lay awake observing this man who was hers, loving him so much that it made her chest ache.

Mary awoke abruptly and stared out of her sleeping room into the courtyard that took up the central portion of the house. Open to the sky, it was shielded from the street by rooms coming off it on three sides and by the wall and gate on the fourth side.

Darkness still shrouded the courtyard. It must have been before sunrise—hours before Ara would return with tales of the night's catch. She tried to sleep again, but it was impossible. Something was not right.

She listened. The wind made wheezing noises that penetrated even into the room where she lay. A storm coming? When Ara had left, the sky was clear. Of course, on the Sea of Galilee that could change as quickly as Joshua could swallow raisin cakes.

Mary sat up on her mat. Even in the short time she had been awake, the speed of the wind had escalated. Soon the rain started. Heavy drops pelted the courtyard beyond her room. The curtain that hung in the doorway swirled in the wind, and the tiny flame from the ever-burning oil lamp on the stand next to her danced wildly.

Kezia will be frightened, Mary thought, and she rose to go to the children's room. In the courtyard, she could see only darkness as the rain drenched her. The storm raged, and Mary remembered again that Ara was not on a trip as usual, but out fishing. Fear gripped her stomach. Perhaps it was not so bad where he was. Ara was experienced on the water and had survived many such storms.

When she reached the room across the courtyard where the children were, Mary discovered Tabitha and Merab were already there. Kezia ran to her mother and embraced her tearfully, ignoring Mary's rain-splattered robe. Joshua was trying to act brave, but Mary knew he, too, was alarmed by the storm, although not from the force of it as Kezia was.

"What will Father do?" Joshua asked anxiously.

Mary reached for him with her other arm. "Father will be fine," she told him in what she hoped sounded like a convincing voice. "He swims well and knows even better how to control a boat. He will be soaked when he comes home and angry as well because the catch will be lost, but he will be all right."

Joshua nodded, and Mary wished she was as sure about what she said as she had sounded. The servants looked worried, too, so Mary sat down, hoping to ease all their minds.

"Tabitha, get us some grapes and dates," she said cheerfully. "I'm hungry. And Merab, bring the lamps from some of the other rooms. We'll have a feast while we wait for the storm to end."

With the food before them, Mary began telling all the stories of their faith she could remember—tales of King David, Abraham, and, of course, Joshua. Her son always wanted to hear about the Israelite hero after whom he was named.

At last the raindrops that pounded the dusty dirt of the courtyard into mud ceased. The wind sank to a whisper, and even the sun flickered in the early morning sky. They were all dressed and preparing for the normal day's activities when a knock came on the courtyard gate. Mary was expecting to see Ara at anytime and jumped up at the sound of it.

"Who?" Tabitha called as her tall thin form hovered by the gate.

"It is I with news for your mistress," a man answered. Mary recognized her father-in-law's voice. She hurried toward him. Eli was stocky like his son, and even though his hair and beard were gray, they were still thick. Mary had always thought she had a good idea of what Ara would look like in twenty years from having seen his father.

"Mary, Mary," he said brokenly, and she noticed his robe was wrinkled, unusual in a man who normally took so much pride in his appearance. "Ara is missing."

The fears she had hidden all night rose within her. "What?"

"The storm was fierce on the sea, and my man Timothy came to me just now to say that Ara jumped overboard. They have not seen him since. One of the waves had washed over Bebai's son . . ."

"You mean Asher? Why, he's not much older than Joshua!" Mary said.

Eli nodded. "It was his first time out on the boats to work all night. He was terrified, and Ara went into the sea to save him. Of course, Bebai did, too, and they have found none of the three."

Mary felt her body tremble, but somehow it seemed as if it was someone else's frame. Ara was all right. He would show up soon. He had been brave to try to help young Asher, and surely the Mighty One would reward him by keeping him safe.

True, Ara was not a religious man, Mary thought as she sank down on a mat by the courtyard's fountain. He felt—and Mary agreed—that attending synagogue and following the major points of the Law was enough. But Ara was a good man, well thought of by his family and friends.

Eli seemed to realize Mary was in her own world, and he left quietly, shaking his head. He feared the chances of finding any of the three alive were slim.

Several hours later, Mary heard the death wail rise from across the village, and she knew that a body had been found. Numbness gripped her body; a buzzing in her ears made her head ache. But she waited calmly on the mat where she had spent the morning. There were three missing. It might not be Ara, but Eli was soon back at the courtyard gate. "Mary, Bebai, Asher, and my son have been found," he told her gently as tears dripped down his gray beard.

Mary knew then that part of her life was over—the part that gave her purpose and contentment. Yet still she sat, unable to get up, unable to weep, unable to even give a death wail to announce that two households mourned this day.

The afternoon passed with the same blur that the morning had. Eli stayed with her, and his wife, Ruth, joined them, along with Ara's sisters and their families. Of course, Joshua and Kezia had to be told, and Mary's father-in-law spared her the task. The neighbors gathered in clumps around the courtyard, and for once Mary felt compassion from them. No more did it matter who had the most servants. Ara was well loved.

The noise in the courtyard was overwhelming. Mary stared at the deserted loom, the motionless millstone, and the forgotten water pitchers around her, trying not to hear the screams of her mother-in-law and Ara's sisters. Naturally, the professional mourners had been summoned, and they groaned and wept the loudest. All around Mary, people were pouring dust on their heads, ripping their clothes, and beating their chests in the traditional signs of mourning. Beside the olive tree, Eli, who had changed into sackcloth, was moaning, "Alas, my son!" Ruth had wept so much that her eyes were red and puffy and her cries hoarse. Her body, only a little shorter than her husband's but not nearly as heavy, slumped listlessly by the cistern in the courtyard. Ara was her only son.

What is wrong with me? Mary asked herself. *I feel no such grief. I feel nothing.* Still she sat on the mat, feeling like a spectator in the midst of the mourning instead of a participant. *Yet, he was my husband,* she thought. *I should be weeping the most.* However, her face remained dry, even when Ara's waterlogged body was carried into the courtyard and then into one of the flat-roofed, sleeping rooms surrounding it.

She could not get up to help strip off his torn robe, anoint the form she had loved, comb the tangled hair and beard, and dress him in his newest rust-colored tunic. She did not see Joshua bravely close his father's eyes—the job of the oldest son. Then the women covered his face with a cloth and bound his feet and hands with linen. At last the body was placed on a bier with a pole at each corner by which it could be carried.

As four of the men, their muscles straining under the weight on the bier that they were lifting, moved passed her, Mary looked at Ara. She still could not cry. This was not the beloved man who had only the day before walked out of the courtyard strong, tan, and upright. This was not the man who had fathered her children, built up the fishing business, laughed, eaten, and shouted. It was a stranger.

"Mary, come," Eli was saying to her. "You must go to the burial."

Like an obedient child, Mary tried to rise, but her legs would not support her. Eli grabbed her arm, and slowly she was able to stand and walk with him out the courtyard gate.

The procession to Ara's family burial cave wound its way slowly out of Magdala to the low hills that surrounded it. The wailing continued full force, and Mary wished she were alone, alone to try to think, to get rid of the numbness and buzzing that followed her everywhere. Vaguely she was aware of Kezia coming to her with eyes swollen and wet, but Mary could only keep walking. At last the child left her. Mary did not even think about Joshua's whereabouts.

The cave had been recently purchased by Eli. It had room for many bodies, and the shelves for them had been carefully carved into the natural rock of the cave by a skilled stonecutter.

Gently, the men lifted Ara's body onto the shelf closest to the entrance. He was the first to lie on it. The friends and neighbors then withdrew to let the family have a last look.

"If only I might have been the one to rest here first," Eli moaned. "My son, my son . . ." Ruth leaned against him, and Ara's sisters moved to either side of the parents, then slowly the four of them left the cave.

Mary, as the widow, was left alone with him. She stood staring, not at Ara but at the shelf above where he was. This is not happening, she told herself. She stayed there until at last Eli came and led her from the cave. A stone was rolled in front of the opening to keep wild animals out, and the procession started back to Ara's home for the mourning feast. Later, Mary remembered nothing of it.

2

"Mother, please have a piece of melon," Joshua coaxed, putting melon into Mary's limp fingers.

She looked at it, but it fell from her hand onto the low table over which the meal was spread.

"Oh, do eat something," Ruth said irritably. "We don't want to have to bury you too."

Eli gave his wife a sharp look. "It has only been a month since Ara's death," he whispered.

Ruth bent her head over the steaming bowl of lentil soup. "He was my son, yet I don't . . ." she began stubbornly, but she stopped abruptly at her husband's angry, "Enough, woman!"

The young widow heard them, but she gave no sign of it. Ever since the funeral, she had not been able to react normally to anything. At night, sleep would not come, and she sat on her mat, her mind blank. Food sickened her, and only by the children's efforts had she been able to eat at all.

Mary's body was paying. Ara would probably not even recognize her now, because the womanly figure he had enjoyed was scrawny and only a little heavier than Joshua. Dark circles rimmed her eyes, and her waist-length hair, once gleaming as marble, was unkempt and dusted with gray, even though she had not yet reached her twenty-fifth spring.

Quite a change in such a short time, Eli thought. Yet Mary still hinted at the beauty which had first attracted his son to her. The slim nose, the even white teeth, and the shapely eyebrows were the same. And if she would begin to eat again, she would regain her looks. But so far, Mary seemed only to get worse as each day passed.

Glancing at her across the table laden with the soup, round flat loaves of bread baked that morning, and fruit, Eli saw she was again staring at nothing. He had to admit he was worried. Grief in the loss of a husband was certainly normal enough, but after so long, shouldn't it be lessening somewhat? Ruth was getting impatient too.

"She doesn't do anything all day," Eli's wife had complained to him. "She even ignores the children."

"Perhaps we should call a physician," he had told her, but they had agreed to wait a little longer before taking that step.

Mary knew they were concerned, but she could not make herself care. Even when Eli told her that he was selling Ara's house, she kept silent.

"We must discuss your future," he said kindly. "Of course, if you wish, you may move in with one of your sisters. But since you have no living parents, we will gladly take responsibility for you and the children. You may stay here until you remarry."

Mary had nodded, though she scarcely heard what he said. *Life has no future for me,* she thought. *I will never again be a wife, and my sisters' husbands would not want the burden of another woman and two children. If Eli will have me, I suppose I will remain in his home.*

Ara's parents' house was much like the one Mary had shared with her husband. It was large and furnished with the best that Magdala had to offer. Upon crossing the threshold, one stood in the courtyard, open to the sky, yet hidden from the street, unless the gate was ajar.

A cistern to collect rainwater, olive and fig trees, and flowers filled the courtyard. Near the sleeping rooms were the loom and the cooking fire. A corner was covered over for the donkeys, and in years past, fishing equipment had been stored in another section. But as Eli had done less with the business, the baskets for transporting fish, the extra hooks, nets, and knives had been kept at Ara's home. Now, however, Mary expected they would soon be brought back to the spot in which they used to lie.

The courtyard was a pleasant place to be at any other time, but for Mary, even the everyday noises of the household bothered her. The large, heavy millstones rumbled as Ruth's two servants sat across from each other, alternately pushing and pulling the wooden handle that rotated the top stone which was almost as wide as the length of Mary's arm. The wheat was scooped into a funnel cut into the stone, and as it poured down through the upper stone to the lower one, it was crushed into flour that sifted out through the bottom onto a sheepskin.

In the past, the rhythmic interaction of the millstones had been soothing. Since Ara's death, the sound of it only made Mary think of her life with him, which she was trying desperately not to do. And since grain was ground for bread every morning except, of course, the Sabbath, the work for a household the size of theirs took nearly all the hours before the noon meal. Mary could hardly stand to be in the courtyard after morning prayers.

But there was no where else to go. When she went inside one of the sleeping or storage rooms constructed to open in the courtyard, the sounds continued in her ears. If she climbed the smooth stone steps that led to the upper rooms built on the roof, the noise followed her.

Even if the girls chose to briefly rest their aching arms and the millstones quieted, their chatter penetrated to wherever

Mary was trying to hide, just as the sound of the children's giggles, the braying of the donkeys, and the slosh of water being brought back from the well. They haunted her day after day.

Then one day, the thought of moving out of Eli's home occurred to her. If she could only have a small house, the one-room kind that the poor lived in, by herself, perhaps over by the sea, Mary would not have to listen to the sounds of everyday life.

The idea grew in her mind, and in another week, Mary was certain that was what she wanted—to get away from everything and everyone. Maybe then she could find some tranquility.

"My lord, I have a request," Mary said softly that evening as she tried to get down a few morsels of chicken.

Eli looked over at her quickly. *Finally!* He thought. *She is starting to recover. Whatever she wants, she shall have.*

"Ask, daughter," Eli encouraged her. Even Ruth and the children brightened at seeing Mary speak.

"I would like a small house to be built for me by the sea."

Eli almost choked. This was not what he had expected. "For what reason?"

"Nothing is lacking in all you have given me. But I find that here I cannot recover from my grief. Perhaps by myself, I can discover the peace that escapes me," she told him.

"Live alone?" Ruth sniffed. "It would not be proper or safe."

Eli tended to agree with his wife, but he hesitated. Nothing else had helped Mary. Perhaps he should grant her wish. She had not asked for anything else since coming to his home.

Mary's eyes were downcast, though she had no interest in the food before her. She felt sure he was not going to do it. Ruth had much influence over Eli, and she plainly thought it was ridiculous. Maybe she was right, but Mary was certain she could not stay in her father-in-law's house much longer.

Finally Eli cleared his throat. "I'll consider this matter, and you'll have my decision soon."

Mary nodded silently.

Awakening with a start, Mary stared around her sleeping room. Only the furniture—the low-carved chest for clothing, the lampstand with its ever-burning lamp full of olive oil, and the mat on which she lay—was there with her, just as it had been when she retired the previous night. No one had entered her room. Again, it was only a dream.

Shivering, Mary rose and slipped a heavy, wool robe over her thin tunic. It was fall, and with the beginning of the former rains, as distinguished from the late-winter latter rains, there was a chill in the air in the early morning hours. However, she knew that was not what made her tremble.

No, it was the nightmare again. Why did she have the same dream every time she slept? It always began with Ara promising her the third servant, but the next scene was of him thrashing wildly in the water. His eyes were wide with terror, such as she had never seen, and his mouth wordlessly called her name. Though she watched in horror, Mary was unable to go to him. Then he swirled away in the waves.

Next the voices started. "Mary, Mary!" they called. She could not identify who they were, but she knew there were a number of them. They became increasingly loud and hostile. "Don't you care at all for your husband?" they mocked her. "How could you insist he get you yet another servant? What do you want? To be a queen?"

At first Mary tried to answer their accusations, but now in her dream, she only covered her face with her hands. *Perhaps they were right. Had I really ever loved Ara? Oh, yes,* she thought she felt it, *but had I sacrificed anything for him?* She had liked the life he gave her for the most part, yet she had done little to contribute to it.

The dream came with increasing frequency, so much that Mary dreaded lying down on the mat. And once, she had even thought she heard the leering voices during the day when she huddled in one of the upper rooms, seeking solitude from the still-irritating grinding in the courtyard. *Perhaps it is only the wind,* she had told herself.

Now, with the blue, wool robe around her, Mary slipped out into the courtyard and then through the gate. The sun was just beginning to send sleepy fingers of dawn up through the dim sky, and the delicate shades of pink, lavender, and gold should have delighted her. Instead, she kept her head lowered. The road was deserted at least for a brief time until Magdala started another day.

Usually fall was a pleasant time of year. The summer heat that had encompassed the land for three months receded, and the former rains brought life to the barren ground. Grass that only weeks before had been brown and lifeless took on the hue of brilliant green, and men smiled as they passed each other on the way to the fields where, hopefully, a bountiful crop awaited them. Tempers improved with the drop in temperature, and the harvest lifted almost everyone's spirits.

Not mine, Mary thought. She walked a little faster. As always, her destination was the sea. The walk from Eli's house to the sandy beach was not far. Although her father-in-law might not do much fishing these days, the sea was in his veins. He could not move away from it. Mary was glad. Being next to the rippling expanse of water they called the Sea of Galilee seemed to help her in ways that nothing else could. She could forget the voices, at least briefly.

Not that the waves always brought calm to her soul. Often enough, she screamed out at them in anger, questioning again and again why they had taken Ara. They never answered her fury, but Mary did not expect that. She only knew that after such sessions, she could weep a little for her husband and their lost life together.

At this time of day, the sea would reach for her with dark blue—almost black—tentacles as she stood beside it. Only as the sun rose higher would it turn a stunning shade of blue.

Though Magdala was located on the western coast, at the point of the greatest width of the sea, it was still only about eight miles to the eastern bank. Yet from where she stood, Mary could not see land on the other side. Hills huddled around the sea and seemed to hold the small body of water in. When Mary looked north, to her left she could make out the distant outline of Mount Herman—so high that it was snow topped almost all year round.

To the southwest of her was the less far-reaching slope of Mount Tabor and then south of it, Mount Moreh. If Mary had turned around, she would have seen the Horns of Hattin, the extinct volcano which rose behind Magdala. It sat on a basalt plateau some eight hundred feet above the town. To get there, one had to make a steep and dangerous climb through the Valley of Doves, the notoriously narrow passageway adorned with cliffs. At the top was Arbela, a village known for its wheat. It was an easy walk from there to the main road that led west to the Great Sea and the port of Ptolemais.

Today Mary was not concerned with the scenery behind her. She kept her eyes on the water advancing and retreating on the sand. It had been a month since she had inquired about having her own house on the beach, and Eli had not yet given her an indication of when she would have his decision. How much longer would she have to wait? And what was she going to do if he refused?

Several times now, Eli had called in physicians to examine

Mary because she continued to lose weight and to spend hours looking into the air. Mary knew Ruth was getting more and more irritated with her, but she could not pull away from her grief the way her mother-in-law expected that she should.

Kezia and Joshua seemed to understand that Mary was not the mother they had known. She noticed that now they went to their grandmother with their joys and sorrows instead of her. While it hurt to feel she was no longer a major part of their lives, Mary accepted it. She was in no shape to care for them; better they grow close to someone who could.

"Mary, Mary . . ."

The voices! They had even followed her here to the beach. She shook her head violently. They could not steal these few times of relative peace from her.

"He did everything for you, even promised you the girl you wanted. What did you do for him?" the voices echoed.

"Leave me alone!" she shouted at them. Their answer was mocking laughter. Mary turned from the water and hurried away from it. *Is no place safe for me?* she thought.

Back outside Eli's courtyard, she leaned against the wall, panting. *Are these voices going to follow me everywhere?* She could not bear to listen to them anymore.

Suddenly from inside the courtyard, Mary heard Eli and Ruth talking.

"She is no better, and we have tried the physicians," her mother-in-law was saying.

"I had hoped by now to discuss remarriage with her, but in her condition that is impossible," Eli replied.

Mary's stomach turned. Take another husband? No! To think of running another's household, of having a husband other than Ara . . . She simply could not do it.

Ruth snorted. "No man would want her the way she is now, barely alive."

"Yet, several have asked me recently about her, and I think they are considering a wife. Of course, they have not seen her since the funeral," Eli said.

"She must remarry," Ruth insisted.

"Of course she shall," Eli soothed. "But first she has to get better. We'll build her the house she wants. There's nothing else we can do for her. And if that does not help, the Mighty One alone can cure her."

Outside the wall, Mary breathed a sigh of relief. She would get what she wanted, and they would not force her to take a husband, not yet.

"Naturally, she cannot live there alone," Ruth was saying.

"Tabitha can go, and the children will stay here. She's scarcely aware of them," Eli explained.

Mary frowned. She had not pictured a servant with her, and she did not like leaving Kezia and Joshua. What would happen to them had not crossed her mind until that moment. But Eli would insist on those terms; she had no choice. *Perhaps it would not be so bad.* She walked to the courtyard gate and went inside.

3

Shortly after she and Tabitha had moved into the one room house that Eli ordered built for them, Mary realized that she had been wrong. Living by the water, away from most of the everyday noises of life, did not help.

Instead, the voices increased, calling her at all hours of the day and night. At the first sound of them, Mary would try to run from them or at least cover her ears with her hands. Then, giving up, she could only moan as they tormented her.

Tabitha watched with tears in her eyes. She had served Mary for many years, having come from her mistress's father's home. She was grieved to see the once-capable woman rendered almost useless.

But there seemed to be nothing Tabitha could do. Mary apparently was hearing things the servant did not, and Tabitha had taken her worries to Eli.

"I will think on it," he promised, touched by the old woman's concern. Maybe there was a priest who could help.

At first, Eli had tried to visit Mary regularly, sending the children or Ruth when he could not go. Their presence did not prove to be beneficial for any of them. If the voices came, Mary would jump up and hurry off, frightening Kezia. If Mary heard no voices, she only sat, appearing to not even listen to her family.

After a month, the old man gave up. "Joshua, Kezia, your mother is still very ill," he told them gently. "We must leave her alone until she is well again. For now, your grandmother and I will be your parents."

The children were relieved. The woman who was their mother bore little resemblance to the one who had so devotedly cared for them in their father's home.

For Mary, not seeing her loved ones was only a small loss. Occasionally she longed to hold her little daughter or to ask her son how his schooling was going, but those times passed quickly. The voices took up most of her days.

Though he did not visit anymore, Eli made sure that Tabitha had money to care for Mary's needs. He was generous in the amount he sent each week, and the old servant used only a small portion of it for food and other necessities. The rest she put in a jar she buried under the raised platform in the tiny house. The women spread their sleeping mats on the platform and kept their clothing and cooking supplies on it.

One morning as Mary sat listlessly on her mat, she heard the voice of Merab outside the house. Now Ruth's servant, she had come to give Tabitha the weekly money.

"Did you hear about the wedding in Cana yesterday?" the younger servant asked breathlessly.

"Something about Cana was said at the well when I drew water today, but I did not pay much attention. Do you know what happened?" Tabitha said.

"Yes, and you will not believe it! My lord Eli took me to the wedding to watch over the children. A Rabbi from Nazareth was there; Jesus, I think His name was. Anyway, they ran out of wine before the feast was over. I was aware of it since I was standing back with the other servants when they realized the jars were empty."

The old servant snorted. "So there was no more wine. They had all probably had enough to drink already."

"Listen to what happened!" Merab told her urgently. "The mother of this man Jesus was there, and she overheard us whispering about what to do. She went and told her Son the problem. When He came over to us, she ordered us to do as He said."

"What did He say to do?" Tabitha asked, now obviously interested.

"Just to fill up with water the jars that had been empty. It was done, all six of them full to the brim. Then He said to dip some out of one of the jars and take it to the ruler of the feast. Tabitha, when he tasted it, it was wine!"

From inside, Mary could hear the old woman gasp. "Well, . . . well, surely it was because the water had the faint taste of the wine that had been in the jar previously."

"No, that could not be. The ruler turned to the bridegroom and praised him for saving the best wine until last. I heard someone say it was unlike any wine he had ever drank."

"What could have happened?" Tabitha asked.

"What do you think? This Rabbi turned the water into wine!"

"But that is impossible! How could He do it?"

"I do not understand it, but magicians can do all sorts of things . . ."

As the servants continued talking, Mary rose and went outside, and started down the beach. Another trickster. What difference did it make to her?

Though it was late morning, the beach was deserted. Eli had built the house on the north side of Magdala, and Mary always walked north away from town. The fishing industry was more to the center and the south of Magdala, and she but rarely came across a fisherman or a woman gathering fuel for the fire. It was just as well; she had no desire to speak with anyone.

Though it was late morning, the air was still cool, and Mary shivered a little as she walked along beside the sea. Now that it was the beginning of the month of Adar, the true chill of winter had passed, but the warmth of spring was not quite a reality.

To her left, Mary could see fields of barley waving in the breeze. It was still nearly two months before the harvest, but the grain was growing well after the winter rains. Behind and above the barley stood the steep cliffs of the Valley of Doves, which ascended to the towering heights of the volcano, the Horns of Hattin. In front of her stretched the rolling hills of Galilee, now green again, though not yet sprinkled with the abundance of spring flowers that would appear in the next month or so. She could just barely see the outlines of Gennesaret and northeast of it, Capernaum, fishing towns that lay on the sea but to the north of Magdala. Although it was not visible from where she was, towering Mount Hermon stood solemnly watching over the province from its position far north of even Capernaum.

Scarcely noticing the beauty that surrounded her, Mary stopped walking and stood facing the sea. Today it was calm, with brilliant blue and green streaks whirling into each other in patterns that would have delighted anyone else's eyes. A few fishing boats bobbed in the current, and doves called to each other as they circled above the expanse of water before they returned to their homes in the nearby rocky cliffs.

Mourn, birds, Mary thought. *Join me in my grief . . .*

"Shalom," a feminine voice called, and Mary jumped. The beach had been deserted when last she had surveyed it. But as she turned, she saw a woman approaching her. Several hundred paces behind the stranger, near the road to Capernaum, Mary saw a group of people resting.

"Shalom." At the sound of the greeting being repeated, Mary

realized that she had not answered the first one. No wonder the other woman looked puzzled.

"Shalom," Mary said quickly, though the word sounded strange on her lips. She was suddenly aware that it had been a long time since she had met anyone new.

The woman now stood before her, panting a little after the walk from the road. She was quite a bit older than Mary, but her hair sticking out from under her head covering had only a trifle more gray in it than Mary's own hair. Wrinkles crisscrossed her face, yet her eyes were bright and lively.

"I am Joanna," the woman told her, and her voice was low and somehow soothing. "The Rabbi I travel with seeks shelter for the night. Is there an inn near here?"

Mary swallowed nervously. How long had it been since she had thought about such things? She honestly could not recall whether Magdala had a place to lodge travelers.

Joanna was looking at her strangely, and Mary knew she had to say something. Before she could, the other woman spoke.

"Forgive me. Perhaps you, too, are not from this area, and you cannot answer my question. I will seek another."

"No, wait," Mary stammered quickly. "I am from Magdala, but I have been, ah, ill. I have not been around others lately, and I find that I forget the simple courtesies of conversation. You ask about an inn. No, we have no such place, but there is one in Gennesaret." Grateful that she had finally remembered, Mary pointed to the north. "It is only about three miles farther."

"My thanks," Joanna said. "I must tell my Master."

Mary nodded, and the other woman started off.

Breathing a sigh of relief, Mary sat down on the sand. She had not known how much of a strain it was for her to simply talk to someone after her months of saying so little.

Back at the roadside, Joanna approached the Rabbi. "My Lord, there is a place to lodge in Gennesaret."

At the sound of her voice, He turned toward her, and once again, Joanna felt the thrill that always touched her when Jesus looked at her. Oh, it was not the kind of feeling she had experienced in her younger days when Chuza, her husband, had kissed her. Nor was it the same as when she had held her newborn baby to her breast.

No, it was a feeling such as she had never experienced before she met the Rabbi from Nazareth. She could not even really explain it. She only knew that when He looked at her, spoke to her, or smiled at her, she would do anything for Him, no matter what the cost.

Jesus had not said anything about the inn, and Joanna wondered if He had heard. Sometimes when someone spoke to Him, He did not seem to listen, as if His thoughts were elsewhere.

"Gennesaret is only three miles . . ." she began again.

"Yes. I know," He said mildly, and Joanna stopped, surprised. If He had been aware of the inn, why had He sent her to ask the woman on the beach? She did not understand, but there were many times when none of those who followed Jesus knew what He was doing. Nevertheless, she was learning more and more that He always had reasons for what He did.

He had turned to someone else, and Joanna moved away from Him to join the other women who, having already served the men their noon meal, were eating themselves.

Joanna glanced over at the Master as she slowly ate a piece of cheese. Melon in hand, He was conversing with Simon, one of the followers. Though Simon was a big man, probably a finger length taller than Jesus and a half talent heavier, it was clear, even from where Joanna was, who was the disciple. As Jesus spoke, the other man listened intently, looking more like a schoolboy than a fisherman who had recently left his nets to follow the Rabbi.

But the Master Himself was who Joanna really wanted to watch. Though His face would not be considered extraordinarily handsome by most women's standards, she found it to be a source of fascination. The heavy hair and beard the color of the sand after a rain; the wide mouth, so often expanded into a smile; the nose, neither too large nor too small; and the eyes, sometimes piercing, other times full of compassion—all of this drew her.

"Joanna," He called, and she quickly moved back to His side.

"We will go on to Gennesaret, but I would have you stay in Magdala for a while."

"Why, yes, Master, as you wish. But what am I to do here?"

Jesus smiled in His special way. "You will think of something. May the peace of the Mighty One go with you."

Obediently Joanna returned to the small circle of women to collect her bag of possessions. *Perhaps He has noticed I am weary from all the walking we do,* she thought. *I could rest in Magdala, so I will be ready for the trip to Jerusalem for Passover. It is only a little over a month away.*

She bid the others farewell. No one asked where she was going; it was not unusual for Jesus to instruct one of them to go off on various errands for Him, though most of the time the women went in pairs.

Looking down the beach, Joanna saw that the woman she had asked about the inn still sat on the sand. She remembered again the unhealthy look on that young face, the dullness in her eyes, and the grey already streaking through her hair.

Jesus had not said where to go in Magdala or when to rejoin Him. Maybe she was to go to the woman and stay with her for the time away from the Master. She could at least ask. If anyone needed the love and hope that Jesus offered, the woman on the beach did. Joanna could tell that with as little as they had said to each other. Swinging the small cloth bag over her shoulder, Joanna set out toward the distant slumped figure. It never occurred to her to feel afraid that she was on her own.

Behind her, Jesus and the others had collected and were slowly beginning to make their way to Gennesaret, but Joanna did not turn around to watch them.

4

"This is madness," Mary muttered, but Joanna only smiled. The older woman was shorter and heavier than her companion, but her step was just as brisk as the two of them walked down the dusty road to Gennesaret.

"If my father-in-law knew of this, he would be furious . . ."

"Ah, but he does not, and so there is no need to fear. When he inquires as to your whereabouts, your servant will tell him you seek solace by walking, which is the truth." Joanna shifted to her other hand the small cloth bag which held several days' food supply.

Guiltily, Mary looked away. Joanna carried both it and the waterskin while Mary herself only had a walking staff, the lighter bag with a clean robe for each of them, and their cloaks for evening. As the younger woman, surely she should be the one with most of their burdens. But Joanna had insisted that Mary let her bear the heavy things.

Of course, they both knew Mary was weak after the months of inactivity and being unable to eat much. To agree to make the trip to Capernaum was a big step for her; one which she expected to tax all her physical strength. *Was it really worth it?* Mary had asked herself again and again.

But Joanna had been persistent. "You must come hear Jesus speak. He is unlike any other Rabbi I have ever seen."

"What do I care?" Mary had told her repeatedly. "I have no interest in listening to Him."

Joanna had shaken her arm gently. "You want to get better, don't you? To be able to return to caring for your children and living a normal life?"

"Of course I do, but even the priest my lord Eli brought said I will always suffer this way. He could not help me."

"But Jesus is different! You must find out for yourself."

Mary had finally given in to her. She had to admit that in the weeks since Joanna had moved in with her and Tabitha, the voices had bothered her much less than before. And the older woman's cheerful smile and considerate ways had brought a manner of peace into Mary's tormented life.

So at last, Mary had said she would accompany Joanna to seek whatever aid Jesus could give her. There was no where else she could turn for help.

"Isn't the sea beautiful this morning?" Joanna was saying, and Mary nodded without enthusiasm. Her companion always saw the good of everything, which was sometimes irritating. But in spite of that, Mary felt she had been blessed by Joanna coming to the little house she shared with the servant. The older woman would not let her sit for hours in one place, staring off into space as she had done so often in the months since Ara's death.

Not that Joanna had tried to push away the memory of Mary's husband. She encouraged the young widow to talk about him, and they had even laughed together at some of the humorous things Ara had said and done. At first, it felt strange to so remember him, but Mary quickly became comfortable sharing with Joanna the good and bad of the life she had had. Her new friend was the first person to whom she had really talked about her spouse since his death.

Now as the two of them walked north on the dirt road that led to Gennesaret, the halfway point to their destination of Capernaum, Mary was as content as she had been at any time since Ara's funeral. Perhaps it was good, getting away from the confining walls of the small house built to comfort her. The voices which had so haunted her seemed to have stayed there, too, even though they had only come to her several times at the house since Joanna arrived. Maybe they were leaving. Somehow, as the bright sunshine stroked her back, Mary felt that could be the case.

"You will like the Master," Joanna was saying. "He is the most unusual man I have ever met."

"Do you realize how many times you have told me that?" Mary asked. "Just what makes Him so special?" She was getting a little irritated at her friend's unrestrained praise of the Rabbi.

Joanna shrugged good-naturedly. "It is hard to say. When you meet Him, you will see. He radiates such warmth, such love. Why, I have never felt more cared for in my life. Even Chuza did not . . ."

Her voice trailed off, as it always did when she discussed her husband. Mary was curious about the man. Joanna had said he was the steward of Herod Antipas, the ruler of Galilee and the son of Herod called the Great by the Romans. To the Jews, the praise was hollow. A cruel man, known for murdering members of his own family, Herod the elder might have brought major building programs and a form of peace throughout the land, but his death was welcomed. In spite of the hopes of the people that their new ruler, Antipas, would be totally different from his father, the tetrarch was developing his own bad reputation.

Yet Chuza served Antipas faithfully in Tiberias, the new capital built by the ruler after he assumed his position in the northern province.

"Isn't Tiberias built on a cemetery?" Mary had asked when Joanna mentioned it.

"Yes," Joanna had answered, her disgust showing in her eyes. "I was never content there. Who would be, living in such a defiled place? It is true, Antipas often travels to Jerusalem or other places. But still, we did stay in Tiberias too much to suit me."

"What of Chuza? Didn't he mind it there?"

Joanna flushed. "It did not seem to bother him much, although he is devoted to the Powerful One, as are a sizable number of other Jews who live there," she added quickly.

"What does he think of your following Jesus?" Mary said softly, watching a small flock of sparrows fly overhead.

"He says I am a fool," Joanna admitted. "Perhaps he is right. I only know that for the first time in my life, I have total peace and fulfillment. At Tiberias, I was bored. The children are grown, Chuza busy with his duties. What was there to do? Then I went to Cana for my sister's daughter's wedding. Jesus was there."

"I heard about the water that became wine," Mary told her, vaguely remembering the conversation outside her room between Tabitha and Merab.

"Yes, it was truly a miracle! I tasted the wine. It was quite extraordinary."

"Does this Jesus have magical powers?" Mary questioned, taking care to step over a broken pot laying in the dusty road.

"I believe He has great power, but it is from the Just One Himself. Jesus is no mere magician." Joanna wiped the perspiration off of her brow with one end of her veil. For early in the month of Nisan, it was extremely hot.

"Anyway, after the wedding, I just wanted to be with the Rabbi," Joanna continued. "Chuza had not come to Cana with me since Antipas was traveling to Caesarea." Mary nodded at the name of the Roman port in the southern province of Judea.

"When I sent him word that I would not be coming back to Tiberias for a while, he was angered enough to ask the tetrarch to give him leave. He had stern words for me," Joanna confessed ruefully. "But I am blessed to have a good husband. I was able to convince him to let me try it for a time. He even sends me money."

Mary stopped and bent down to retie one of her sandals. "You are married to an unusual man. I have never heard of a husband permitting his wife to do as you are doing."

Joanna nodded. "I know. But Chuza has heard Jesus speak and feels He is a good man. And he hopes that soon I will get my fill of living on the road and return home."

"Will you?"

"I plan to follow Jesus until the day I die. Or the day He dies! Why don't we rest and eat a bit under these oak trees? It is not often there is so much shade along the side of the road."

The idea was appealing, and the women sat down, resting their backs against the tree trunks.

"Does your Rabbi know about Chuza?" Mary asked, still thinking about Joanna's story.

The older woman handed her a bunch of grapes and pulled one out of the food bag for herself. "He does, and though He has not said it, I think He does not approve. But I am not following Jesus against my husband's orders."

"Yet it sounds as if Chuza is not pleased."

"No," Joanna said shortly. "How about some bread?" She made it clear she had no wish to continue the discussion.

Mary did not ask anymore, but somehow she felt sorry for

Antipas's steward, waiting in vain for his wife to return home. *I could have never left Ara to follow even a man like Jesus,* Mary thought.

Though the five-mile journey to Capernaum would have taken a man only three or four hours to walk, Joanna and Mary found it took them quite a bit longer. The late afternoon shadows were stretching across the countryside as they came into the town. Like Magdala, Capernaum's main business was fishing, and the distinct smell of the silvery-scaled creatures brought tears to Mary's eyes.

How well she remembered the days Ara spent mending nets, preparing the boats to be seaworthy, and cleaning freshly caught fish. Of course, in the last few years of his life, most of that kind of thing had been done by the hired men while Ara supervised and worked out trade agreements. But Mary still pictured her husband more with a fish in one hand and a knife in the other than as the successful businessman in charge that he had become.

If Joanna noticed her friend wiping her cheeks with the end of her veil, she said nothing, and Mary was grateful. Perhaps it was good that she could cry a little at the thought of Ara. Could the grief which had so crippled her be healing?

"If only I knew where to look for the Master . . ." Joanna was saying.

"You have no idea where He is? He set no place for you to meet?" Mary hoped her voice sounded normal and not like she was weeping.

Joanna shook her head. Surveying the nearly deserted beach, for most fishermen were home preparing for their night of work on the sea, she pointed to a man sitting on the sand some distance from them. "We will ask him."

At their approach, the man looked up from the barrels into which he was sorting fish according to their sizes.

"Shalom, my lord. We seek the Rabbi, Jesus of Nazareth. Have you heard where He is?"

Though Joanna spoke, Mary noticed that the man was looking at her and not the older woman. His stare made her uncomfortable.

"Yes, I have heard of this man. I believe He was at the home of one Simon, a fisherman, but I do not know if He is still there."

Even Joanna noticed the way the man was watching Mary, and she instinctively took a step back away from him. "Where might this house be?"

He gave her directions, and the women quickly moved on.

"I hope we find Jesus soon," Mary whispered, and Joanna nodded.

"But don't worry," she said. "I know Simon. Even if he and the others are not here, surely Simon's family will let us lodge with them for the night."

"Your Rabbi might not be in Capernaum?"

Joanna shrugged. "With the Master, one never knows. He does not always end up where He is expected. Besides, it is getting close to Passover, and Jesus is surely planning on going to the Holy City for that."

Though Joanna kept her voice calm, she had to admit to herself that she was concerned. Had she dragged poor Mary all this way, only to find the Rabbi already gone? The young woman so needed to meet Him.

Nevertheless, Joanna led Mary through the winding streets of Capernaum until they found the fisherman's house. At her knock, a stern-faced older woman came to the courtyard gate.

"Simon is not here," she told them, and then, apparently suspecting they thought she was only a servant, she explained that she was Leah, Simon's mother-in-law.

"Have they left for Jerusalem?" Joanna asked, trying to sound as if it did not matter to her.

"Oh, no. The Rabbi is not planning to do that for several more days."

Joanna sighed with relief. *Thanks be to the Mighty One we did not wait until later to come to Capernaum,* she thought. "Where is the Master now?"

Leah pointed to the west. "He has taken all of them out to the hills, I suppose to teach them something. But they are coming back here for the night. You could wait here for them," she invited, but Joanna could tell she did not want them to accept.

Her first impulse was to refuse, but then she glanced at Mary. The long walk had obviously exhausted her, and Joanna knew her companion needed to rest. Even though staying here would be awkward at best, they had to do it, in all fairness to Mary.

"Why, thank you for your generosity. It has been a long walk from Magdala . . ."

"But we are most anxious to see Jesus," Mary interrupted. "Could you tell us more exactly where He is?"

Joanna turned to her. "But you must sit down!"

Mary smiled at her too broadly. "I feel refreshed. We must find the Rabbi at once."

Leah must be blind not to realize Mary is lying, Joanna thought, but she gave in to the silent pleas the younger woman was making.

"I hope you will not regret this foolishness," Joanna said as they started back down the street. "It would have been much more sensible to wait there for the Master, so you would have been rested when you meet Him."

Mary did not look at her. "I will not stay in a house where I am not wanted. I would sooner go back to the beach."

Remembering the stares of the lone fisherman, Joanna doubted that Mary meant it, but she kept on walking. *It will be good to see Jesus again,* she thought. *I have missed Him.*

Simon's house was near the middle of Capernaum, and it did

not take the two women long to continue walking west to the
outskirts of town. From there, they could see the hills which
surrounded Capernaum, except on the side where the sea gently
lapped up onto the beach. Now with the approach of evening, the
brilliant green of the spring grass had dimmed somewhat, and
the blooming trees like the almond with its tiny pink blossoms
had blurred into shadows. Though the sky was still light, the
sun was no longer visible in it.

Mary waited silently as Joanna peered around. *I did not need
to make this trip,* she told herself. *I am feeling so much better
that surely, soon, I will be able to go home and get Kezia and
Joshua.*

At the thought of them, Mary suddenly realized how much
she wanted to see them. *I wish I had stayed home. Then I could
have gone to be with them tonight,* she told herself.

She pictured the surprise on Eli and Ruth's faces when she
appeared at their courtyard gate. *Why, I am ready for that,* she
thought. *I have no need to meet this Jesus.*

Mary was just about to tell Joanna that when suddenly the
older woman pointed to the right of them.

"There they are!" she exclaimed, and Mary had never seen
Joanna look so happy. "Come on, let's go to them."

"Joanna . . ."

But she was ignored. Joanna had picked up the end of her robe
and was actually running toward the small group, looking more
like a young girl than a mature woman of fifty. Mary could do
nothing but follow her.

5

Nothing has changed, Mary told herself miserably. Joanna was so sure that meeting Jesus would make a difference in my life, but she was wrong.

Rolling over on her mat, Mary squeezed her eyes shut. At the other end of the raised platform, Tabitha snored, oblivious to her mistress's turmoil. She must not be awakened. But how difficult it was to keep from crying out in the darkness.

Yes, of course, she was tired after the trip to Capernaum. But Mary knew that was not the real problem. It went much deeper.

She remembered again her introduction to the famed Rabbi. He had seemed no different from any other man of the Torah, and when Joanna had excitedly pushed her forward and murmured her name, the Master had only smiled in her direction. That was all.

Well, what did you expect? Mary chided herself. *Trumpets blowing? Him sitting down and devoting His evening listening to your woes? He is human, like anyone else. He would have no way of knowing what troubles a heart.*

Still, Mary could not deny the disappointment she had felt. After all Joanna had said, it seemed as if the Rabbi would at least have given her some words of encouragement. But there was nothing like that the night the two women had discovered Jesus and His followers in the hills of Capernaum.

He is tired too, Mary had told herself at the time. *In the morning, we will speak.* She had joined the group heading back to the house of Simon the fisherman.

But at daybreak, Mary awoke to find that the Rabbi had decided to start for Jerusalem that day. Joanna urged her to go talk with Jesus before the men left, but for a reason she could not explain, Mary refused.

"I have nothing to say to Him," she whispered.

If Joanna was disappointed by Mary's refusal, she did not indicate it. But Mary suspected that her friend had also been surprised by Jesus' cool response to her the previous night.

"I suppose we should go back to Magdala," Mary said as the men finished their preparations for the trip south to the Holy City.

Joanna did not look at her. "I shall go to Jerusalem too."

"Of course," Mary said quickly, pretending she had anticipated her friend going with them. Actually, she had assumed that Joanna would return to the small house by the sea. But why would she do that? She, too, was a follower of Jesus, and she no longer had a reason to stay with Mary.

"You may travel with us to Magdala," Joanna suggested, and Mary had agreed. She was obviously unable to make the trip there herself.

Back at home, Mary wordlessly hugged Joanna after the older woman had put down Mary's bundles. As she hurried to rejoin the others, the young widow stood alone by the courtyard gate.

I will miss her, she thought. *How dull life will be without Joanna.* She watched her friend's short, stocky body walking purposefully toward Jesus. There was no hesitation, no reluctance. Clearly Joanna did not feel the same way about their parting.

She wants to be with Him more than anything else, Mary told herself. *Why can't she see that I need her here? In just the short*

*time I've known her, I have grown to care for her, and now she is
walking out of my life.*

Long after the dust had settled from the feet of the small
group continuing south, Mary stood by the gate. She hardly noticed when Eli arrived, looking angrier than she had ever seen
him.

The things he spoke—words like "irresponsible" and "insan-
ity" and others, more fierce—all passed over her like the afternoon breeze. She barely heard his ranting or even the
resounding slap he gave Tabitha for not stopping Mary from
traveling to Capernaum. When at last he had finished and left,
Mary remained at the same place.

Then the voices returned. "Mary, Mary!" they taunted. "Now
there is no hope that you will ever recover . . ."

"No!" she whispered. "I am better now."

Their laughter was obnoxious. "You fool yourself! Even the
Rabbi from Nazareth would not help you."

Long into the night, the voices tortured Mary. Somehow
they were even stronger than before, and Mary trembled at the
thought of enduring them day after day. What had happened?
She had felt almost well again, and now she seemed worse than
ever before. Perhaps she was doomed to a life of torment.

As the fall rains beat on the roof, Mary leaned back against
the wall. Even the sheepskin around her did not keep the chill
from penetrating her bones, and she was weary after the previous week. She and Tabitha had been required to return to Eli's
house for the Feast of Booths, held in thankfulness to Yahweh
for the recently gathered harvest. It had not been a good experience for any of the family.

As always, the servants had constructed the small hut made
of branches in which the family would spend the week. The law

specified exactly how the hut had to be built, with a height of at least ten hands but of no more than thirty. Three of the walls had to be made of boughs, covered yet open enough for the sunlight to penetrate.

Just as in previous years, Eli had explained to the children that they lived in the hut to commemorate the tents in which the Israelites had dwelt during the years of wandering in the wilderness. Some disagreed, he knew, and said the huts merely symbolized the shelters made in the fields during harvest. The farmers took up residence in them to protect their crops from those who might be tempted to steal the ripe fruit or grain. But Eli preferred the more spiritual view.

Though the putting up of the hut and moving into it was a festive occasion, Mary felt none of it. She sat dully on the ground, longing only to get back to the little house on the sea. Even the children's excitement meant nothing to her, for in the six months since her trip to Capernaum, they had become complete strangers to her. She rarely saw Kezia and Joshua, and when they were together—as for the feast—they ignored her as she did them.

Though some of the more religious men in town traveled to Jerusalem to celebrate the feast, Eli did not. Anyone further than one day's journey from the Holy City was permitted to keep it at the local synagogue, and Eli did not have the desire nor the health to make the long trip.

But from previous visits there for the feast, also called the Feast of Tabernacles or Ingathering, Eli knew well enough what went on there. Special offerings were presented in the temple, and just before the morning service, a priest went to the nearby pool of Siloam to fill a golden pitcher. He was accompanied by a joyous procession, complete with musical instruments. Others, Eli himself in his younger days, went to gather willow branches from the valley of Kidron. They were tied to either side of the altar, then bent to form a sort of canopy over it.

As the sacrificial animals were placed on the altar, the priest with the water returned and poured it into two silver basins which had been put to the left of the altar. At the same time, a drink offering of wine was poured into the basins. Then the temple music began, and the worshipers waved their branches in the air. It was a time of rejoicing, yet also of earnest prayers for the life-giving fall rains. The first day of the feast ended with each person having a torch or lamp lit from the holy fire of the altar.

Each evening during the feast, Eli had joined the other men who filled the temple courtyard for a night of dancing. Carrying torches, they had chanted psalms until it was nearly daybreak. Even when Eli was not at the temple, during the week of celebration, reminders of the feast surrounded him.

Each person he saw held a lulab, the switch of woven branches from palm, willow, and myrtle trees which was waved in the air as one walked. Also in every hand was an ethrog, fruit only to be eaten when the festival was over and the lulab was taken apart. In addition, the booths of travelers were all over the city—in courtyards, open squares, even in the streets, and on rooftops. The feast was a popular one, and many Jews from all over the country, as well as from distant parts of the Roman Empire, made their way to Jerusalem to celebrate it.

Eli carefully explained the ceremony to his grandchildren, who listened attentively. They even convinced him to promise that he would take them to the feast in Jerusalem the following year, so they could see it themselves.

Perhaps by next fall, we can make the trip, the old man reasoned. Unless something remarkable happens, Mary will not be on this side of the grave by then. Another reason he had not wanted to travel away from Magdala was his daughter-in-law.

Now that it had been almost a year since Ara's death, Eli had reconciled himself to the loss. The death of his only son had been a bitter blow, totally unexpected, of course, and Eli had wondered if he would be able to endure the devastating pain that filled his heart. Ruth, too, had been crushed with grief, and Eli had forced himself to be strong to help her. Then there was Mary and her sorrow, as well as the children, who mourned their father's passing too.

Yet Eli had had to deal with his own loss in order to be there for the others. It had meant many nights of slipping out of the courtyard gate to walk down by the sea. There, sometimes he wept. Other nights, he shouted at the waves, and, once, he had blindly struck at them with his stick, ordering them to undo the damage they had inflicted on his family. But gradually, peace and acceptance had come, and life had gone on.

One of Eli's sons-in-law had stepped in to manage the business, and though it was not doing as well as it had when in Ara's hands, it was surviving. And the presence of the children in his home had given some new life to him.

But while Eli had withstood Ara's death, and Ruth and the children also seemed to be adjusting, Mary was more ill than ever. For a while the previous spring, Eli had thought she was improving. But after that sudden unexplained trip to Capernaum, his daughter-in-law had declined rapidly.

Eli had quizzed Tabitha extensively about what might have happened on that journey, but the servant could give him few answers. She only knew that her mistress and the woman Joanna had gone to see the Rabbi who turned the water into wine at Cana. For what reason, she could only guess. Perhaps it had to do with the voices Mary had been hearing. But after the time away, everything grew progressively worse.

Eli had made sure that Tabitha realized the seriousness of not letting him know about Joanna's coming. Even though Mary had ordered her not to tell him, the old man stressed, the servant had to look out for the welfare of a woman in Mary's condition. Tabitha promised that she would keep Eli aware of what her mistress was doing, and especially if anyone came to visit her.

"We simply cannot have her running off at any time," Eli reminded her. "In her frame of mind, she could do anything, even hurt herself or others. We must protect her from herself."

"Yes, my lord," Tabitha answered meekly, although she hated the thought of informing him of each move Mary made.

It did not help. Mary became more and more locked into her own world, and the voices came on a daily basis. Eli had to admit that she would probably be permanently ill. Though he did not tell anyone, he toyed with the idea that her death would be the best thing that could happen. Watching her from a distance, he could not feel hopeful about either her mental or physical condition. She continued to eat almost nothing and to sleep either most of the time or next to none of it.

Even if Mary was awake, she was usually unaware of what was going on around her. She huddled on her mat or stood next to the sea, always silent, even when the voices moaned in her ears. Tabitha soon could not remember the last time her mistress had spoken, as she remarked to Merab one morning when the younger servant came with the week's money from Eli.

"I wonder how much longer she will last. My heart breaks to see her so. Yet sometimes I do wish I could leave her. Living with the insane can make one that way too."

Merab giggled. "You, my dear Tabitha, continue to sound perfectly sane, but, believe me, I will let you know if you start to resemble the mistress."

Tabitha smiled. She missed having someone to talk to, and it felt good to hear something even remotely humorous. "Enough of my life here. What is happening in Magdala? I hear so little.

Even when I go for water, I must hurry back from the well so as not to leave her alone for too long."

"Well, my lady Ruth continues to try to teach Kezia to weave, but I think it is a waste of time. She has no interest, and the robe she has started is a disaster."

"She will not soon earn the fame of the skilled weavers of Magdala, huh? She is only a child."

Merab snorted. "And a spoiled one at that. Not that she was so good before her father's death, but now she is even worse. Her grandmother gives her more than her parents did . . ."

Sitting on her mat on the raised platform at the back of the house, Mary heard the sound of their voices. But they meant nothing to her. Even at the mention of Kezia's name, she felt no different.

". . . and Jesus told those fishermen to let down their nets into the water. Well, one of them spoke up and told the Rabbi that they had been fishing all night and never caught one thing," Merab was saying.

At the name of Jesus, Mary felt a sudden chill. She knew that name. How?

"What did He do?" Tabitha was asking.

"I hear the fishermen took one look at the Nazarene and decided to obey anyway. When the men had lowered the nets, they were suddenly completely full, so full they tore. Another boat had to come over and help them get all the catch to shore."

"Are you sure?" the older servant asked breathlessly.

Merab's answer was quick. "Yes! My brother was there and saw it all. He said there were fish all over the beach after they pulled the nets in. Not just tiny worthless ones, either. And this Jesus had preached to the people first. Dan told me that it was unlike any other teaching he had ever heard."

"How?"

"He said it was done with authority . . ."

Jesus . . . Jesus . . . ah, yes, Mary remembered. A long time ago, perhaps years before, she and someone else had gone to meet a rabbi named Jesus. He had seemed ordinary enough. But now He was doing extraordinary things. Oh, well, it did not really concern her. Feeling only relief that the Feast of Booths was over and she was back in the house by the sea, Mary stretched out on the mat and closed her eyes.

6

"... but I must see her!"

Mary roused at the sound of the vaguely familiar feminine voice. As the woman at the courtyard gate again spoke to Tabitha, something inside of Mary stirred. She stepped down off the platform at the back of the house and walked toward the courtyard.

"I'm sorry, but I cannot let you near my mistress," Tabitha was telling the visitor. "She has been very ill, not at all like the person you knew. Her mind . . ."

"I know, and that's why I have come. I want to help her."

Mary heard the old servant sigh. "If only you could . . ."

"You care about her very much, don't you? I can tell you do," the woman said. "Please then, let me talk to your lady. I know someone who can make her well again."

In the doorway of the sleeping room, Mary stopped. The voice of the visitor drew her, but she still had no idea to whom it belonged. She only knew that the speaker was from the dim shadows of her past.

Tabitha was shaking her head. "I would truly like to admit you, but I have my orders from the master."

The visitor glanced past the servant and saw the dark form in the doorway. "I too have orders from my Master," she said and darted around Tabitha, who did nothing to stop her. Reaching Mary, Joanna flung her arms about her.

Startled, Mary gasped but did not pull away.

"Mary, Mary, it's me, Joanna. Don't you know me? I have returned." She took a step back from her friend. "You look terrible. What have those demons done to you? But don't fear, Mary. You can still recover, I know you can."

She waited for a response, but there was none. Puzzled, Joanna turned to Tabitha, who had joined them.

"She doesn't talk anymore," the servant whispered.

"Oh, my poor Mary," Joanna said. "I never suspected you would be in this state. You must go to Jesus. He will heal you."

"Don't tell her these things!" Tabitha told her quickly. "If my master were to find out . . ." She remembered again the blow Eli had given her, the only one she had ever received from him, when he had heard of Mary's trip to Capernaum the previous year.

Suddenly understanding, Joanna nodded. "Quickly, go fetch water from the well. If you do not hear me, you will not have to lie to your lord about my talk with Mary."

Tabitha hesitated, obviously wanting to trust Joanna but wondering if she could.

"Please go, Tabitha."

The words were clear, but it took Joanna and Tabitha an instant to determine who had said them. Mary had spoken! They both stared at her in disbelief.

Then huge tears began rolling down Tabitha's face. "My lady! Oh, my lady, you have finally spoken again!"

"You see, your mistress wants to hear what I have to tell her. Do go and leave us alone. I want only to help Mary. I could never harm her," Joanna pleaded.

The servant studied the visitor's lined face. She looked like she had only good in store for the mistress, but still, Tabitha knew little of Joanna. She would never forgive herself if anything happened to her charge. Yet what could take place? What could possibly render Mary more useless than she had been the past few months? Tabitha made her decision. She reached for the water pitcher and the leather bucket to lower into the well.

As she was leaving, Joanna gently pulled Mary down on the ground next to her. "Mary, much has happened since last we were together. Why, Jesus is becoming known all over. He has healed many people, and that is why you must go to Him again."

Mary sat silently, but she watched Joanna's face intently. Encouraged, Joanna took one of the pale thin hands into her own.

"You remember Leah, don't you? The mother-in-law of Simon, the fisherman, who follows Jesus? She was the one at Simon's house who sent us to the hills to find the Master. Several months ago, when we were in Capernaum, we again stayed with her. One morning while Jesus was out teaching the people, some of the women and I remained there at the house with her. Leah fell sick."

Though she had not spoken again, Mary was still listening, so Joanna continued.

"We guessed that Leah did not feel her best that day as her tongue was especially sharp. But we suspected nothing like the fever that gripped her. All at once she took to her mat, and her brow was fire under my hand. Truly I feared that she would be dead before Jesus returned."

Joanna shivered at the memory. "Though she was moaning and helpless, she was alive when the Master came back. I was ready immediately to tell Him, but some of the other women held back.

"'She has hardly been even cordial to Him,' they said. 'He may not want to heal her.'

"'We cannot just let her die,' I told them. 'Besides, her son-in-law is one of Jesus' closest followers. Perhaps He will do it for Simon's sake.'

"So I approached Him and was a bit surprised to see Him hurry to her mat. I was even more surprised to see the love for her written so plainly on His face. Even with the way she had treated Him, the Master cared about her, and not just because of Simon. Mary, are you listening? He merely touched her hand, and the fever was gone!"

The younger woman did not speak, but she was obviously concentrating on what Joanna was telling her.

"Would you believe that Leah got up immediately, and the next thing I knew, she was carrying out trays of fruit to the Master and His followers? But Mary, the change was more than just the fever. Leah has become the picture of warmth and hospitality. She is a different person! That's why you too must go to Jesus. If Leah could be thus transformed, so can you!"

At this, Mary hung her head, and Joanna saw tears drip down onto her robe.

Compassion for Mary filled Joanna's heart, and she reached over to embrace her. "I know you met Jesus before, and you must have been disappointed that He did not help you then. I was, and I still don't understand why. But you must give Him another chance. Mary, you have no other choice! You know that."

Mary moaned as the tears continued to make damp splotches on the robe.

"Leah is not the only one who has been healed. Why, just before we went to the Holy City for Passover last month, some men brought a paralytic to the Master. But when they reached Simon's house, it was packed to overflowing with those who wanted to hear His teachings. They ended up having to take the sick man on his mat up to the roof. Then they lowered him down through a hole right to Jesus' feet. At the Master's word, the paralytic rolled up his bed and carried it home himself! And Mary, there have been countless other people who have also been healed. Jesus can help you too. Please tell me that you will come see Him again."

Though she kept quiet, the sobs that had shaken Mary's thin body ceased. She tried to think about what her friend was saying, but her mind had not been clear for so long that she found it difficult to make it focus on one thing. Yet in the mist that shrouded her consciousness, one name echoed: *Jesus, Jesus, Jesus.*

"Mary, will you go with me to see the Master?" Joanna was asking. "Will you go?"

"I will go," Mary said clearly.

Tabitha walked slowly back from the well. True, the full water pitcher was heavy, and at her age, she did not have the quickness of step she had had in her younger days, but she purposely retarded her steps even more. She wanted to give Joanna plenty of time to convince Mary to go with her.

Perhaps I am foolish to trust her, the old servant thought. I do not really know her, and I am disobeying my lord Eli's orders. But this may be the last chance my lady has to recover. And if seeing this Jesus does cure her, I will not mind the beating I will surely get for allowing her to escape.

At last Tabitha reached the familiar courtyard. As she had hoped, it was deserted. Smiling, Tabitha put down the water pitcher and the leather bucket and went over to the loom where she was weaving her mistress a new robe. She would wait until the morning to tell Eli of Mary's disappearance.

As Mary and Joanna neared Capernaum, the voices increased the intensity of their shrieks in Mary's ears. They shrilled accusations and obscenities at her like the rotten fruit that was pelted at wild dogs to chase them away.

Though Joanna could not hear them, she was aware of what was happening. She kept a gentle but firm hand on the younger woman's arm as they walked. This time, Mary must get the help from Jesus that she needed. *And I am not leaving her until she is made well,* Joanna promised herself. *I will not let her run away like before.*

She did not have to worry. The voices were determined to stop Mary, but from deep within her, an equally strong conviction had risen up. *Jesus can help me,* Mary kept thinking in her phases of coherency. *I will beg Him for His help. He will be merciful to me.* So in spite of the voices, she continued to walk.

Sometimes Mary's mind emptied, and she was unaware of the glimmering sea to their right, the bright hues of the spring hyacinths and anemones, the delicate blossoms on the flowering trees, or the vivid green of the grass. An almost trancelike state enveloped her.

Other times during the journey, distorted memories crowded in on Mary. She saw two children running along the beach, a tiny girl with long hair the color of ripe dates and a boy not much bigger. Laughing, they fell into the arms of a stocky man with a small scar on his cheek. She could smell the scent of fish on the man, taste the salt in the kiss he planted on the girl's forehead, and hear the low murmur of their voices, voices of contentment and caring for each other. But she could not recall who they were.

Then the picture at the beach faded as the demoniac voices returned full force to assault her. The recollections they brought were horrifying—the man from the beach drenched and silent, the children crying, and a grinding stone turning relentlessly, crushing her hopes into dust.

Nevertheless, Mary kept on pushing her feet in front of each other. Sensing her determination, the voices would occasionally recede to low mutterings, only to return to their attack all too quickly.

The next time the voices relented, Mary had another memory. This one she knew involved herself walking the same path to Capernaum. But she could hear her thoughts from that forgotten trip the previous year: *I am well now. I do not need this Jesus. I will soon return to my children. How surprised they will be to see me standing at the courtyard gate, healthy and ready to care for Joshua and Kezia again.*

"No," Mary whispered. "No, those were lies."

At her words, Joanna anxiously turned her face towards the younger woman. It was the first thing she had said since they had left the courtyard. She tightened her grip on Mary's arm. Her companion was not going to back off now from Jesus and the help He could give her, was she? Joanna would not let her.

But the distraught figure beside her said no more. Gradually Joanna relaxed a little.

Mary did not. Inside of her, the voices had softened and were telling her that she was again nearly whole. That the Rabbi would not have to do anything. That they were leaving.

But Mary knew this time that the voices did not speak the truth. *I must have Jesus' help,* she told them silently. *You cannot deceive me again. I will get better, but it will be by the Nazarene's touch.*

"Today we do not have to ask a fisherman for directions as to where the Master is," Joanna said, though she was not certain Mary had any memory of the last journey the two of them had made together. "Look, see the crowd over there by the water's edge? Surely that is Him teaching the people. He is so popular now that sometimes He gets into a boat to speak. More can hear that way." She steered her charge in the direction of the mob.

As she had done for the entire walk to Capernaum, Mary let

herself be led where Joanna wanted. They moved off the road onto the beach, and the sand, hot from the afternoon sun, worked its way between her feet and sandals.

". . . not everyone who says to me, 'Lord, Lord,' shall enter the kingdom of heaven, but he who does the will of my Father . . ."

At the sound of the strong masculine voice, a shudder shook Mary's body. Joanna felt it and quickened her steps.

". . . many will say to me in that day, 'Lord, haven't we prophesied in Your name? Haven't we cast out demons?'"

The word that identified them sent the voices inside Mary into a frenzy. Screaming, they bombarded her with such noise that she was aware of nothing else. Though the two women stood on the outskirts of the crowd, no one turned to stare at the Magdalene. Only Mary could hear the battle that raged within her.

". . . then I will say to them, I never knew you. Depart from me, you who work iniquity. Whosoever hears these words of mine and does them, he is like a wise man who builds his house upon the rock . . ."

As Jesus' words continued, the voices began striking at Mary with blows that felt as real as if Joanna had wielded them. Groaning in pain, the object of their rage sank to the sand.

"Mary! Mary! What is it?" Joanna cried, suddenly realizing that her companion was in agony. But she could not answer.

The older woman peered around in desperation, praying that one of the disciples she knew was near enough to assist her. Yet she saw no one. "Oh, Merciful One, help me!" she silently called out to her God.

Almost instantly, Simon appeared beside her, and she realized that Jesus had finished speaking and the crowd was breaking up.

"Joanna, what is it?" he asked, and then noticed the writhing woman at her feet. "We must get her to the Master."

But as Simon reached down for her, Mary suddenly sprung to her feet with a supernatural strength. Before the big fisherman could grab her, she darted off down the beach.

"Stop her!" Joanna screamed, and Simon took off after the crazed woman whose feet barely touched the sand as she ran.

Never had the voices been so loud in Mary's ears as they continued raining down blows inside of her. She had no control over her body already bruised and battered by the powers which tormented her. She would run forever . . .

But her foot caught on an abandoned net, and when she fell, Simon was able to catch up with her. Though he was muscular, he could not hold Mary as she struggled to get up.

"Release her, Simon," a voice said behind him, and the big man turned to see the Master. At the sight of Him, the woman ceased fighting and went limp. Simon let her arms go and rose.

"Jesus, . . ." Mary panted, weak from the wild run down the beach. Sand cascaded through her long hair as she lifted her head in His direction. Her eyes were only half open, her face streaked with perspiration.

"Come out of her," the Rabbi said, and though His voice was not loud, there was no mistaking the authority it conveyed.

The roaring in her ears was so loud that she could not hear His words, but she knew what He was saying.

"No, no, no!" an unnatural voice screamed. Horrified by the eerie sound, Mary did not realize at first that the words came from her own mouth. But the voice was not hers—it was low and gutteral—and it sent chills down her back.

The others felt it too. She saw even Simon take a step back away from her.

But Jesus was not intimidated. "Out!" He said.

This time there was no argument. Immediately, Mary's body began to heave, again and again. The force of it shook her entire body.

Although it was happening to her, Mary felt like she was merely an observer to the whole situation. She could not understand how that could be, but in some way, she was detached from it. It was as if she were only watching the great power which was causing her body to react so violently, waiting with the rest of the people to see what would occur next.

Finally the heaving gave way to coughing. It was so strong that Mary could barely breathe, but it lasted only a brief time. All at once, it stopped, and at that exact instant, Mary felt a release as the demons departed.

The difference was staggering. She looked around her to see vivid colors, the bright blue of the sea, the rich brown of Simon's robe, and the brilliant green of the grass on the hillside nearest the beach. Everything seemed clean and fresh and new. Mary laughed out loud, joy bubbling up inside of her.

"Get up, Mary," Jesus said, extending a hand to her.

"Yes, Master," she answered softly. As she stood before Him, the silence around her bathed her with more joy. The voices were gone! She glanced at the people near her, Joanna, her face wet with tears of relief; Simon, grinning broadly; others she did not know, looking equally happy. And Jesus, in front of her, His eyes gentle.

"My Lord!" Mary murmured, and bowed before Him, her tears dripping onto the sand.

7

"But I too want to follow Jesus!" Mary told her again.

Joanna only shook her head. "Be reasonable, girl! You cannot!"

Sitting up on the mat where she had spent her first truly restful night in years, Mary brushed the hair out of her eyes. "Why? The Master has set me free from the voices. I long to serve Him now."

Joanna continued to recline on the mat she had spread next to her friend's. "You don't understand. To follow Him you must have a call. It isn't enough to just desire to be with Jesus out of gratitude for what He's done for you."

"I have such a call," Mary persisted. "My whole heart yearns to be with Him. I know this is the only thing for me to do."

"But life on the road is not easy. You are used to living in a grand house, with servants to do the work. Out here, we all are equal. The women from well-to-do backgrounds cook and wash just as do the ones who have come from a life of poverty."

The younger woman nodded emphatically. "I know. I am willing to do these things along with everyone else."

"But have you the physical stamina? Be realistic! You have done little but sit for the past year," Joanna told her.

"Already my strength is returning. And I am young. Somehow I will be able to do what must be done."

Joanna sighed. Mary's arguments were persuasive, and she had to admit she would enjoy her friend's company on their travels with the Nazarene.

"So, you do see my side, don't you?" Mary said, a smile playing at the corner of her lips. "You really would like me to come!"

Joanna reached over to give her a hug. "Of course I would! But I'm not sure it would be best for you . . ."

"Yet you won't protest if I ask the Master, and He permits me to join His followers?"

Joanna smiled. "Certainly not. He will know the right thing to do."

Suddenly Leah strode into the room. "I am serving the mid-morning meal in the courtyard now. Would you two care to eat now?" she invited warmly.

Realizing that she was actually hungry, Mary immediately jumped up. Again she marveled at the change in Simon's mother-in-law. Just as Joanna had said, Leah had been healed of more than the fever.

As the two women folded up their mats, Leah lingered in the doorway. "Mary, as I was coming in, I could not help but overhear what you said just now. It is certainly admirable that you want to follow Jesus. But don't you have a son and a daughter?"

The mat in its place in the corner, Mary straightened up. "Why, yes, but I plan to take them with me. They, too, will love the Master, and surely they would enjoy the travel, the excitement . . ."

"No children come with Jesus," Leah said softly.

"What about Joshua's schooling? Do you think your in-laws would allow such a thing?" Joanna asked.

Her hunger forgotten, Mary stood perfectly still in the middle of the room. They were right. Living on the road was no place for youngsters, especially ones like hers, used to servants and whatever they wanted. How could she have thought otherwise?

"I'm sorry," Leah murmured, breaking the awkward silence that stretched across the room. "I did not mean to . . ."

"It's all right," Mary assured her, and she and Joanna followed Leah out into the courtyard. "I will be leaving for Magdala after our meal," she whispered to Joanna.

Joanna did not realize how much she had looked forward to Mary joining them until she saw the younger woman walking out of the gate into the street. Several others were also going south, and Mary would not have to travel alone. Joanna felt a little better knowing that.

But already she missed the Magdalene. Perhaps part of it was that having only sons, Joanna had always longed for a daughter, and in Mary, she sensed an outlet for her motherly instincts. In addition, since the Rabbi had cured her, Mary had displayed a sweetness of spirit that drew Joanna. She had guessed that her friend would be totally committed to the Master, and she even felt that somehow Mary would be significant in her service to Him.

But I must have been mistaken, Joanna told herself as Mary's figure became smaller and smaller. A tear wound its way down her cheek.

Suddenly an arm went around her shoulder, and Jesus stood next to her. "She will be back," He told her quietly. Joanna hoped He was right.

"Mary! Why, Mary!" Shock spread across Ruth's face. "Come in, child. You look . . . well, wonderful! What has happened to you?"

"I am whole again," Mary began as her mother-in-law pulled her inside the gate and motioned for Merab to fetch Eli.

"You know we had no idea where you had gone. When Tabitha

told us you had disappeared again, we were certain it would mean your death," Ruth told her, her relief at seeing Mary turning to irritation.

"I'm sorry for any concern I caused you," Mary said quietly as Eli ran out of his sleeping room.

"Mary, Mary, I thought we had lost you too!" the old man cried, and she was touched to see tears fill his eyes. She returned his warm embrace.

"Father, I have been cured. I went to Jesus of Nazareth . . ."

"Yes, yes," he interrupted. "We will have plenty of time to hear all about it later. For now, it is enough that you are here. Merab, food for your returning mistress. Come, come, Mary. Sit here in the cool corner of the courtyard."

Obediently Mary let herself be ushered to the place of honor usually reserved for guests. Why had she worried about how Eli would respond to her? Could he be any warmer, any more compassionate?

As the servant handed her a cup of wine, Mary looked around for signs of the children. Especially on the way back to her hometown, she had realized how much she missed Kezia and Joshua. Now she could hardly wait to see them.

"You seek the children, of course," Eli said, noticing her darting eyes. "They are not here now. Joshua is at synagogue school, and Kezia is at the market with Tabitha."

Mary nodded. Well, perhaps it was better this way. She could talk with her father-in-law undisturbed.

But every time she tried to explain what had happened to her, he changed the subject.

What is wrong? Mary thought. *He does not seem to want to find out where I have been or what I have been doing.* At last she gave up trying. *Perhaps he needs to first see that I am well. After living here with him for a few days, I will have shown him. Then I can talk about Jesus with him.*

Outside the courtyard gate, giggles floated into where Mary sat, and she rose quickly. Kezia! Little Kezia was home!

The gate swung open, and in danced the child, pulling on Tabitha's arm. "Grandmother, where are you?" she called. "We saw a beautiful piece of shiny cloth at the market. I must have a new robe from it . . ."

"Kezia," Mary said softly, moving toward the girl.

". . . Tabitha said she would not get it unless you said it was all right," the child continued, having seen Ruth in the corner of the courtyard. "Is it, Grandmother? Please say that it is."

"Kezia!" Mary called, a little louder.

Reluctantly, Kezia faced her mother.

When was the last time I saw her? Mary asked herself. *She looks so much older!* Her hair was still long and thick, but the baby face had matured to that of a girl. Unable to hold off any longer, Mary ran the last few steps to her daughter and flung her arms around her.

"See, Kezia, your mother has returned," Eli said weakly as he came up from behind them.

The child remained stiff and silent in Mary's arms. Gently the mother released the girl. It had been a long time since Kezia had seen her and longer still since Mary had been a real mother to the girl. How could she expect her daughter to respond normally to her?

Ruth awkwardly cleared her throat. "Come, child, you can talk to your mother later. Now it is time to help Tabitha put away the food from the market."

"Why? I never do that," Kezia began, but after thinking about it, she meekly followed the servant.

"She is only a child," Eli told Mary gently. "You cannot expect . . ."

"I know," Mary said quickly. "Please don't worry. I won't force myself on her."

Eli nodded and turned away.

It will take a while to undo all the damage I have inflicted on her, Mary thought. *But I will do it if I accomplish nothing else in my lifetime.*

The reunion with Joshua was much less strained than Mary's meeting with her daughter. When he returned from school and noticed his mother sitting in the courtyard, he immediately went to her.

"Mother?" he asked hesitantly, not knowing what to expect.

"Joshua!" Mary cried, and at the sound of her voice, the boy dashed into her arms.

"Mother, are you well again? You look like you used to."

"Yes, my beloved, I am cured, and I have come home to you. How I have missed you!" She gave him another hug.

"Truly, Mother? You do not hear anything?"

"The voices are gone, and they will never come back. Have you heard of Jesus of Nazareth?"

The boy nodded impatiently. "Of course! We talk about Him in school sometimes. Besides, I was at that wedding in Cana when He turned the water into wine."

Obviously that had given Joshua some manner of importance in the eyes of his peers, Mary realized. She looked at her son again, studying each feature. *How he looks like Ara,* she thought. Though he was still slim, and his hair darker than his father's was, he had the features and even some of the mannerisms of Ara, more so than he did even a few years ago.

"Have you seen Jesus, Mother?" Joshua was asking.

"Yes, yes, that is what I want to tell you about. He was the one who healed me!"

Joshua's eyes grew huge. "How did He do that?"

"Joshua! Joshua! Come here!" Eli called.

The boy gave Mary an agonized look.

"Obey your grandfather," Mary told him, trying to smile. "We will have many other times to talk about the Rabbi."

"But . . ."

"Joshua!" Eli's voice was stern.

"Go now," Mary urged. "Do not anger him."

Reluctantly Joshua left her.

In the two weeks since she had returned to Magdala, Mary had not seen the sea so restless. While she hurried along beside it, it cast up jagged blue fingers from its depths, as if it was reaching for her.

Maybe it is foolish to go back to where I suffered so much, she told herself. She knew, however, that at some point she had to return to the small house she and Tabitha had shared in the height of her illness. She had realized that for over a week now, but only today had she finally felt she could do it.

Arriving at the deserted courtyard gate, Mary pulled the key out of the sash at her waist. She had convinced Tabitha to give it to her last week, though at that time she was not sure when she would be able to go to the house.

Swinging open the gate, she stepped inside. Everything looked normal enough, dusty perhaps, for no one had been here for a month. But nothing unusual.

What did you expect? she asked herself. *It is just a house.* Yet within herself, she knew what she had feared to find inside these walls: the voices! Somehow she felt she had to come back here to be certain that her healing would last. If the voices that had tormented her did not bother her at the place where they had had the most power over her, she would be certain that never again could they harm her.

She listened. All was silent except for the water violently washing up on the sand outside. Briskly Mary moved into the sleeping room the servant and she had shared. Everything remained as it must have been when they lived there, though she could not say she remembered much.

The mats stood in the corner of the raised platform to the back of the room. The lamp still sat on its stand, olive oil filling it, though the flame had been put out. The clothes chest held several of Mary's robes, but Tabitha had removed her own.

Quickly the woman began packing up the household items. *I will never live here again,* she thought. *We can move out these things and sell the house.*

Of course, now that she was well again, she did have the future to consider. Living with Eli and Ruth was satisfactory for the present, but she could not conceive of remaining there on a long-term basis. For one thing, her father-in-law remained indifferent to her attempts to explain her healing or what Jesus meant to her. He even seemed to block her chances to talk privately to Joshua about the Nazarene. Surely by now, Eli could see that Mary was back to her old self. In fact, she was better than what she had been before Ara's death, for she had a song in her heart that had never been there before. Yet Eli clearly did not want to talk about Jesus.

His reluctance to hear about the most important thing in her life made Mary uncomfortable enough to want to leave his home. Of course, her first choice would be to go to the Nazarene and follow Him. But she suspected that would result in estrangement from Eli. And she had no money with which to support herself on the road.

Naturally, the usual way a widow left her parents' or in-laws' house was to remarry, Mary knew. But at this point, that still seemed distasteful to her. She carried some bowls over to the clothes chest and tucked them inside.

Not that she never thought of marriage. During the past few weeks, she had to admit that she had yearned for a man's touch more than she had expected. But in spite of it, she could not help feeling that taking another husband was somehow disloyal to Ara.

The problem was that if she wanted to leave Eli's home, and did not remarry, there were really no other respectable options. It occurred to Mary that living here in this small house with the children might be what she wanted, but she knew her in-laws would never agree. It was one thing for a mentally ill woman to live alone with only a servant, but it was quite another for one who was perfectly well.

Sighing, Mary took the broom from the corner of the room and began sweeping the floor. What should she do? There seemed to be no answer.

At least Kezia was warming to her. She still came to her grandmother with her childish wants, but she had responded to Mary's hug several days ago. And no longer did the little girl go the opposite direction when her mother appeared. She had even sat quietly beside her the previous evening as they rested in the courtyard after the evening meal.

A noise from the courtyard startled her, and Mary peeked out of the doorway of the sleeping room.

A man stood at the gate, his back toward her. She could tell at once that he was a fisherman. His sheepskin hung over his broad shoulders, his brown tunic was girded up to his knees in the way of working men, and his hair was still damp with the spray of the sea, from which he had obviously just returned.

Mary gasped. Ara! It was her husband! *He didn't really die,* she thought, half fearful and half longing to run into his arms. *Ara has come home to me!*

8

Could it really be Ara? Mary took a step closer to the man by the courtyard gate. He still did not seem to be aware of her presence, and she studied his back. Wasn't Ara taller than that? But she was across the courtyard from him, and maybe he would look shorter at a distance. The shape of his head did not appear to be quite what she remembered.

Let it be him, she thought desperately. *Tell me it was not my husband we buried in that cave.* The breath in her throat threatened to choke Mary as she stood suspended between hope and despair.

Though she remained motionless and silent, the man suddenly swung around to face her. He was not Ara.

"Shalom," he greeted her, and Mary stammered a reply. How could she have actually believed that her husband had returned? How foolish! *No one comes back from the dead . . .*

"I beg your pardon for disturbing your work here," the man was telling her. "But I had to talk to you."

At Mary's blank expression, color crept up his ears. "Don't you know me? I am Jedidiah."

"Of course. Forgive me. It's just that it's been so long since I've seen you . . ." Mary murmured, embarrassed that she had not recognized the first man that Ara had hired to help in the business.

He glanced out the courtyard gate nervously. "It's not proper for me to be here alone with you"—at this his ears became even more red—"but I had to see you by yourself."

Mary nodded at him encouragingly, and he continued.

"I don't know how to tell you this, but when I worked for Ara, the last year I mean, he trusted me to start selling loads of fish for him."

"I remember. He had great faith in you."

At the compliment, Jedidiah looked all the more miserable. "His faith was not well placed. What I mean to say, is, ah, I did not give him all the money I received for the catch." The man stared at his hands. "Sometimes I told him I had received a certain amount when actually I had more. I explained the lower price away: 'The merchant had just purchased a load from another fisherman.' Or, 'Some of the fish underneath were spoiled, so he gave me less.' Ara always believed me."

For once Mary was glad her husband was not present. His anger would have been unappeasable. But at this point, she did not particularly care about Jedidiah's dishonesty.

"What do you want from me?" she asked.

Stepping closer, the man reached inside his sash and withdrew a money bag stuffed with coins. "I wish to return to you what I took that was not mine." He put the bag into her hands. The weight of it was such that she almost dropped it.

"But, why me? This should go to my father-in-law."

"I know, but for a reason I cannot explain, I felt you personally should have it."

"I have no need . . ." Mary began, but suddenly she thought about Jesus. Why, the money could help support the Rabbi and His followers. Her protest died on her lips.

"Thank you for taking it," Jedidiah told her. "I have been

haunted by what I did for a long time. Recently I knew I had to make things right."

"Oh? What brought about this change of heart?"

"Well, I heard a Rabbi from Nazareth speak . . ."

"Was His name Jesus? The one who travels all around these parts and does miracles?"

He nodded.

"Then I understand, for I too have been changed by Him."

"I have heard of it. Most of Magdala knew of your sickness, and when you came back, well again, I knew it was then time for me to give you the money." Jedidiah looked embarrassed again, but he did not turn to leave.

"What is it, Jedidiah? Have you something else to confess to me?" Mary asked him lightly. How refreshing it was to meet someone who did not doubt her experience with Jesus.

"It is only that I find you very attractive," he said. "The last time I saw you was at the funeral, and then . . ."

Quickly Mary turned from him, not wanting to hear such things from the lips of any man. "Ah, yes, the funeral. It was a long time ago."

Silence stretched between them, and Jedidiah awkwardly licked his lips.

"Well, shalom," he said abruptly and started toward the gate.

"Thank you again for the money," she called after him. "I am certain the Mighty One will bless you for your honesty."

He nodded and was gone.

Fighting the urge to go after him, Mary returned to the sweeping. But what would I say to him? she chided herself. That I also find him attractive? That we have a common bond in our interest in the Nazarene? That I was wondering if he was looking for a wife?

Yet in her heart, she knew she was not interested in Jedidiah as a husband. *Perhaps it is because he reminds me of Ara, with the smell of the fish, and his appearance being so much like Ara's,* she thought. But whatever the reason, she determined to ignore those thoughts.

Sitting on the low stool in her sleeping room, Mary drew the comb through her hair again. While the gray which had mingled with her natural brown color after Ara's death remained, her hair had regained the shine and body it had before.

Actually, I look better than I did two years ago when I was a married woman, she thought, looking at herself in the bronze looking glass. The weight she had lost in her mourning had come back, and instead of being rimmed by dark circles, her eyes had a certain sparkle that had only come since her deliverance from the voices. Even Joshua had commented on her appearance lately.

But that beauty is part of the problem, Mary reflected. Jedidiah had already come to Eli requesting a betrothal, and Ezra, a carpenter, had asked about the same time.

When Eli had approached Mary about the two offers, he had been more than reasonable. "Of course, Ezra would provide for you better, but Jedidiah is also a good man. Whichever you think you would be most content with, you may marry."

"But, Father, I am not ready to become a wife again. Not yet. Please give me a little more time."

"Mary, you have been widowed for almost two years now. It isn't good for you to be alone for so long. You should be married. You should be having more babies."

"I know. But I desire another springtime by myself. I beg you, don't force me to make this choice."

Eli had sighed. "You know as well as I that I cannot make you take a husband, Mary. I can only suggest, and I feel you should marry one of these men. They won't wait forever. They will select other women, and perhaps you will have to pick someone not as good." The old man laid a gentle hand on Mary's arm. "Promise me that you will at least think on it."

Mary had nodded, but inside, she rebelled against the idea of taking either Jedidiah or Ezra as husband. *It's not the men themselves,* she thought. *Neither seem unkind or unappealing to me. It's just that I'm not ready.*

But how long can I hold out against the pressure Eli and Ruth give me? she asked herself, as she tried to get the comb to go through a tangle. *What can I do?*

As soon as she asked the question, the answer came: *Go and follow Jesus.*

With the comb in midair, Mary froze. Well, why not? She could not stay here much longer. And her heart was really with Him anyway. She now had money, the bag the fisherman had returned to her last week. In addition, just the previous day Tabitha had given her the coins she had buried in the floor of the little house by the sea.

"Your father-in-law sent money faithfully when you were sick, but I never used all he gave us. I saved the extra. Here, take it. You may need it." The old servant wiped a tear from her eye. "You will not be staying here much longer."

Touched by Tabitha's honesty in not keeping the money for herself, Mary had not asked what Tabitha meant. Did she expect her mistress to accept one of the marriage proposals, or could she have other ideas of where Mary might go?

But now, with the coins she had, there was no reason to remain with Eli. Except for the children.

Since Mary had been home, she had been pleased to see Joshua and even Kezia get to know her again. In fact, she felt that their old relationship had been almost reestablished, but not quite. Something still hung between them, something Mary could not name. Most of the time it was not obvious, but every once in a while, Mary knew that everything was not right. It was as if they did not quite completely trust her yet.

Well, that will come, she told herself. In spite of Eli's obvious disapproval, Mary had been able to take Joshua aside and explain to him about Jesus and her new life. He had listened, awed, and she hoped to tell Kezia the same story soon.

She had just put away the comb when suddenly she heard Eli clearing his throat just outside the woven hangings that was over the doorway to her sleeping room.

"Father?" she called.

His voice stern, her father-in-law asked if he and Ruth might enter to speak with her. "It is a matter of gravest concern," he assured her, as if he expected her to refuse to listen to him.

"Of course. I always value your opinion. Come in." Rising from the room's one stool, she motioned for him to take it. *Now he is going to insist I choose Ezra or Jedidiah,* she thought. *What will I tell him?*

But Eli did not have Mary's marital state in mind. "I have decided that you are to move back into the house by the sea."

Mary stared at him. "But . . ."

"Don't argue," Ruth said quickly. "You must do what my lord thinks is best."

"I only wonder why."

Eli would not look at her. "I have your interests in mind. You were very ill, you know. It takes time to recover from such sickness."

"But as you can plainly see, I am well now." She could not understand what he was trying to say.

"So it seems in many ways. But there are still things that bother me. For example, your interest in this Nazarene. And your refusal to marry again, as any proper woman would want."

Shocked, Mary could not speak.

"Do not think that once you are back in the small house, you will be able to run off to do as you please. I will have you locked up until I am convinced you are completely healed." The old man licked his lips, and Mary felt compassion for him. He really did not like doing this to her, she could tell. But he sincerely thought it was the right thing to do.

"What will indicate to you that I am ready to return to society?" she asked quietly. "That I be willing to take a husband?"

"Perhaps. I do not know yet. But prepare to move in the morning."

"What of the children? I am certainly well enough to care for them now."

"Mary, it is difficult for me to tell you this, but I feel that for the sake of Joshua and Kezia, I must forbid you to see them."

"What?" Mary could not keep the shriek from her voice. "Not see them? Not ever?"

"No, no, of course not. Just until you have completely regained your health."

Tears stung her eyes. "Father, how can you do this to me? My heart will break from grief."

"I am sorry, truly. But it is best for all of us for things to be this way for a while. I must confess I do not feel you have been a good influence on the children. Filling Joshua's head with the doings and teachings of this Jesus . . ."

"I merely told him about what had happened to his mother! Surely at his age, he has a right to know that!"

Stubbornly Eli turned from her and started out the doorway, Ruth following him. "The decision has been made," he told her firmly.

After they left, Mary collapsed on the mat. *How can this be?* she asked again and again. *How can they do this? I will be a prisoner, and everything I have accomplished with the children will be lost. They will never trust me again.*

Soft footsteps approached, and Mary looked up to see Tabitha's sympathetic figure hovering over her.

"Did you hear what they are planning for me?" she asked the servant brokenly.

"Oh, yes, my lady. I do not understand it. Surely anyone can see you are restored, yes, even better than your old self."

"Tabitha, what am I to do?" Mary let the older woman drape her arms around her mistress as the tears left a wet path on her cheeks.

"Why, you must go to Jesus. That is what you wanted to do anyway, isn't it?"

"Yes. Yes, you're right. But I cannot leave my babies."

"Then bring them with you!"

Joanna and Leah's words about children traveling with the Master came back to her. *But surely the Rabbi will permit it under these circumstances,* Mary thought.

"Certainly my father-in-law will not object to my seeing Kezia and Joshua this evening to say good-bye to them before I move in the morning," Mary said.

The servant smiled at her. "But actually you will take them tonight and flee?"

Smiling back at Tabitha, Mary nodded. "If you help me. Perhaps get some food together for me, a few robes, that sort of thing."

"I will do anything for you, my lady. I only wish I were young enough to go with you." Guessing Mary's thoughts, Tabitha shook her head. "No, I cannot go. I will not leave Magdala now, and I have neither the strength nor the desire to live the kind of life you will have with the Rabbi."

"Are you certain?" Mary asked. "If you remain here, you may be beaten for allowing me to escape again."

Tabitha shrugged. "What happens, will. My place is here, just as yours is with the Nazarene."

9

As she had hoped, the courtyard was quiet and dark when Mary slipped from her sleeping room. Clutching the small cloth bag of food and clothing that Tabitha had packed, she tiptoed across the hard-packed dirt floor to the children's room.

Once inside, she was surprised to see Kezia stretched out on her mat. Joshua sat next to her, and neither child looked ready to leave.

"My dears, get up," she whispered. "We must go at once."

Both remained where they were, and Mary then noticed Tabitha huddled in the corner. "Haven't you explained to them what we must do?" she asked the servant. It was important that they get away before Eli or Ruth were aware of their plans. There was no time to linger, she thought, feeling a trace of irritation.

"I did, my lady, but . . ."

"We cannot go," Joshua finished for Tabitha.

"What do you mean?" Mary asked quickly. "If I stay here, I will be imprisoned. You will never see me. Don't you understand? We must leave now."

"Mother, we do not want to go with you."

"Sometimes we must do things we do not wish to do," Mary said briskly. She picked up one of her daughter's robes from the clothes chest and stuffed it into the bag. "Come, Kezia. Get up."

Obediently, the little girl rose, but Mary saw in the flickering lamplight that tears were rolling down her cheeks.

"What is it, darling?" She reached down to hug the child.

"I can't leave Grandfather and Grandmother. I do not want to live on the road with no house and nothing to eat. I will cry the whole time."

"Kezia, there is plenty to eat, and you will have many new friends to play with. It will be an adventure! You will forget your tears. And we will again see your grandparents. We'll just be apart a short time . . ."

Joshua stepped over next to her. "We know that you must go, Mother. But please do not force us to join you. Grandfather would never speak to us again if we deserted him. And what about school?"

"You would be taught by the great Rabbi Himself," Mary assured Joshua. *Why does the boy sound more like an old woman too set in her ways than a youth ready for a chance at new excitement?* "Your life will be better than here." She stretched out an arm to him while she continued to hold Kezia with the other.

Leaning against her, Joshua shook his head. "But . . . but although you are our mother, we really don't know you anymore."

So that was the real reason for their reluctance! Mary could not blame them; the past few months that she had been well could not have completely made up for all the time she was ill. Yet she had to keep trying. "But if you won't go with me, I, too, will have to stay. Don't you see? I can't begin the trip without you two," Mary told them.

"You must," Tabitha said, stepping forward. "You will be separated from them whatever you do, and how much better it will be to be with the Rabbi than imprisoned in the little house by the sea."

Mary shook her head. "If my children will not come, I also will remain in Magdala."

"My lady, think! You will be of no use to them if you stay. Please go on your way. You will be reunited some day."

Mary's tears dripped on Kezia's hair. "They need me now, while they are young."

"No, my lady. They have done without you for a long time. You will help them more if you go to Jesus. You can leave with the assurance that my lord Eli will give them the best of care. And I will devote myself to do for them as I have always done for you."

Reluctantly Mary stepped back away from the two small forms. Tabitha was right, of course. She would be separated from the children no matter what. It would not solve anything to stay in Eli's house, only to be moved to the little house in the morning. And if she forced Joshua and Kezia to go with her, they would either run away, back to Eli, or be so unhappy that she would not be able to stand it.

Mary gently placed a kiss on each of their foreheads. "Remember, my darlings, that I love you, that I will always love you. I leave tonight only because I have no other choice. But, someday, I will come back, and we will be a family again. Promise me that you will remember."

They both nodded solemnly, and Tabitha whispered, "I will not let them forget. But you must flee now. Morning is not far away."

Without thinking, Mary gave the servant a hug. Highly improper, she knew; however, no one but the children saw it, and Mary felt she had to show Tabitha that she considered her more than just a servant. "I entrust to you my most precious possessions," she said softly, motioning at the children. "Guard them well." Tabitha nodded.

Picking up the cloth bag, heavy with the coins in the bottom of it, Mary stepped out into the courtyard and was soon on the road. The night seemed very dark.

Bright sunlight in her eyes awakened Mary, and drowsily she stretched, unaware of where she was. But quickly she realized that she was not in Eli's house. No, she had spent her second night in the little house by the sea.

Where would they not think to look for me? she had asked herself when she had left her father-in-law's residence. It is not safe to travel all the way to Capernaum at night by myself. I must find a place to sleep and wait for daylight.

So Mary had made her way to the site of her confinement. *They know I do not want to return here,* she had told herself. *Eli will not look for his escaped daughter-in-law at the house at which he wants to again keep her.*

At first she had been a bit apprehensive about going inside. Could the voices possibly find her again? But after she had hesitantly made her way into the sleeping room and unrolled one of the mats which still remained in a corner, she had felt comfortable enough to sleep immediately.

Now, as she awoke, refreshed, she did not even think about all the torment she had experienced in this very room. Instead, excitement tingled throughout her body. Today was the day that she would join the group of Jesus' followers! Finally she would be where she wanted to be more than anywhere else. Even the fact that the children were not with her only hurt a little in light of her actually being with the Rabbi.

Soon she was making her way north to Capernaum on the familiar road which followed the sea. *Perhaps it would have been less risky to wait until dusk to leave,* Mary reflected. But she did not want to arrive at her destination in the darkness of night, even though she planned to go straight to the courtyard of Simon, the fisherman, where she knew Leah would admit her.

Besides, now that she had been gone since the night before last, maybe Eli had given up trying to find her. She suspected that as soon as he had realized she had disappeared, Eli had summoned some of the hired men to search for her.

Of course, he would not have known exactly where to look for her, and though he might have discovered Tabitha's involvement in helping her mistress, he would get no assistance from the old servant. Mary trusted Tabitha completely, but she had not told the woman her plans. It was safer if no one knew where she was going. Even a beating, which Mary prayed Eli would not resort to, could not make Tabitha reveal her mistress's location since she honestly did not know it.

Nevertheless, Mary's father-in-law would guess that she was bound for Capernaum. It was common knowledge that the unusual Rabbi from Nazareth had made the fishing town to the north His headquarters. Though Jesus still traveled all over Galilee, as well as to Jerusalem for the feasts, He always went back to Capernaum. And Eli surely would know that Mary would choose to follow Jesus above anything else.

But as Mary walked along, she could not dwell on gloomy thoughts. The road was nearly deserted, and the sea was gentle and full of sparkles. Somehow she knew she would make it to the Rabbi. How wonderful it would be to see Joanna again! She pictured the look of pleasant surprise on the older woman's broad, wrinkled face at the sight of her friend.

A man's song interrupted Mary's thoughts. She turned and saw a masculine form bent over a small flickering fire on the beach. The smell of fresh cooked fish made her stomach growl. Not knowing how long she would be on her own, she had rationed her food supply and was eating as little as possible.

The man was still unaware of her, and he continued his song, his deep voice barely hitting the high notes. Now Mary was close enough to hear the fish sizzling. How good it would taste . . .

The singing stopped abruptly, and she knew he had finally seen her. Her face averted from the man, Mary hurried on past him. Too many people in Magdala recognized her and could report her whereabouts to Eli.

"Mary, is it you? Mary?" the man called, and she realized with a sinking sensation that it was Jedidiah.

Perhaps if she pretended she did not hear and just kept going, he would think he had been wrong in assuming it was she. Still not looking in his direction, Mary continued walking.

The fisherman was not to be deceived. Leaving the food, he caught up with her in only a few strides. "Mary, I thought it was you. Didn't you hear me call?"

Giving him a weak smile, Mary shook her head. *If only he would go back to his fire . . .*

As if he heard her thoughts, Jedidiah motioned back toward it: "Would you share my meal with me? I have plenty of fish caught just last night."

Mary longingly pictured the flakey filets which had to be just about done. Her empty stomach growled again. But she had no time to stay here and eat with him. And what about if someone saw them? It would be thought that she had no morals, even if Jedidiah had asked Eli if he could marry her.

"Please, Mary, it won't take long. You look as if you have to go somewhere, but surely my good fish will sustain you as you walk."

Go somewhere? *He must not realize what I am doing,* she thought, trying not to panic. *Obviously he has not heard I am missing from my father-in-law's house, so he must think I am merely about everyday business.*

She forced a laugh. "Traveling? No, I only go . . . go to the dyer's up the road." She forced herself to think of some reason which would require her presence. "I . . . I wish to match my daughter's robe," she said, pulling it out of the top of her bag.

Even when Kezia had refused to come, Mary had brought the robe, as if somehow it being with her made the children close. "It is to be a surprise for the family. I want to have robes dyed the same color for all of the women." Even to her, the excuse sounded made up, but Jedidiah only nodded politely.

"A bit of fish then before you reach the dyer's?" he encouraged.

Perhaps she should accept. Then he would have no suspicions about what she was up to. She peered up and down the road. No one was in sight.

"Thank you, Jedidiah," she finally answered, giving him her most dazzling smile. "I am a little hungry. I was so anxious to take care of these robes before my family awoke that I have not eaten yet."

Jedidiah grinned at her but did not speak. When they reached the fire, the fish were indeed cooked to perfection, and the big man carefully took two of the largest pieces off the stones placed near the flames. Wrapping them in a leaf, he handed them to her.

"Why, thank you, Jedidiah, but my appetite is not that large," she protested; however, he would not take them back.

"Perhaps you can eat the rest of it by the time you reach Gennesaret."

Gennesaret? How did he know? "Why, as I told you, I am not going any great distance. Only to the dyer's." She hoped she sounded casual.

"Of course. Forgive my mistake." He winked at her as he stuffed some of the fish into his mouth.

He knows where I'm going, Mary thought. *But he doesn't seem to want to do anything to stop me. Why? Is he planning even now to tell Eli?*

"I must get started," Mary told him, backing away from him. "I do appreciate the fish."

He nodded. "And, Mary, remember that I will wait for you as long as it takes."

Color flooded her cheeks, and she turned from him quickly.

But Jedidiah was beside her before she reached the road. "Learn of Jesus and His ways. But when you are ready to again become a wife, I will be here. I only wish I had the courage to also follow the Rabbi."

Wordlessly, Mary hurried on, and Jedidiah let her go.

You are an unusual woman, Mary of Magdala, he thought. *It is all I can do to allow you to walk away from me. Old Eli would reward me handsomely if I were to return you to him. He would probably even force you to marry me.*

He remembered again how the old man had stammered a refusal when, for the second time, Jedidiah had asked to become betrothed to Mary. "She is not completely well, you see. That is not to say she will never marry you. I believe she thinks favorably of you. But she craves a little more time to recover more fully from her ordeal."

Naturally Jedidiah had been disappointed. When he had given her the money in the house by the sea, he had been certain he had seen something in her eyes. And he had responded. It was only by using every bit of his will power that he had been able to leave her there.

The only thing that had made going away from the little house possible was the assurance her expression gave him that she would consent to be his wife. But now she was leaving, and Jedidiah was sure she would not be back for a long time. Oh, she could lie all she wanted about the dyer's, but he knew Mary was going to follow Jesus.

Jedidiah had heard about her disappearance the day after it had happened. Not that Eli was informing the town about the loss of his daughter-in-law. On the contrary, Eli had merely told

Jedidiah that Mary had another one of her spells and had wandered off.

"If you happen to see her, bring her back, despite her protests. She is no longer herself. Blessed be the Mighty One that you did not yet marry her!" Eli had said.

But Jedidiah had overheard the servants talking and knew what had really happened. He did not blame Mary for leaving, although he had hoped to get to tell her of his love before she went. His prayer had been answered when he had seen her on the road. Now, as he put out the small fire that had cooked his meal, Jedidiah pictured again her smile, her hair, and the sparkle of her eyes. *Someday she will come back to me,* he told himself firmly.

10

The group of people gathered around the small fire in the dark courtyard was quiet. Occasionally a man leaned over and whispered with his neighbor, or Simon stood to put another stick into the flames. But Jesus remained motionless, His bowed head and arms resting on His bent knees.

"He is weary tonight," Joanna finally murmured to Mary. "It's no wonder, with all the excitement lately."

"What has happened? I've heard nothing."

Joanna stared at the younger woman. "Truly? You don't know about the widow's son in Nain? Or the centurion's servant?"

At the shake of Mary's head, her friend moved closer. "We were in Nain the day before last Sabbath when we passed a funeral going out the city gate as we were coming in. It was for a young man who had died after an illness, and his mother was devastated from the loss. We didn't know it at the time, but her husband had been killed in an accident only a few years ago, and this boy was her only son."

"You say he was dead? How could the Master help in that case?"

"Just wait until you hear! He must have been a well-loved young man, for it seemed like most of the people of Nain were part of the funeral procession. Jesus stopped as they went by, so, of course, we all stopped too. Then as the mother passed, tears sliding down her cheeks like beads on a string, she looked right at Jesus. Who knows what went through her mind? She reached out her hand to Him in a silent plea for mercy."

Several of the men near Mary were glaring in Joanna's direction, silently ordering her to be quiet, but she ignored them. "Suddenly the Master spoke just to her: 'Weep no more.' He told her. I wondered what He meant. Who wouldn't sob at a funeral? But Jesus was already moving over to the bier where the body lay. And, Mary, He reached out and touched it! He told the boy to rise."

Mary gasped, imagining the shock of the people in seeing this obvious breaking of the Law in touching something as unclean as a corpse's bier.

"Would you believe the young man sat up and began to talk? He was alive again!"

"Are you sure?" Mary said, forgetting to keep her voice down.

Joanna nodded emphatically. "Jesus took his hand and helped him off the bier. The men carrying it had almost dropped it in their surprise at seeing the body sit up. It gave them a scare, let me tell you! But then it was all I could do to keep from letting out a scream myself. Can you imagine? A corpse—suddenly a living man! Anyway, the Master led the youth over to his mother. I couldn't hear what was said, but she threw herself at his feet. You should have heard all the people! They were ecstatic! Everyone was praising the Powerful One for such a miracle!"

Mary sat in shocked silence. What kind of rabbi could do that? Healing a blind man or a paralytic was one thing, but giving life back to the dead? The whole thing was so incredible that she could hardly believe it. Her thoughts were interrupted by the voice of Jesus.

"Joanna, who do you have with you?" He asked suddenly, sitting up straight again.

"Why, you remember Mary, Master," Joanna answered. "Mary of Magdala."

"Of Magdala?" one of the men said skeptically, and Mary knew he thought of the number of Magdalene women who were paid for their services to men.

Mary stiffened. "Though my hometown has a reputation of immorality, not all from there live in that way," she responded tartly before she thought. Immediately, Mary regretted her words. She wanted to follow Jesus, and antagonizing His disciples was no way to go about it.

But the man said nothing more, and Jesus Himself ignored her comment. "Why do you want to join us, Mary?" He asked gently.

She felt her face flush and was thankful for the dim light the fire provided. At least no one would notice. But how was she to answer? She had not expected to be questioned by the Rabbi in front of the others.

Naturally she had not thought He would just let her join His followers. She had been prepared to speak to Him from her heart, to tell Him of the voices, to tell Him how grateful she was that He had healed her, to tell Him she longed to follow Him. She would have appealed to Him that she had no where else to go. But she had pictured it taking place with just her and the Master, not with this group of people, at least some of whom were already hostile to her.

Joanna nudged her, and Mary realized she had not yet responded to Jesus' question.

"Master, I wish to follow You, to . . . to serve You," she murmured.

"But, why?" the Rabbi persisted.

"I . . . I am whole again, and it is because of You, my Lord. You have made me well."

"She is worthy to be one of Your followers, Master," Joanna added quickly, "She will work hard."

"I will do anything for You," Mary told Him earnestly. She wished she could see His face better, to have some kind of indication of His response to her. What if He refused to let her stay? Where would she go? If she could only talk alone with Him, perhaps she could make Him understand how she felt.

"Anything, Mary?" Jesus was asking. Somehow she sensed pain in His voice.

Without thinking, she rose and ran to His side. "Oh, Master," she cried, kneeling next to Him. "I desire to serve You with my whole heart. I will do all You ask of me." Unexpectedly, the emotion of the past week—Eli's ultimatum, leaving the children, Jedidiah's confession of love, and coming to Jesus—all of it overwhelmed her. Her sobs echoed in the quiet courtyard. Yet above everything else was the assurance that following Him was worth it, and it no longer mattered that the others watched.

Jesus' voice was soft, but she heard each word He said: "And so you shall serve Me, precious Mary."

In the morning, Mary went with Joanna to the well to get water. If she was going to be permitted to follow the Master, she wanted Him to be convinced from the start that she would contribute to the group.

"Oh, you don't need to worry," Joanna reassured her. "Now that He's accepted you, you won't have to prove anything."

"I know, but just the same, I don't want to be thought of as idle, especially by some of the men."

Remembering the comment about Magdala the previous night, Joanna nodded. "I didn't see in the darkness who said that, but it sounded like Simon the Zealot. As you can see, he has little use for women." She shrugged good-naturedly. "But who else is going to put food in his stomach and clean clothes on his back?"

"Who but the hardworking women who follow the Master?" The masculine voice behind them made Mary jump, and she turned quickly to see one of the disciples.

"Have you met Matthew, Mary?" Joanna said. Her voice sounded normal enough, but something in her eyes told Mary that she did not quite trust this man.

"No, I have not," Mary murmured, noticing at once his handsome dark features. "Shalom, Matthew."

"We are blessed to have you join us," he replied.

Mary felt herself again blushing. "Thank you."

"We are going out on the sea today," Matthew told them. "I must make arrangements to hire a boat."

Mary smiled at him. "It's a perfect day to be on the water. When do we leave?" It had been a long time since she had been in a boat, but the rare times she had gone with Ara had been pleasurable. It would be good to feel the wind against her face as they floated over the waves.

Matthew cleared his throat. "Well, ah, the Master said we are to go as soon as I can get things worked out. But . . ."

Joanna gently interrupted. "The women do not go on such trips. We must stay and prepare the day's meals."

Mary turned to her friend in surprise. "But how do we learn of His teachings if we do not go where He is? How can we witness the miracles He does?"

Embarrassed, Matthew fumbled with the small coin bag hanging from the band of cloth around his waist. "Excuse me, but I will be expected back soon. I must be off on my errand." With a nod to the women, he hurried on before them.

"I'm sorry," Joanna said, as soon as he was out of earshot. "I thought you understood. Our purpose is to care for the men's food and clothing, that sort of thing. Often we do miss the teachings and the healings. But it's worth it to me, just to be of use to the Master."

"But don't you long to understand more of what Jesus says? How can you sit and grind grain, knowing that just over the hill the Rabbi speaks of truth?"

Joanna did not look at her. "Someone must grind, or He would not speak at all."

"Forgive me, Joanna," Mary said quickly. "Of course, you are right. I know it is a great honor that the Master has accepted me to follow Him, and I will gladly cook or mend or do whatever is necessary."

They had reached the well, and Joanna moved up next to the last woman in line. "Perhaps there will be times when the work is done and you—ah, we—can sit and hear the Master."

Mary handed her the leather bucket that would be lowered into the water to fill the pitchers. "I hope so, but if not, I will be satisfied anyway."

"Perhaps the women have been satisfied with too little for too long," Joanna said softly, stepping up in line.

Mary did not hear her, but she soon realized that Joanna had talked with Leah and the other women, as well as perhaps to Jesus Himself. The result was that Mary and the others found they were having more opportunities to sit behind the men and hear the same words of new life. Joanna, who as the eldest woman, appeared to be in charge of them, began to send several of them over to the Master when He taught.

"Mary and Susanna," she would say, "go with the men today."

They would hurry to catch up with the disciples, thankful that the other women would take care of the food and other chores. It meant the ones left had to work harder to get everything done, but there were no complaints. Even Joanna occasionally let herself listen and learn from the Rabbi, which was a change, Mary heard. Jesus seemed to welcome the women's presence, always smiling at them as if He was glad they wanted to hear. The other men did not acknowledge them, but they did not object either.

A week after Mary had joined the group, they were still in Capernaum. As the days passed, she felt more and more at home with the Master, His followers, and the life-style they embraced. The crowd of people in the courtyard that had intimidated her when she had wanted to tell Jesus of her desire to be with Him had now turned into individuals.

There were a number of fishermen in the group, John and James, and Simon and Andrew, and being so familiar with their occupation, Mary felt comfortable with them. Philip and Bartholomew, Thomas, another James, and Thaddaeus, all were known to her now. In spite of his first reference to the prostitutes of Magdala, Simon the Zealot had not been unkind, and Judas Iscariot, the man who handled the money for the group, was more than polite to her.

Then, of course, there was Matthew. The day after she had met him, Mary remembered the bag of coins she had brought. Since Matthew had a money bag and had gone to hire the boat, she assumed he was the one to whom her money should go.

She had approached him after the noon meal. "Excuse me, my lord," she had began, noticing again his thick dark beard and hair the color of basalt, the black volcanic rock that surrounded Capernaum, Magdala, and much of the area around the sea.

Matthew looked up at her; she saw his even white teeth and his kind smile. "No one here but the Master is your lord, Mary."

"Yes, of course. But it is you to whom I wish to speak."

At that Matthew rose and motioned her to a corner of the courtyard, away from the others. As she followed him there, Mary was impressed with his powerfully built body. He was of medium height and weight, about her age, and the lack of a deep tan like the fishermen had indicated he had, until recently, worked at an inside job.

From the other women, Mary knew he had collected taxes, explaining Joanna's distrust of him. It was difficult to break with the preconceptions of the past, even for Joanna, and everyone knew tax collectors were betraying their homeland by working for the Romans. So hated were they that they could not testify in court, nor tithe their money to the Temple.

"Sit here," Matthew was telling her, giving her that warm smile again. Mary smiled back. She could not let Matthew's previous occupation bother her; it was plain the man had also had a life-changing experience with Jesus and was no longer the same man who had cheated whenever he had the chance.

"Now what can I do for you?" Matthew asked her.

Quickly pulling out the bag of coins, Mary explained to him her desire to give the money to him to help support the group of followers.

"I am not the one to give the offering to," he told her. "Judas handles the money."

"But you hired the boat that day . . ."

"Oh, yes, I did. No wonder you thought it was I to whom you should come. That was just for one day. With my background, I do sometimes help out with the funds, but the Master put Judas Iscariot in charge of the treasury. Why don't you talk to him?"

Mary almost blurted out that she would rather continue speaking to the one who sat with her, but she was able to control herself and merely agree. When she handed the money to Judas, he was pleased. Tall and dark, with a carefully trimmed beard, he immediately reached for her gift.

"The funds were getting low," he told her in his strong Judean accent. The only disciple from the southern part of the country, Judas would always find his voice standing out against the coarser Galilean speech of the rest of the disciples. "Chuza has not sent Joanna any funds lately, and your coins will be put to good use. Thank you for sharing them with the Master."

She nodded and returned to the other women, who were cleaning up the remains of the meal. But Mary's mind was not on Judas. Instead she was picturing Matthew's smile.

"Mary, did you hear me?" Joanna said, a trace of irritation in her voice.

Mary looked up at her. "Oh, were you speaking to me? I'm sorry. My thoughts were elsewhere."

"Obviously! I wanted to tell you what happened with the centurion's servant. Remember I mentioned him to you the night you joined us? But I never got to tell you the story."

"Yes, I would like to hear it," Mary replied, reluctantly drawing herself away from thinking about the former tax collector.

"Well, we had just entered Capernaum when, suddenly, this centurion approached us. It was apparent he was a worried man, and he told Jesus the problem at once. One of his servants was deathly ill, and the centurion wanted Jesus to help him."

Joanna scraped some leftover grapes into a basket. "At the time, I thought that he certainly must be a kind master to care so much for his servant. Jesus felt it too and said He would come and heal the servant. But the centurion immediately asked Him not to."

"Why? Hadn't he wanted to get such a response?"

"Yes, certainly! But the man, though a Gentile, was aware of our customs. After all, he had the synagogue built here in Capernaum. He knew for the Master to go in his home would mean great disapproval from the Jews. So the centurion said, 'I'm not worthy for You to come home with me. Just say so, and my servant will be healed.' He explained that he, too, was a man under authority. He had orders to obey, and those under him had their orders to follow."

"What did Jesus say?" Mary asked.

"He was impressed, believe me. He even said something about not finding such faith even among His own people! And, Mary, that servant recovered right then!"

Picking up the clean cups she had just finished washing, Mary rose to return them to their place. Surely the Rabbi from Nazareth was an unusual man.

11

"The Master told me that we leave for Nazareth tomorrow," Joanna announced as the disciples and Mary were walking out of the courtyard onto the road. Selected earlier in the day to go with the men, Mary, nevertheless, slowed at her friend's words.

"That means we have food to prepare for the trip, clothes to wash, and this house to clean," Joanna continued. "Since we have all shared Leah's hospitality for several weeks now, it's only fair that we should leave her home spotless."

The other women nodded in agreement and gathered around Joanna to divide up the necessary work.

Mary quietly slipped back to join them. She had known at once she could not sit at the Rabbi's feet while her companions had that much to do, but even so, disappointment washed over her.

Although she did not always understand everything Jesus said, listening to Him brought the greatest contentment she had ever experienced. Mary longed for the days when it was her turn to spend time soaking in what the Master said and did. But since today would not be just the usual chores, she surely had an obligation to help Joanna and the others.

"Mary, I thought you went with us today," Matthew said. He was the last of the disciples to leave, but he stopped when he noticed her heading back toward the other women.

Still unaccustomed to the freedom Jesus allowed His followers to talk to members of the opposite sex, Mary felt herself blushing. "Yes, but since we are traveling tomorrow, there is much to be done. I am staying here to help the others."

Matthew nodded approvingly. "How generous of you. I doubt if the other women would have thought to do so."

Mary lowered her eyes at the frank admiration in his face. He was wrong, of course; any of the others would have done the same thing. But she treasured him saying it.

"I must go," Matthew said, glancing in front of him. The rest of the disciples were already quite a way down the road. "But when we return, I'll tell you everything that happened."

She nodded and waved at him, then turned to Joanna. The older woman's welcoming smile told Mary that she had made the right choice about where to spend the day.

Jesus and the men had not yet returned by the time the women wearily unrolled the sleeping mats. "Just as well," Susanna mumbled, laying down beside Mary. "We got much more done with them gone all day."

Smiling at the girl, Mary nodded. Only recently had she begun to get to know the only other younger woman in the group. Susanna was only nineteen winters old, but she too had already been widowed. However, she had no difficulties in following the Master. Childless and with parents who were also believers in Jesus, Susanna had joined them shortly after Joanna had. Her mother, Naomi, also sometimes traveled with them, Mary had been told, although she had not yet met Naomi.

"May I ask you something? I mean, ah, perhaps it is too personal . . ." Susanna was saying. She was small and slim, but her face was blemished and her hair a pale brown. Mary suspected she might have trouble finding a second husband.

"Please, speak," Mary encouraged. She wanted to get to know Susanna better.

The younger woman bit her lip. "It's just that I wondered, ah, if you've thought about your husband lately. But you don't have to say." She suddenly got busy smoothing her mat down.

"I don't mind at all," Mary assured her quickly. She had hoped that at some point they would be able to discuss their common loss. "To answer your question, I guess I haven't. Since I became a part of the group, he hasn't been on my mind much." It was the children to whom her thoughts turned almost constantly.

"I remember Attai mostly at nighttime," Susanna confessed. "I . . . I miss him holding me." The girl sounded embarrassed to say it.

Mary reached over to touch her hand. "But it's only natural to feel that way. You would be abnormal if you did not long for him. I do too."

"Sometimes I want to have a man's arms around me so badly that I think of running up to one, Jesus, or . . . or one of the others, and just hugging him . . ." In the dim light, Mary saw Susanna blink back the tears. "But I would never do it," she added immediately.

"Of course not," Mary assured her. "But I know just what you mean."

"You do? You too want to remarry?"

"Well, perhaps some day. But not now. Following Jesus is what I want to do most. Don't you want to be here, Susanna?"

"Oh, yes," the girl said at once. "I do wish to be with the Master's friends. But . . . but I also long to have a husband. And a baby . . ."

"Have you spoken to your parents of this?" Mary asked gently. "Do you have someone in mind who pleases you?"

"Well . . ."

"Who is it, Susanna? Perhaps something can be worked out."

"I don't think so." Susanna turned her face away.

Suddenly Mary understood. "It's the Master Himself, isn't it?"

Susanna nodded miserably. "But please don't tell anyone. He just seems like the most wonderful man in the land."

"Maybe it is possible. Simon has a wife. Doesn't she travel with the group sometimes?"

"Yes, Hannah did before her sister had twins and needed her help. She has been in Cana since then, but she will probably rejoin us soon."

"See? It might work. Why not ask your father to speak to the Master? It couldn't hurt."

"Thank you, Mary," Susanna whispered. "Perhaps the Gracious One will answer my prayers. A woman could have no greater honor than to be wife to such a man as Jesus."

Susanna was still smiling when she fell asleep soon afterward.

Once again, Mary rolled over on her mat. It was useless; she simply could not sleep. Her talk with Susanna had been over for probably an hour, and Mary was certain the others had been dreaming before the two of them had ceased their conversation. But in spite of her weariness after all the day's work and the lateness of the night, sleep would not come.

Outside the courtyard, the wind had picked up, and Mary shivered a little as the raindrops started. Soon the light tapping on the roof had changed to pounding as the storm increased in intensity.

It was on a night like this that Ara died, Mary thought suddenly. Though it had been over two years before, she could still feel the dampness of the robe she had worn to rush across the courtyard to the children's room. She could taste the grapes they had eaten that night as they waited for the torrent to end, and she could see the devastation in Eli's eyes as he told her about the discovery of Ara's body.

No, I won't think of that now, Mary told herself sternly. *That is in the past. I am safe, I am with Jesus.*

But Jesus and the disciples were in a boat on the sea, she suddenly realized. The knowledge sent chills down her back. They, too, could drown if the water chose to claim more victims this night. "Oh Merciful One, guard over those who serve You," Mary whispered. "Don't let the nightmare of losing Ara be repeated tonight."

Slipping from the mat quietly, so as not to awaken the others, Mary tiptoed out the door into the central courtyard. There, large puddles had formed, and the olive and fig trees were twisting in wild contortions from the wind that reached into open space between the walls of the house. Even from where she stood under the overhang of the roof, Mary felt the icy fingers of the rain.

Where were the men? Had they landed the boat yet? Or perhaps Jesus somehow knew about the coming storm and planned to spend the night wherever they had been docked for the day. Mary had to find out.

Ignoring the wind which pressed her robe against her body and drew it out behind her, Mary ran around the cistern, past the loom and the cooking fire, and over to the smooth stone steps which led up to the flat roof. They were slippery, but she managed to climb them.

Naturally, the roof was deserted and nearly empty, except for the washing, laid out to dry that morning and forgotten. She considered folding it up and taking it out of the rain, but the tunics were already soaked, so she left them.

Stepping over to the edge of the roof, Mary passed a few stalks of flax, evidence that the previous month the harvested crop had been spread out at this place to dry before it was made into cord and linen cloth. Not until early fall, three months away, would Leah need the rooftop again for such a purpose; at that time, drying figs would cover it.

On top of the roof, Mary stood peering off in the direction of the sea. The night covered the water as a blanket; she could see nothing. Quickly her hair and robe became soaked by the rain, but Mary hardly noticed. So that an especially strong gust of wind would not blow her off, she braced her legs against the low wall, mandated by the law, which went around the edge of the roof. Mary waited.

Jesus must return, she told herself. *They must all come back safely.* She again saw Ara's water-soaked body as it was carried into her house to be prepared for burial. No, no, no! The same thing could not happen to the Master!

Sinking down, Mary was almost unaware of the rainwater in which she knelt. She again stared off into the distance, trying to part the darkness with the intensity of her desire to discover the men's fate.

It was useless. The gloom would not yield to her; she could see no further than the courtyard walls. Pushing her dripping hair back over her shoulder, Mary huddled on the roof, still watching, still praying that somehow everything would be all right.

I will not go in until I know something, she told herself. *Even if I sit here the entire night, I will wait.* But even as she said it, Mary wondered if she meant it. Yes, the determination was there, but she was soaked and shivering. How long could she stand the chill?

The storm showed no sigh of abating, and Mary slumped down closer to the low wall, craving even the little shelter it could give. Once again, her thoughts turned to Ara.

Why had they argued so about getting another servant? Had

he realized how much she loved him? When was the last time that she had told him she admired him—his skill as a businessman, his strong stocky body, and his devotion to the children?

The questions haunted Mary. Then she saw again Ara's lifeless body on the bier, being carried to the cold cave where it would remain, turning to dust what had once been Ara ben Eli, the fisherman of Magdala.

Suddenly the tears which had been stored since the day of the funeral, over two years before, could not be stopped. Oh, she had wept before, after the initial shock of Ara's death had worn off a bit. But this, this was different. These sobs tore at Mary's heart, crept down inside of her, and came with the force of the storm which raged around her.

And yet, as Mary cried, mourning the loss of her husband and the comfortable life she had with him, lamenting the wasted years she had been chained by the voices empowered by her grief, there was no bitterness, no devastation. Instead there was release as if, finally, now that she was more whole than she had ever been, Mary could turn away from her past. It was painful, this final parting from Ara, but there was also a degree of sweetness, like the last rope connecting them was being cut, totally freeing her for a new life.

As Mary's sobbing ceased, she noticed that the storm had stopped too. The wind had dropped, the rain no longer attacked her with its icy fingers, and even the dark of night seemed less black.

How strange, Mary thought. *I have never seen a storm be over so quickly. If the puddles around me were not here, I would guess I had dreamed the whole thing.*

She looked out toward the sea and could make out the waves, now benign as they gently rolled up on the beach. *Amazing,* Mary told herself. One would never know that only a short time ago, the water was as a wild animal fighting its capture.

Had there really been a storm? Mary was beginning to wonder. But her robe was drenched, and she could ring water out of her hair. Mary lowered herself into a sitting position. There, drowsiness overwhelmed her along with a sense of peace and well-being. Even though there was not yet any sight of the Master, Mary rested her head against the wall and slept.

The low murmur of voices awakened her. Surprised at her location, Mary had to think briefly before she remembered the past night. But now it was midmorning. In the courtyard below her, the other women were packing food and clothing for the trip to be made that day to Nazareth.

Horrified that she had slept so late, Mary ran down to join them. "Joanna, I'm sorry. I didn't mean to leave you to work most of the morning."

Her friend just smiled. "We were worried at first when you were not in the sleeping room as we got up. But Susanna found you, and it was more important that you rested."

"Did Jesus ever come back?" Mary asked, suddenly remembering her reason for being on the roof in the first place.

Joanna shook her head, and Mary felt her stomach twist. Could her worst fear, that of losing the Master during the storm, have happened?

"Don't look so worried," Joanna told her. "They'll be back. Often they don't return when they say they will. Maybe we won't even leave for Nazareth today."

"But the storm last night . . ."

Joanna shrugged. "Yes, I heard it. It was a bad one, that's true. But even the worst storm could never harm our Master."

"How can you be so sure?" Mary asked, as Joanna handed her some bread and cheese to eat. "I would have expected Ara to be completely safe from such a death. He was a strong swimmer, an experienced fisherman, yet . . ."

"Oh, that's why you are so concerned. I had forgotten how your husband died."

The rest of the morning passed quickly as the women hurried to finish the travel preparations. Mary tried to concentrate on mending holes in the men's robes, but she often found herself stopping to pray for Jesus' safety. If His absence bothered the other women, they didn't show it, and Mary began to feel irritated at them. Most of them did not know, as she did, how vicious the sea could be.

Just then, she heard the sound of masculine voices and footsteps outside the courtyard.

"It's the Master!" Susanna called from where she stood looking out of the gate.

Relief flooded Mary's heart. They were safe! *Oh, the Mighty One be praised!* The storm had not harmed them.

Forgetting the pile of mending, Mary hurried toward them. "Shalom, Master," she called as she reached the gate. "How thankful we are to see Your return! Many a man has died on the sea during storms like that we had last night."

She had expected to see exhaustion on His face, but Jesus greeted her with a wide smile. "We were in no danger," He told her as He strode across the courtyard to His sleeping room where fresh clothing awaited Him.

"Mary, Mary, you should have been there!"

"It was a miracle . . ."

"All at once the storm stopped . . ."

"The dead girl was alive . . ."

The disciples crowded around her, all speaking at once. On no face did she see weariness; rather, each one held a boyish enthusiasm. What had happened the previous night?

Suddenly aware that the other women were busy preparing food for the returning men, and that she alone was standing there listening to them, Mary broke away. "Please sit by the fire," she invited them, pushing aside her curiosity. "We will serve you a meal at once. You must be hungry after being out all night."

"Mary, I must tell you what happened last night," Matthew said as she went by. She had never heard such intensity in his voice.

"I must help the others now," she told him quickly. "But later I would like to hear."

Matthew nodded, and Mary left him. As she hastened to pile dates, grapes, and melon on trays for the men, she wondered if Matthew had sought her out to tell her what had happened. Perhaps in his excitement, he had only spoken to her because she was there. Or had he come to her because he wanted specifically to tell her? Mary wondered.

12

As she waited on the men, refilling their cups and making sure they had as much fruit and cheese as they wanted, Mary could not help but listen to snatches of their conversations. What she overheard frightened her while at the same time it intrigued her.

How could the wind and waves just cease? Storms tapered off; Mary knew it as well as anyone. And the parts she had listened to about a demonic they met on the other side of the sea were equally troubling. Something about an entire herd of pigs drowning. Then there was even a comment about a dead girl coming back to life.

When at last the men were full, most of them made their way to the sleeping rooms. They had been up nearly the entire night, and Jesus had decided they needed a day of rest. As Joanna had suspected, the journey to Nazareth would not be until the next day.

When Mary saw Matthew joining the others, she was not surprised. *He, too, is tired after everything that's happened,* she told herself. *He would be foolish if he were to miss getting his rest just to speak with me.*

Still, Mary was disappointed. She had hoped to hear the whole story herself instead of having to try to piece together the bits she had overheard.

Mary had to admit she had looked forward to spending some time with Matthew. *Perhaps I have been talking with Susanna too much lately*, she thought. I think I am beginning to feel something for this former tax collector that I do not feel for the other disciples.

The concept was tempting. *Maybe marriage itself is not what I found so difficult to accept*, Mary reasoned, remembering her reluctance to consider the offers of Jedidiah and Ezra. It could have been who the men were, rather than just the idea of returning to being a wife. Then again, perhaps the final release from Ara the previous night made the difference. Mary gathered up the empty cups to wash them.

"Mary, can you stop your work for a while?" a familiar voice asked, and she turned to see Matthew. Joy rose within her.

"Of course," she murmured. "But I thought you were going to sleep."

"There will be time for that later," Matthew said, and he motioned her over to a corner of the courtyard. "I knew you would want to hear all that went on."

They sat next to each other on low stools, in sight of the other women who still were at work in the courtyard but far enough removed from them that their conversation would not be overheard.

"You look beautiful today," he said softly, once they were settled.

Mary felt herself blushing. While she had found a chance to slip into a clean robe, her long hair felt as dirty and matted as an old rope. "Please, I would like to hear what took place on the boat."

Matthew looked embarrassed. "Yes, of course." He cleared his throat. "Well, after a day of teaching, the Master took us on board to get across the sea. He said He wanted to go to the country of the Gadarenes. I have to admit I was surprised He chose that for our destination. After all, they're Gentiles, and what have we to do with them? But I guess we've learned not to question the Master by now, so we said nothing as we set sail."

Mary agreed that the Rabbi's feelings toward non-Jews were extremely unnatural, but she remained quiet as Matthew continued.

"We were tired—it had been a long day—and I think most of us expected Jesus to return here to Simon's home instead of taking off on another trip. But we figured we could at least get some rest on the boat. Most of us were asleep when the storm hit. I awoke at a crack of lightning that illumined everything within sight. When I saw the waves, I felt like sleeping no more, believe me! I am not used to being on the sea during a storm, but even John and the others who used to fish became frightened as it continued to escalate."

The man next to Mary twisted his hands together, and she could not help noticing his long slim fingers and uncalloused palms.

"What did the Master do?" Mary asked quickly, grateful that Matthew was willing to share even his terror with her. Not many men would so expose their feelings to a woman.

Matthew gave a low laugh. "He slept, that's what He did! By then, every one of us was up and trembling as the waves increased. But Jesus was in the back of the boat, sound asleep! I couldn't believe it! How any man could be oblivious to all that crashing of the water against the hull, the lightning, and the wind . . . Why, if I hadn't known otherwise, I would have thought He was deaf."

The image of the Rabbi asleep as the others panicked suddenly struck Mary as amusing, and it was all she could do to keep a straight face. Surely Matthew would not think her giggles appropriate.

He was studying his hands. "Simon and the rest of them tried everything to secure the boat, but the water just kept coming up onto the deck. Our arms throbbed from bailing, but the boat just kept sinking lower and lower. Then the wind tore down the mast, and we knew for sure that we had little chance of getting to shore. Finally James said we would have to wake the Master, that only He could save our lives. It was that serious."

Her amusement evaporated; Mary shuddered as she pictured the soaked men frantically trying to keep the boat from capsizing while Jesus continued to sleep peacefully.

"James and I made our way back to where the Master lay, which was no small task with the deck pitching like a bee-stung donkey, and the waves threatening to sweep us overboard.

"'How can He be oblivious to all this?' James muttered when we reached Him and saw He still slept. 'Master, Master,' James called, trying to make his voice heard above the storm. 'Don't You care that we are about to die?'"

"What happened?" Mary asked breathlessly.

"Jesus heard him. Almost at once, He stood up, raised an arm out over the sea, and said, 'Peace, be still.' He didn't shout, and I don't know that any heard exactly what He said except for James and me since we were next to Him. We were clinging to the side like fearful children. But Mary, as soon as Jesus spoke, at that very time, the waves retreated. The wind howled no more. I tell you, I have never seen anything like it! I looked around in wonder. The sea looked as calm as on a sunny summer day. If the deck had not been littered with pieces of the broken mast and other debris from the storm, if water had not continued to coat the deck, I would have thought I had dreamed the entire storm."

Mary remembered again her night on the roof. Hadn't the same thing happened? In the midst of the wind and rain, all at once, there was no more storm. Now she understood why, and the Master's obvious power overwhelmed her.

Matthew was watching her face. "I know it sounds impossible, but believe me, Mary, such a thing did take place."

She quickly realized that Matthew had misunderstood her silence. "But I do, Matthew, I do! I was up on the roof that night, and the storm stopped suddenly there too . . ." She stopped. What if he asked her why she was awake on the roof in the middle of the night? Even though Mary felt something special for the disciple, she was not prepared to share with him such an intimate experience.

But Matthew had no questions for her, only a relieved smile that she did not doubt him. "When we realized the storm had ceased, we just stood there, looking at Him, the enormity of what He'd done rendering us speechless. Jesus shook His head a little, and I saw a hint of a smile on His face. 'Why were you so fearful?' He asked us. 'Where's your faith?' I had no answer for Him, and neither did anyone else. But James whispered to me, 'What kind of man is He, that the waves and wind obey Him?'"

Mary flung her hair back over her shoulder. "He is truly extraordinary. How does He do such things?"

"But that's not all. We reached the shore near Gadara as dawn was breaking." He seemed glad to go on to talk about the rest of the day. "When we were approaching the land, we passed some tombs, and I noticed a man running along beside them. Actually, you could not help but be aware of him. He was screaming, and he was . . . ah, without clothing."

Mary lowered her eyes but not in time to miss Matthew's ears turning red.

"When we came off the boat, the man was on the shore, staring at us. He was obviously demon possessed, his flesh cut and marred and filthy, and I tried to step away from him. His eyes were wild, like an animal's. He came right at the Master. 'What have I to do with you, Jesus, the Son of the Most High? I beg you, don't torment me!' The voice was such as I have never heard before, gruff and unearthly sounding."

"How did he know the Master's name?" Mary asked.

"I have no idea. I didn't think about that."

"Tell me what happened then."

"Yes, ah, well, Jesus just said for the unclean spirit to come out, and He asked what its name was. That same gruff voice answered, 'My name is Legion, for we are so many. Please don't send us out of the country,'" Matthew said with a yawn.

Mary could see that her companion was growing weary, and she knew she should encourage him to join the others in the sleeping rooms. But she had to hear what came next.

"And Jesus did as they asked?"

He nodded. "There was a large herd of swine feeding on one of the slopes nearby." Matthew wrinkled his nose in disgust. "Odious creatures. I can't understand why even a Gentile would keep them. Anyway, the demons asked to go into the pigs, and the Master permitted them to do so." Matthew shook his head. "You should have been there! As soon as the demons left that man, the fire came out of his eyes. He noticed his nakedness"—here again the disciple looked away from Mary—"and was embarrassed by it. In a normal voice, the stranger asked for my cloak. I still didn't want to have anything to do with him, but one look from Jesus, and I gave it. At least he didn't look quite so bad with a robe on."

"Perhaps you should go rest now," Mary suggested, not wanting this time together to end, but realizing that it must.

"But I have to tell you the rest!" Matthew said. "When the demons went into the swine, they went wild! They started running in every direction, knocking each other down, trampling the little ones. The herders tried to calm them, but it was no use. Every last one of them took off as if it had been burned with a flame, and they ended up falling down the slope into the sea. We just stared at them, shocked, but the Master acted as if nothing unusual had happened. He invited the man who had had the demons to join us for a meal."

Remembering the force of the demoniac voices which had tormented her, Mary was not surprised by Matthew's story. It made her grateful that she had been afflicted no more than she was, for, obviously, the man Jesus healed had been much worse off than she.

"Later, as we were resting on the beach," Matthew continued, "some men from around there came over to us. When they saw the former demoniac sitting with us, clothed and sane, they couldn't stop staring at him. They had heard what happened to the swine too. They begged us to leave." Matthew chuckled a bit. "I guess they wanted nothing to do with the kind of power the Master has. And they didn't even know about the storm!"

Mary smiled at him. Surely, the disciple would agree with her that following the unusual Rabbi from Nazareth was the best place in the world to be. Watching the miracles (or at least hearing about them directly from someone who had), listening to the teaching about a new kind of life, and having the opportunity to be with the Master each day—could anything be more fulfilling?

Matthew was giving her a puzzled stare. "Mary, did you hear me? I said that when we started to board the boat to return here, the man who had been a demoniac asked to go with us."

"Forgive me," Mary said quickly. "I was just thinking . . . but go on."

"Jesus gave the Gadarene a long look, and I was certain we were to have a Gentile disciple join us this morning. It was a horrifying thought! But when the Master at last spoke, He told the man to go to his own people and tell them about what great things the Holy One had done for him in making him whole."

"Was the Gadarene disappointed not to be permitted to join you?"

Matthew shrugged. "I suppose, but he went off to do as he was instructed. I must confess I was glad he was not permitted to follow us. Unless, of course, he was willing to convert to Judaism."

The disciple was looking more and more tired as the excitement of the day wore off, and Mary stood up. "You have been most kind to take so long to tell me each detail. But I can see you are weary. Please go get some sleep now."

"But there is more—Jairus's daughter and a woman with a flow of blood . . ."

"I can hear about them later," Mary said gently. "You must rest."

This time Matthew agreed.

But Matthew was only to have a short time for leisure, because not too much later, when Mary returned from the well with a jug of water, she discovered the Master and the men were gone.

Joanna was trying to finish a new robe on Leah's loom before they left the next day, but she stopped long enough to tell Mary about it. "Right after you left, a crowd started gathering right outside the courtyard. They were asking for Jesus, and I was a little worried they would all try to come in here. We wondered whether we should call the Master, but before we had decided, He was up, motioning the men to follow Him. I think He took them over by the water."

Mary nodded.

"Since we're not taking the trip until tomorrow, I sent some of the women with them. I know you missed your turn yesterday, but I wasn't sure when you'd be back," Joanna continued as she resumed sliding the shuttle over and under the threads stretched between the upright wooden posts of the loom.

Before Mary could say that she wished her friends would have waited for her return, a knock on the courtyard gate startled them both.

"Who?" Leah called from where she was working in one of the sleeping rooms.

"It is I, Chuza," a masculine voice answered.

At his identification, Joanna jumped to her feet. "My husband is here!" she told Mary. But she did not look pleased at his arrival.

And as Joanna talked with him, sitting on the very stools where Mary and Matthew had been earlier, neither of them seemed to be in good spirits.

Mary served Chuza a cup of wine and some honey cakes, but she guessed from what she overheard of the conversation that Chuza was no longer so patient with his wife's travels. After he finally left, Joanna was sullen.

"Has he ordered you to return home?" Mary asked her gently.

"Not directly," Joanna said, shoving the shuttle back and forth with much more force than necessary.

"What are you going to do?"

Joanna's mouth was a hard line on her face. "I will stay with the Master, no matter how risky it gets." She would say no more.

13

"You fool! I pay you good money, and this is what I get in return? Nothing!" Eli did not often get angry enough to lose his usual composed manner, but this time, he was dangerously close to releasing a shower of blows on the servant in front of him.

"My lord, I assure you, I have searched everywhere for her. It's just that this Jesus of Nazareth travels around so much that it is impossible to keep up with Him," Micah said, taking a step back away from Eli. A small man, Micah had always worked at the house for Eli and Ruth instead of on the boats, and the fire in his master's eyes made him nervous.

Eli tried to control the fury rising within him. "Yes, He moves around, but the man draws crowds wherever He goes. All you have to do is look for a place where the people gather. Are you too stupid to do that?"

"Is it certain that she is with Him?" Micah asked, unwilling to admit that he had not sought Mary as diligently as he had reported.

"Of course, you donkey! I know my daughter-in-law, and she would go no place else except to His side." Eli shook a short, stubby finger at the servant. "You will go out again, and this time you will not come back until you have Mary."

"But what if she will not accompany me?" Micah anxiously stroked his thin beard.

By then, Eli could feel the blood pounding in his head. "You will bring her back!" he shouted. "I don't care how. Hire some of your friends to help you abduct her. You are paid enough to afford that. Bind her with ropes. But at whatever cost, get her here!"

His objections dissolving while yet unspoken, Micah bowed. Better not tempt the master to beat him. But he did not like the idea of trying to steal Mary away from the miracle worker. Who knew what power the man had? Almost constantly, there was word of some person who had been healed by the Rabbi. It was even said several had been brought back from the dead by His touch. Of course, that could not be true, but just the same, Micah did not like to risk irritating such a man.

He was almost out of Eli's courtyard gate when his master called to him. "Do not hurt her," Eli said. "Remember you must not hurt her."

Micah nodded and strode away.

Coming up from behind her husband, Ruth slipped an arm around Eli's waist. Highly improper outside of the sleeping room, she knew, but they were alone in the courtyard, and Ruth sensed he needed her comfort. "Do you really expect to find her?"

Eli continued watching Micah's retreating figure, but he was not displeased with his wife's open affection. "Of course, I do. Micah will succeed."

"It's been over a month since she left."

"I know, I know. But I'm convinced she's with the Nazarene. It's only a matter of time until she's discovered and brought back."

"I'm not so sure. She will resist." Ruth turned towards the children's sleeping room. "Besides, perhaps it's not so bad having her gone. I find satisfaction with the children here, and it is less of an embarrassment with her away. Many remember

Mary's illness. I think some even still avoid me, so they won't risk getting it."

With shocked eyes, Eli faced his wife. "How can you turn on her? She is your daughter-in-law, the widow of our dear son."

"I would not have chosen her for Ara," she said stiffly.

"You didn't object when he expressed an interest in her."

"You never asked me my opinion. Perhaps now I would tell you regardless, but then, I would not have dared."

Eli shook his head. "Well, it is no matter. They did marry, and now she is part of our family, regardless of how ashamed she makes you."

"I did not mean I don't love her as a daughter . . ." Ruth began, realizing she had said too much.

Eli was already walking out the gate. "Just make certain the children never find out your opinion of their mother."

"My lord," she called, but he did not turn around.

Tabitha picked up one of the small silvery-scaled fish, sniffed it, eyed it critically, and then replaced it in the pile. Choosing another one which she put through the same process, Tabitha finally nodded with satisfaction.

"I'll take this one," she told the shopkeeper, who wrapped it in a leaf and handed it to her. "It's a bit larger."

Giving him a coin, the elderly servant started off. But before she had reached her next destination—the market stall that sold fresh vegetables—she was halted.

"Tabitha! That is your name, isn't it?" a man called.

She turned to see a stocky man, obviously a fisherman, coming up from behind her.

At her blank look, the man smiled. "I am Jedidiah. I used to work for your old master, Ara."

Tabitha relaxed. "Oh, yes, of course. My ancient eyes don't work for me like they did years ago, and I did not recognize you."

"May I speak with you briefly?"

Tabitha looked dubious. "It isn't proper . . ."

"Oh, come on. We will go back behind this stall, and no one will see. I must find out about Mary."

At her mistress's name, the servant nodded, and the two slipped in back of a deserted booth which had at one time sold spices. The faint scents of oil of nard, cinnamon, and garlic mingled in their nostrils.

"Have you heard from her since she left?" Jedidiah asked anxiously.

"Why would I have?" the woman replied curtly. "I am only a servant."

"Please, you don't understand," Jedidiah said. "I . . . I love her. I have no wish to harm her." Tabitha still looked suspicious, and the fisherman tried again. "I tell you, I am glad she follows Jesus. She must do what she is called to do."

"I don't know that she is with the Nazarene."

The man impatiently brushed his dark hair out of his eyes. "Don't play games with me! I know why she left. She passed me on the road to Gennesaret. I guessed where she was going then. But I told no one, though Eli would have probably rewarded me handsomely if I'd come to him with the news of her whereabouts. I gave her food for her journey."

Tabitha sighed. "I believe you, but that changes nothing. I have not heard from her; I do not know where she is or what she does."

Jedidiah's face dropped. "I just wanted to make sure she is well. I have hopes . . ." He looked away, "hopes that perhaps when she returns . . ."

Tabitha started past him. "I am truly sorry I cannot help you. Now I must get back. It is almost time to begin the evening meal."

"Of course. I'm sorry to have delayed you."

The servant stopped. "There is one thing . . ."

"Yes?" Jedidiah asked quickly.

"Well, I did overhear just yesterday my master Eli talking to his manservant. He ordered Micah to find Mary and to bring her back, even if it meant abducting her. He said to use ropes to bind her if she resisted. Perhaps I shouldn't trust you with this, but . . ." Tabitha's eyes filled with tears, "I can't bear the thought of my lady being dragged back here like an animal."

"I must warn her!" the fisherman said. "Thank you—for trusting me. I promise you that I will get the message to her, and I will keep her safe."

"But what of your business? You can't just leave it! It could take you weeks to find the Miracle Worker . . ."

Jedidiah was already back in the street. "The fish will still be here when I return!"

"Have some more wine," Azor said, motioning the shopkeeper to refill Micah's cup.

The servant shook his head. "No more, not when there is business to discuss."

"We have settled the business. Sadoc and I accept your offer to help you find the woman and bring her back to Magdala. The three of us will leave in the morning. Now we drink to seal the agreement of working together. After you pay us, of course." The man grinned, revealing ugly diseased teeth. He was not much taller than Micah, but he probably weighed twice as much, not in fat but in muscle.

Micah took a step back from him. Why had he ever come to this wine booth, seeking help for his task? These men were not the type with which he wanted to work.

"The money!" Sadoc growled. Azor's friend towered above the other two, and he also had enormous shoulders and upper arms. His heavy black hair and beard, obviously without the services of a comb for some time, made him bear more resemblance to some sort of wild animal than a person.

"Of course, but first you must find the woman," Micah said quickly.

"What does she look like?" Azor asked, picking at a tooth with his fingernail.

The servant shifted uncomfortably as he tried to describe Mary. "She is no young girl, you know. She is a widow with children."

Azor shrugged. "No matter, we'll find her."

"The money!" Sadoc growled again.

"I told you, find the woman first!" Micah said, not liking the expression in the man's eyes.

Azor stepped between his friend and Micah. "Have another drink," he said to Sadoc. "I don't believe the young man here understands much about business. After all, he is only a servant."

Micah nodded, "But . . ."

"Let me explain a few things to you about businessmen. You see, when arrangements have been made between men, such as have been done here today, the party who wants the service—that is you, my friend—pays the party who will perform the service—that is Sadoc and me—in advance."

"But how will I know the job will be done if I pay you now?" Micah asked.

Azor gave the servant a hurt look. "Why do you ask such a question? Can't you tell that you are dealing with men of honor? Of course, we will fulfill our end of the bargain. You have nothing to fear. You have our word! And now if we might have your money, everything will be settled."

Micah reached for the coin bag tucked inside his sash. "I will pay you half of what I owe you. The rest you will receive when the woman is safely home."

Sadoc gave Micah a menacing look, but Azor touched his arm, silently ordering him to keep silent. "Why is this? Have you doubts about our ability to do the job? If you do, speak."

"I do not wonder if you can handle it, but I will still only give you half. And remember, my master says she must not be hurt."

Azor sighed. "All right, all right! Whatever you want. Here, another drink for each of us."

Several hours later, Micah slumped by the booth, unaware of the fingers that reached into his sash to pull out the rest of the coins there.

"He is a fool," Sadoc muttered. "A good business deal we have made this time, huh? A few drinks, and the job is done."

"You are the fool," Azor told him. "We will search for this woman, as we have agreed. Aren't we men of honor?"

Sadoc laughed as they started off down the road. "What if we find her?"

Azor grinned as he replied, "We will think of something to do with her. If nothing else, we can always actually bring her back here. If she is as ill as he says, she won't realize what is happening to her. Even if she does remember, who would believe a demoniac?"

"What if this Micah catches up with us?"

"He won't find us. Even if he did, what can he do? Both of us will swear we understood him to say that we alone were to go for the woman, not that he was to go with us. He must have been robbed of the rest of his money after we left with the half of our fee he gave us." Azor gave a short laugh. "This is the kind of business I like."

On the north side of Magdala, Jedidiah was walking briskly toward Gennesaret. Beyond that was Capernaum. He had heard Jesus was there. In fact, it seemed that the Miracle Worker had made that His home. Perhaps it would not be so difficult to find

Mary. Surely people everywhere would be more aware of where the Nazarene was, now that His popularity was growing so. Why, Jedidiah had heard of some from Jerusalem itself who had traveled to Galilee seeking Jesus.

The fisherman shifted his walking staff into his other hand. *I should have followed Him long ago,* he thought. And though he wanted to be near Mary, Jedidiah knew there was more to his desire to be with the Rabbi than just her.

If only I were more bold, Jedidiah chided himself. *But leaving my job and everything for such an uncertain life-style was too much of a sacrifice. Now, at least, I have a legitimate reason to go—to warn Mary.* He smiled at the thought of her.

In front of him, a child darted after another, and Jedidiah grinned at them. He had always liked youngsters, and he had looked forward to the day when he would have his own. But when he was only fifteen, his father had died. He had immediately hired on Ara's fishing crew, and his entire salary had gone to support his mother and four younger brothers and sisters.

Ara was a demanding master, Jedidiah remembered. He tolerated no idleness, and the work was long and hard. Somehow there was never time for Jedidiah to think of marriage, not with all his coins going to feed and clothe the five who depended on him. Even after his sisters married and his brothers assumed their own positions on fishing boats, Jedidiah had been too busy to consider taking a wife. By then, he had left Ara's employment, and with the money he had stolen, he had bought his own boat. His brothers and he had begun a small business. Of course, in no way did it compete with the amount of trade that Ara then had, but it was satisfactory for Jedidiah. At least he was his own master.

After a while, of course, even Jedidiah's mother had started to question him about his marital state. As she served his meals, she would suggest this girl or that, but Jedidiah was not interested. They seemed to be decent choices, but somehow he knew they were not right.

What exactly Jedidiah wanted, he was not certain. And so he waited, content in living with his mother, yet yearning for something else. About the time Ara had been lost in the storm, Jedidiah's mother had also died. At that point, he had become even more alone, often going out to sea for days at a time, landing in different cities besides Magdala, and often just sitting in the boat watching the water. Jedidiah's brothers soon tired of his bizarre behavior and found other jobs.

From that point on, Jedidiah worked largely by himself. Occasionally, for a time, he would hire the services of a deaf-mute man who was not annoyed or troubled by Jedidiah's life-style. The two established a comfortable employer/employee relationship. But more and more, Jedidiah preferred to make his living by himself.

Then one day, his boat had landed near a crowd of men, and Jedidiah heard Jesus for the first time. It was shortly afterwards that Jedidiah took the money he had saved to Mary, to replace what he had dishonestly taken from Ara. Though he had gone with no plan but to return the coins, Jedidiah left with the certainty that he was ready to marry and that Mary was the one he wanted.

It was strange, he realized, to suddenly find a woman he wished to make his wife. But somehow, just in his brief contact with her, Jedidiah sensed that she could give his life the meaning he had been seeking.

And now perhaps that dream will become reality, Jedidiah thought. He would ask for nothing else.

14

"Where is He going?" Mary asked, panting from climbing the ascending path of the road they were on. "There's nothing this far north except that heathen city."

"You mean Caesarea Philippi?" Susanna said. "But surely the Master would not go there. It was built by the tetrarch Philip, wasn't it?"

Joanna came up from behind them. "No, his father, Herod called the Great, first constructed it. He built a temple and dedicated the whole area to Caesar Augustus. Only later did Philip rename the town after himself."

Mary wrinkled her nose. "Then why is Jesus taking us here? What possible good can it be to travel to an area so pagan?" She looked around in disgust. In front of them, Mount Hermon filled the sky. Over nine thousand feet high, it was visible even far to the south in the Jordan valley, and only recently had the snow which topped it most of the year melted in the midsummer sun.

Now as the small group of travelers reached the foot of the mountain, they were forced to watch carefully where they walked. Numerous rocks of all sizes were scattered around the riverbank they followed. Gurgling in their ears was the icy water which flowed in countless small streams as well as the four larger rivers in the area that joined to form the beginnings of the Jordan River.

Joanna sighed. "Well, I guess you know we can't question what the Master does. He has His reasons. You didn't have to come with Him, you know."

"I'm sorry," Mary murmured quickly. "I didn't mean to complain. It's just that this trip is so different from the others we've taken since I joined you." Catching a glimpse of a carved stone idol which had been placed in a niche in the rock wall to their left, she turned her head to avoid continuing to look at it.

Susanna nodded sympathetically. "Perhaps we will not remain this far north for long. I confess I do not like it either."

"Look, Jesus is motioning for the men to stop," Joanna told them. "I wonder if He plans to spend the night here."

The rock wall which they had followed intermittently for the past few hours' travel had given way to an open space big enough to pitch the tents in. Soon the men were, indeed, setting them up.

The women began unpacking the food and cooking supplies. Since there were only the three of them, they would be extremely busy caring for all the men. But they expected as much. Before they had left Capernaum the previous week, the Rabbi had warned that the trip would be exhausting. Any who chose not to go could wait at Leah's home for their return.

Of course, Joanna would not leave the Master, nor Susanna, who still blushed when Jesus looked at her. Mary had thought only briefly about staying. But she decided against it; somehow, it was important that she continue to be with Jesus.

In the past several months, Mary had noticed times when the Man they served seemed especially quiet and even perturbed about something. Why, she had no idea. Crowds continued to follow Jesus, miracles were done, and His teachings fed her spirit. What more did He want? Of course, she had heard He had enemies, but Jesus was too popular with the people for anything to happen. And He had done nothing to trouble the Romans, nothing that could be interrupted to mean revolt against the hated foreigners who controlled the land.

As much as there was for the women to do, none of them could sit and listen to the Master as they had taken turns doing when more were there to share the labor. But Mary did not mind too much.

For one thing, Matthew took it upon himself to keep her informed about what Jesus was saying and doing. Almost every night, when the work was done, Matthew found her and explained all that had taken place that day. Often Joanna and Susanna listened too, but sometimes it was just Matthew and Mary.

She looked forward to the evenings. Naturally, she sincerely wanted to know what the Master was teaching, but Mary had to admit that she had grown to welcome the disciple's attention. More and more often, marriage did not seem as distasteful as it had once been. She did not tell even Joanna, but Mary could picture Matthew in the role of husband.

She wondered if Jesus was aware of her feelings toward the disciple, and she considered going to Him to make sure He was not displeased. But once as she sat with Matthew, Mary glanced at Jesus and found Him smiling at her. Then she felt more confident that the Master understood and did not mind their deepening relationship.

More and more often, their talks included not just Matthew describing the day but Mary giving her opinion on what a particular parable might mean. At first Mary had been shy about going any farther than asking what happened next, but as her feelings for Matthew grew, so did her boldness in telling him her thoughts. Matthew did not seem to mind in the least, and he even confessed that he had not considered things the way she had.

Once Jesus had said that He did only what the Father told

Him to do. "We too must learn obedience," Mary told Matthew. "It should be an instant response. He speaks, we obey."

"But we cannot blindly do everything. We must reason things though, make sure it is the right step to follow," the disciple replied.

Mary shook her head. "Would you consider a man to be a good servant if when you asked him to do something, he questioned within himself if it was worth obeying? No, the servant must do as the master says, even when he does not understand. He must trust the one above him to have the wisdom to know what is best."

"But I am not a servant. Our people have a proud tradition of being free, free to make our own decisions about how to live our lives," Matthew replied.

"Perhaps it is time to give up such 'freedom,'" Mary told him calmly. "For me, it is like children who must obey their parents. When I tell Kezia she may not have more honey cakes, she pouts and does not understand. But I realize that if she eats too many, she will be sick. She must trust me that because I love her, I do only what is in her best interest. So, too, can't we have faith that the Father loves us and will have us do only what is best?"

Matthew nodded slowly. "I suppose that is the difficult part, believing that anyone beside yourself can know what is right for you. I find that hard to do." He gave her a reluctant smile. "Sometimes I think you understand the Master better than I do, Mary."

She had thrilled at his praise, she remembered as she bent over the cooking fire and stirred a pot of thick lentil stew. But did Matthew feel anything in her presence? If only there was some way she could tell. True, it seemed his eyes sought her when the men returned from a day of teaching. No one could debate that he openly talked with her almost every evening. But was there only friendship in his heart, or was there something else, something that might match the emotions in her soul, which were already forming words of love?

The lentil stew was ready, and Mary ladled it into bowls for the waiting men. All of them were tired and hungry after the day's long walk. They took the steaming dishes gratefully.

Perhaps I should ask the Master how Matthew feels about me, Mary thought, handing Jesus His portion. *He knows everything. But would He tell me?*

She looked up at the Rabbi, hoping that His sensitive spirit would see the questions in her eyes and ask the reason. But tonight Jesus was weary, and somehow Mary realized it was not just from the traveling. Again she felt a quiver of apprehension within her. Something was going to happen. She did not know how or what or when, but the life they led was not going to continue indefinitely. She sensed it deep within herself, and suddenly her questions about Matthew seemed unimportant.

What can I do to minister to the burden I see within You? she asked Jesus silently. She remembered how Ara had liked his back rubbed when he felt weak and depressed. How she wished she could offer the same comfort to the Master, but she knew it was not proper.

Jesus had settled Himself beside a large rock, but His stew sat cooling in His lap. He seemed unaware of the people around Him.

Suddenly His dusty feet caught her eyes. Of course! She could wash His feet! Here on the road it was not customarily done since the next day would bring only more grime. But perhaps it would be a welcome comfort to the Master.

The last man had taken his serving, and Mary left her bowl untouched beside the cooking pot from which she had served the stew. She had no basin, but she could at least pour the cool water over His feet and dry them.

"Mary, aren't you going to eat?" Susanna called from her position on the grass.

Picking up a bucket, Mary nodded. "In a short time I will, but I must do something else first." She started toward the stream nearest them.

"May I help you?" the younger woman offered, but Mary saw she had no desire to leave her meal.

"No, finish your stew. I can handle it myself." She glanced over at Jesus, sitting motionless. He was still sitting this way when she returned with the full leather bucket, a towel, and some olive oil.

"Master?" she said softly, feeling awkward as she stood before Him. Perhaps He would have preferred to be left undisturbed. She considered backing away from Him and forgetting the whole idea.

But Jesus was looking up at her, no longer in His own world. "Yes, Mary? What can I do for you?"

Again she saw the exhaustion in his eyes, and she had to blink away her tears. If only she could wrap her arms around Him as she had done to Joshua when he had fallen . . . She immediately rejected the thought. Certainly it was wrong to think of comforting the Rabbi as she had a child, even if He did look as though He needed it.

"Lord, I . . . I came to wash Your feet, if You will permit me," she murmured, almost afraid of what His reaction might be.

But He only nodded quickly, and she knelt beside Him. As she poured the water over His soles, He leaned back against the rock and closed His eyes.

Lightly Mary massaged the calloused toes before rinsing them again and drying them with the towel. Then she pulled out the small vial of olive oil and emptied it on His feet. As she worked, Jesus said nothing, but she could feel His body relaxing. Her instincts had been right.

When at last she was finished, the Rabbi opened His eyes and smiled at her. "Thank you for knowing what to do," He said to her alone. Picking up the by-then-cool bowl of stew, Jesus finally began to eat.

By the time the Master had finished His meal, the other men were sprawled around the fire, and the women had cleaned up the clay cups and bowls and replaced them in the bundles they carried.

Mary settled down near Jesus. She was pleased to see some of the old sparkle in His eyes and even more pleased to think that she had had some small part in restoring it. She moved a little closer to Him as she saw Him prepare to speak.

"Who do men say that I am?" He questioned.

The disciples eyed each other warily. They preferred it when He explained parables to them or taught about the kingdom of God. His questions were difficult, and the one who answered them usually ended up looking less than brilliant.

"Who do men say I am?" Jesus repeated, staring at the men who had chosen to follow Him.

"Some say John the Baptist," James finally replied. There seemed to be no trick in this query.

"Others say you are Elijah," Matthew put in, and Thomas added, "Or Jeremiah or one of the other prophets."

Nodding a little, Jesus sat quietly for a while. Mary could hear the stream behind them gurgling and the flames of the fire crackling. Was that all He would say?

Finally the Master spoke again. "But who do you say that I am?"

What did He want for a response? Mary wondered. She saw several of the men exchange puzzled looks. Why, He was Jesus of Nazareth, the great Teacher, the Miracle Worker, the Leader of their small group. But He knew that. What kind of answer was He seeking? Mary had no idea.

But somehow Simon did. "You are the Christ, the Son of the Holy One of Israel."

Mary gasped. The Anointed One? The Messiah? Did Simon realize what he had just said?

"You are blessed, Simon Bar Jonah, for flesh and blood did not reveal that to you; my Father did."

Mary's breath again caught in her throat. Jesus was agreeing with the disciple! The Master was admitting that He was the promised Deliverer for which the Jews had been waiting. Mary could hardly believe she had heard correctly.

"You are Peter, and upon this rock I will build My church, and the gates of hell will not prevail against it" Jesus was saying, but Mary was not really listening.

She was not just following a great man, the one who had set her free from the tormenting voices. She was in the service of the actual Son of the Mighty One. Awe swept over Mary. And to think, this very night she had touched Him, washed His feet, wanted to cradle Him in her arms to wipe away His grief . . .

"But do not tell anyone this news," Jesus instructed. "It is not yet time."

Again Mary was startled. If it was true, if the Master was who He had just confessed to be, why shouldn't everyone know? She did not understand.

But Jesus was talking again, and the words He said this time were of suffering, and death, and life again after the third day, words that Mary did not want to hear. Was this the burden that she had sensed He carried?

"No, Master, no!" Simon objected. "This shall not happen." The glow Simon had had when he said Jesus was the Christ had disappeared, and in its place, Mary saw harshness.

She had expected the Master to tell Simon he was wrong, but the rebuke that came out of Jesus' mouth was more stern than she had ever heard Him speak to one of the disciples. "Get behind me, Satan! You think in the way of men, not the way of the Almighty."

The glint in Simon's eyes dissolved. "But, Master, . . ."

Jesus rose, and Mary was saddened to again see the weariness in His face. Wordlessly He left the warm circle of light around the fire. No one tried to stop Him.

15

After only a little over a week in Caesarea Philippi, Jesus announced that it was time to go south again. Mary was relieved to hear His decision, and she and the other two women packed food and cooking utensils with eager hands.

"It will be good to be back in Capernaum," Susanna admitted.

"What makes you think we are returning there?" Joanna said. "I don't know, not for sure, but I feel the Master has reached some sort of a turning point in His ministry. I wonder if following Him will continue to be as it has been so far."

"What do you mean?" the younger woman asked.

Placing a few remaining loaves of the flat round bread she had baked that morning in a cloth, Mary joined them. "I feel it too. Things are going to change for us."

Susanna drew closer to the others. "You mean because the Master said He is going to die?"

Mary nodded, and Joanna busied herself with packing the bowls and cups. "I cannot imagine such a thing," she murmured. "But if Jesus said it, then it will happen."

"Some of the men don't feel that way," Mary told her, remembering Matthew's words the previous night. "They think He does not mean physical death but some other kind. You know the way much of what He says is hard to understand. Perhaps they are right."

Joanna only shook her head grimly.

Later as they were walking, Susanna brought up the subject again. "Mary," she whispered when Joanna was in front of them talking with Simon, "Do you think Jesus will die?"

"I don't know," she admitted. "Yet if Joanna feels He will, I am inclined to believe it. She has great sensitivity to the Master."

"But He is too popular with the people! Everywhere we go, they love Him; they bring their children to Him to bless; they bring their sick for Him to heal. They come to hear Him teach. How could Rome or anyone else hurt Him? A riot would erupt."

Susanna wiped away a tear, and Mary remembered again how she loved the Rabbi, in spite of the fact that there could be no marriage. After their late night talk, Susanna had, indeed, asked her father to see if Jesus would consider a wife, without mentioning her as interested.

Her father had returned reluctantly. "Please don't cry, daughter. The Master has said He cannot marry, even one as lovely and kind as you."

"You told him I . . ."

"No, no, but He knew. And He loves you, dear child, but not as a man loves a woman. Someone else will come to be your husband; I'm sure of it." He had given his daughter an awkward hug.

Though Mary was concerned that the crumbling of Susanna's hopes would crush her, the younger woman went about her tasks with her usual gentle and loving attitude. Only once did Mary see her weep as they lay on their mats late at night.

"It's all right," Susanna told her when Mary had reached over to comfort her. "Truly it is. I can accept that He will not marry me. But I will follow Him everywhere; I will love Him always, no matter what. Even if it means having no husband or child."

Mary admired her fortitude. *I could not be like that,* she thought. *If the one I cared for rejected me, even as lovingly as Jesus did Susanna, I would fight for him.*

Matthew's face came into her mind. *Would you fight for him?* something inside her asked. The answer came immediately: *Yes. Oh, yes! For I love him as dearly as I loved Ara.*

The realization of what she had vowed struck her full force. Mary was in love again. It had been growing, like a mustard tree that starts out small and hidden by the branches of the bigger trees. No one was aware of such a tree until, one day, it pushed through the boughs of the surrounding oaks or willows—a scrawny tree, yes, but one strong and confident of its place in the world.

My love is like that, Mary decided. *I was not even sure if it was there until this moment when it has burst forth. I love Matthew.* The words sounded good, good enough to make her want to reach over and hug Susanna.

Of course, what Mary felt for the disciple was not exactly like what she had experienced with Ara. But it should be different because Matthew and she had the shared commitment to the Rabbi. *How happy we could be together,* she dreamed. *Kezia and Joshua could join us, and we would follow Jesus together. As a family, we could learn about the new life He teaches.*

But what about Matthew? Did he also feel toward Mary what she had just realized she felt? If he did not, her situation was just as bad as Susanna's was.

"Oh, Mighty One," Mary prayed, desperate enough to forget the formal prayers to which she was accustomed, "tell me in some way how Matthew feels. Does he care for me the way I do for him? Please let me know."

Just then Matthew came up from behind her on his way to the front of the group. He gave her a warm smile and a wink. "I must talk with you tonight," he said softly just to her as he passed.

Mary smiled and nodded. This was her answer! Why would Matthew have walked by at the time she was praying about him, unless the Holy One was giving her a response? And the way he grinned and winked, didn't that show all the more that he shared her love? Further confirmation would come that evening, Mary was sure of it. Matthew must be planning to ask her to marry him. Why else would he make sure to say he had to talk to her? Of course it was irregular to ask her directly, but Mary had no father, and her father-in-law would certainly refuse.

Mary fought the impulse to whirl around. She was in love, and surely anyone who looked at her could tell. *It is ridiculous for a grown widow to feel this way,* she told herself sternly. *I will act dignified. Besides, such behavior can only hurt Susanna. She is the one who really wants to remarry.*

Somehow Mary managed to keep walking down the narrow path south, following the Master. But joy rang again and again in her mind, and she memorized each rock formation, each small stream, each grove of trees she passed. *I don't want to ever forget this day,* she told herself. *I will remember the smells of the ripened grapes, the gurgle of the water, and the blue of the sky. For I am in love.*

That evening, after hungry stomachs had been filled, and weary bodies clustered around the warmth of the fire, Mary sat nervously waiting for Matthew. With the fading of the daylight, her certainty of his feelings had dimmed. She wondered if perhaps she had been premature in supposing Yahweh had answered her prayer so quickly.

Not that her feelings toward the disciple had changed any. On the contrary, Mary was as sure as she had ever been that she loved Matthew. But suppose he did not share that special caring for her? Had their relationship over the past few months been mere tokens of friendship on his part?

No, Mary told herself quickly. Too many times, things have happened that had convinced her otherwise. Even Matthew's eyes lately had seemed to say he wanted to kiss and hold her. Matthew had to feel as she did.

Though the group was a day's journey south of Mount Herman, the cool night air chilled Mary. Soon the cold winter rains would descend upon Galilee. How nice it would be to have the marriage take place before springtime. Mary had always craved the comfort of a man's arms when the temperatures dropped. Surely at their ages, the usual betrothal of a year would not be necessary.

Mary glanced over at the place where she had last seen Matthew, but he was no longer talking to Judas. In fact, she could not find him anywhere around the dimly lit circle of men. But suddenly Matthew broke through the night to stand next to Jesus. Another man stood slightly behind him, and Mary was surprised to see Matthew's hand firmly gripping the forearm of the stranger, as if he did not trust him. Mary could not quite see the newcomer's face.

"Master, I found this man creeping up on us through the darkness. He claims . . ."

"Release him," Jesus said, and Mary thought she detected a note of humor in His voice. "He comes in peace."

Reluctantly, Matthew let the other man go. He immediately knelt at Jesus's feet.

"Master, I have been trying to find you for weeks. I seek one Mary, of Magdala."

Mary's heart jumped within her at the sound of the man's

voice. It was Jedidiah! How had he found them? She had not even thought about him since she had taken his fish and left for Gennesaret.

"She is here," Jesus was saying, pointing in her direction.

"Master, Mary is in danger," Matthew began, taking a step between the newcomer and where Mary sat. "This man says he is here to warn her, but how do we know that he isn't planning on taking her back to her father-in-law?"

Mary felt herself blush, and she was glad it was too dark for anyone to notice. Very few of the people around the fire knew her background, and though she was certain Matthew meant only to protect her, his words embarrassed her. Already curious eyes had turned to her from every direction.

"Matthew, sit down," Jesus told him. "You have a right to be concerned, but I can assure you that this man has no such intentions." He gestured to the fisherman to rise, which he did immediately.

"Thank you, Master," Jedidiah said as Matthew grudgingly stepped away from him and joined the seated disciples. "Might I speak privately with her?"

Mary heard Susanna gasp. The fisherman was asking for something normally quite improper, and he even suggested it in front of every one of them. Several of the men had troubled looks on their faces, and Mary wondered if the Rabbi might be angered at such boldness.

Obviously Jedidiah knew what he was requesting, and she could tell from the nervous twisting of his hands that he was not at all certain he would get what he wanted.

"Are you agreeable to this, Mary?" the Nazarene asked, sounding totally unaware of the inappropriateness of the request.

Mary thought briefly of Eli and what her life back in Magdala would be like. Jedidiah had let her go once, but perhaps since then, her father-in-law had convinced him of the importance of her return, especially if he still hoped to marry her. Could she really trust him?

But then why not at least listen to him? She had no doubt that Matthew would not be far away, and if Jedidiah did or said anything she did not like, she could always find safety back with the disciples. Simon even had a sword.

She nodded at Jesus, and a greatly relieved Jedidiah escorted her out of the circle of light. She could not help but smile a little at Matthew's suspicious face.

They settled down on some large rocks not far from the group of disciples.

"I have come to warn you," the fisherman told her abruptly.

Mary felt a shiver go down her back. "My children . . . are they . . ."

"No, no, they are very well. It is for you that I am concerned." He quickly shared what Tabitha had overheard.

"Thank you for telling me, but I am safe with Jesus."

Jedidiah shook his head. "You don't understand. Your father-in-law is determined to find you and have you brought back to Magdala. He even told the servant to bind you, if necessary. He is to hire others to help him. This is no small matter."

Mary stood up. "I appreciate your trouble to inform me about this, but I am constantly surrounded by the Rabbi's followers, and you know there are always crowds coming to listen to His teachings." She saw the worried look in Jedidiah's eyes, and her voice softened. "I will be careful."

"That is all I ask," Jedidiah said, also rising. "Because you see, Mary, I . . . I meant it when I said I love . . ."

"Please, you must not feel this way," she interrupted.

"But . . . but the last time I saw you, you said . . . at least, I got the impression that perhaps at some time you could care for me."

Mary turned to face the circle of men still sitting around the fire. How could she explain to him that everything had changed since she left Magdala that day which seemed so long ago?

"I'm sorry if I gave you that idea," she began carefully. "I did not mean to convey it."

"What has happened? You must tell me! I at least deserve that much. For the past few weeks, I have traveled all over Galilee, looking for you."

The sudden anger in Jedidiah's voice made her take a step back away from him. "If that is the case, I am truly sorry you wasted so much time on me." She paused to control her own rising anger. Who did he think he was? There had been no betrothal between them; she had not expressed feelings for him. He had no right to think as he did.

Jedidiah was silent for a moment, and Mary was just ready to start back to join the others when he finally spoke. "You are right, of course," he said softly, the fury gone from his eyes. "I had no business expecting so much of you. And my time was not wasted, for I had to warn you. Jesus has many enemies, you know. Just on this trip, I have heard there are a number in the Sanhedrin who wish to kill Him. You may not be as secure as you think you are."

Mary nodded and began walking toward where Matthew was waiting for her. "Thank you again."

"Please wait! Don't you want to hear about how your family is?"

"I do, but . . ."

Jedidiah hung his head like Joshua used to do when she scolded him. "I promise I will not let my emotions get out of hand again. Sit back down," he urged.

Though something told her not to stay with him, Mary found herself back beside Jedidiah. *I must at least hear about the children,* she thought. *Even as contented as I am with the Master, still there is a hole in my heart as long as they are away from me.*

By the time Jedidiah had finished telling all he could remember about what Kezia and Joshua were doing and saying, how Tabitha was, and what was happening in Magdala, it was late. But Mary was satisfied, and she had to admit her feelings toward the fisherman had mellowed. *He cares for the children, and he really is a kind man who would make a good husband,* she decided. *Just not for me.* As they parted, Mary gently told Jedidiah again that she could never be his.

"Have you found someone else?" he asked.

She nodded, and wishing him the Holy One's peace, Mary hurried back to the fire, by then almost burned out. Only a few men remained awake, and though Matthew was among them, she knew it was too late to talk to him.

There will be an opportunity to do that tomorrow, Mary thought sleepily as she moved toward the tent she shared with Joanna and Susanna.

16

As Mary passed out slabs of cheese to the disciples the next morning, she was disappointed—but not really surprised—to see Jedidiah in the line.

After all, it had been late when they had finished talking the previous night. It would have been foolish for him to begin the journey back to Magdala in the dark. Besides, the nearest inn was several hours' walk away. Better that he should remain with the Master's men until daybreak.

But seeing him again was something Mary had hoped to avoid. At best, it was awkward to feel his eyes on her, to still catch the look of devotion he had for her. His smile was brilliant as he took his cheese from her.

Perhaps he believes now that morning is here, I have changed my mind about him, Mary thought, a little irritably. *If he only knew how wrong he is! I will never love him, and if he so much as says one more word about his feelings toward me . . .*

But the tall fisherman merely moved down the line to receive a loaf of bread from Susanna and a cup of water from Joanna. Mary noticed that Matthew and several of the others kept a close eye on the intruder, and she took comfort in that.

"Where is the Master today?" Susanna whispered to Mary as the last disciple found a seat with his meal. "He should eat something."

Mary shook her head. "I haven't seen Him."

Joanna joined them, handing each woman her cup of water. "He left early to pray. I wasn't even up yet."

Since Joanna was always the first one awake, in her diligence to care for the men, Mary knew that Jesus must have risen when it had actually still been night.

"He may not be back for hours. I guess that means we won't be traveling much today," Susanna said.

"Just as well," Joanna muttered. "This old back of mine is ready for a day of rest."

Mary studied the portion of cheese in her hand. Ever since Chuza had come to Capernaum and expressed discontent with his wife's being gone for so long, Joanna had seemed different somehow. Oh, not significantly, but she complained more and seemed to feel worse.

She should go back to Chuza, Mary thought. But she suspected Joanna was not yet ready for that step.

Finished with her food, Susanna rose from the small circle of women and began to gather up the now empty cups. "Well, I have great plans, if we will be here for a while. I will wash my hair!"

"Oh, that sounds wonderful!" Mary told her quickly. "I'll join you." It had been ten days since she had been able to feel really clean, and the thought of shiny hair again was more than appealing.

Of course, they were all supposed to be completely cleansed for the Sabbath, but last week Mary had not had a chance to give herself a thorough washing. Besides, the mountain streams near Caesarea Philippi were frigid. So she had settled for merely a good brushing. She had been thankful her veil hid most of it.

By the time the women had cleaned up the remains of the meal, the Nazarene still had not returned. The disciples broke into small groups, some discussing the latest topic Jesus had shared with them, others going off to rest or pray. Mary even saw Judas preparing to cut Andrew's hair and trim his beard.

To Mary's disgust, Jedidiah made no move to depart. He had eaten with James and John, and she watched, biting her lip, as he continued to sit with them.

At last, the visitor from Magdala rose to his feet.

Mary gave a quick sigh of relief. Certainly he would start his trip now, and she would not have to be with him anymore.

"Mary?" Jedidiah's voice was soft and low. "May I speak with you once more before I leave?"

"There's really nothing more to say, except peace to you as you travel." Mary struggled to keep her voice level.

"Mary, I still think of you as special."

"I don't want to hear such things. I thought I made that clear last night."

Jedidiah licked his lips. "I know you would feel differently if you would just get to know me. It would be in your best interests. I could provide for you and the children; the children already care for me." A trace of a smile crossed his lips. "I have taken the boy to synagogue and the market with me. And Kezia likes the little toys I carve her."

So, while she was gone, he was endearing himself to Joshua and Kezia! "Stay away from my children!" Mary hissed, surprising even herself by the anger in her voice.

Fury flared in Jedidiah's eyes. "You have no authority to tell me that. Your father-in-law approves of my being with them. I will see them every day, if I wish. Their own mother is not there to care of them."

Rage propelled Mary's feet away from him. How dare he talk to her like that? Praying for self-control, she hurried past the curious stares of several of the disciples.

Jedidiah ran after her. "I said, their own mother does not care for them."

The repetitious words tore at her. "Stop! Leave me alone!"

Jedidiah caught up with her, grabbing her arm, and leering in her face. "Their own mother does not . . ."

Without thinking, Mary raised her free hand and slapped Jedidiah's cheek as hard as she could. The unexpected pain made him release her, and she slumped to the ground, almost oblivious to the presence of Judas, Andrew, James, and John who had come running when they saw what was happening.

"You must go now," James told Jedidiah, stepping between him and Mary, who was being helped up by Andrew.

"I'm leaving," the fisherman answered, gingerly touching the red welt on his cheek.

"What has happened?" Matthew shouted, coming toward the group. He broke into a trot when he saw Mary in the midst of them.

"Nothing, brother," Judas told him, giving Jedidiah a little push in the opposite direction. "There is no problem."

But Matthew was not satisfied. He immediately took in Jedidiah's bruised cheek and Mary's tears, which were now running unchecked down her face. "What has this dog done to you?" he asked her.

"Matthew, it is not your concern," Andrew told him.

"It very much is. This woman is important to me, to all of us . . ."

Through her tears, Mary almost smiled. If nothing else, Matthew's statement confirmed his love for her. Surely today he would ask her about marriage. "I am all right," she said quickly. "A mere disagreement, that's all. I'm sorry." Embarrassed, Mary pulled away from the concerned circle of men. She hoped most of them had not seen her slap Jedidiah.

Judas had hustled the fisherman over to the tents and was stuffing some food into his sash in preparation for the journey, which was apparently to start immediately.

Mary took a deep breath. At least he would bother her no more. She could hear Matthew talking with Andrew.

"But what happened? What did he say to her?"

Andrew's reassuring voice was too low for Mary to pick up the words, but she could hear every syllable of Matthew's reply.

"If he so much as comes near her again, I will beat him senseless."

"You know the Master says violence is not the answer," Andrew told him. "Pray for your enemies . . ."

Matthew broke away from him. "Do not talk to me of such things!"

To the left of her, Jedidiah started down the road toward Magdala.

Somehow Jesus knew. When He returned from His hours of prayer, Jedidiah had long since disappeared, and the disciples were back at whatever tasks they had been doing. But just the same, the Master was aware of what had happened in His absence. Mary was sure of it.

She was the one to blame. Why had she let herself get so angry? All Jedidiah had done was to make those unkind comments. If she had only ignored them . . . Surely, if she had really experienced the new life the Nazarene taught, she would not have reacted with such fury. Would Jesus make her leave His group? He had every right to; she had failed Him. And what of Matthew? He, too, had let his anger get out of control. Mary had ruined things for both of them.

An hour after the incident, when Matthew had calmed down, and he had a chance to talk with Mary away from everyone else, she had been tortured by her deed. She hardly noticed him taking her into his arms and patting her back, as one might comfort a child. She could not appreciate the gentle stroke of his hand on her still-dirty hair, even though it was the first time he had touched her.

Now Jesus was back, looking straight at her, His eyes challenging her. Yes, there was love there, and compassion, as she always felt in His presence, but today there was more. There was disappointment. She had disappointed the Master.

Fresh tears clouded Mary's vision as she finally approached Him. "Master, forgive me," she murmured.

He reached out for her, and Mary bowed her head over His calloused palm, letting her tears dampen it. "What have you done?" His voice was gentle yet firm.

"You know, Lord."

"Tell me."

Miserably Mary sat down beside Him. "I . . . I sinned. I got too angry. I struck a man."

"What do you want from Me?" Jesus' eyes remained fixed on hers; she could not break away.

"Why, Master, I want Your forgiveness. I'm sorry I reacted that way. I don't want to do it again."

"You have My forgiveness. But your determination alone will not keep you from sinning again. Let My power flow through you, Mary. You can't do it yourself."

She bent her head. "I know, Lord. I know."

"What else is it?" He asked, when she made no move to go.

"Just . . . just I wondered if You would have me to leave Your followers. I know I'm not worthy."

Jesus smiled a little. "If all who sin had to depart from Me, I would have no one left. Each man and woman here has done as you have, in one way or another. But with the Everlasting One, there is mercy, there is always mercy for those who will accept it."

"Yes, Master."

"Mary?"

"What is it, Lord?"

"You must also go to Jedidiah and ask his forgiveness."

She nodded slowly. It would not be easy to admit to Jedidiah that she had been wrong, but she realized Jesus was right. At least she would not have to face the fisherman in the near future. Many months could pass before she saw Jedidiah again. In the meantime, she was back in the good graces of the Master. That was most important.

As Mary moved from Jesus, the peace that usually enfolded her when she spoke to Him returned. Wiping away the last of the tears, she went to find Susanna. She would be finished with her hair by this time, but perhaps she would sit by the water with Mary while she washed hers.

Susanna readily agreed, and Mary soon stood in the stream, her long hair floating out in all directions from her head. How wonderful it felt to be in the water!

Rubbing the soap over her body, she thought with pride how no one could fault her figure. She wanted Matthew to be proud of her. Mary thought of Matthew, of his hand on her back earlier in the day, of his fingers in her hair. She smiled.

"You look so happy, Mary. What pleases you so?" Susanna asked, breaking into Mary's thoughts.

"Why . . . why, nothing. Just the feel of the water." Mary stepped out of its chilly depths and into the towel Susanna offered. "Do you have some perfume I could use? Perhaps work it into my hair?" Surely tonight Matthew and she would talk.

"Of course," Susanna said simply. She asked no more questions, but the women smiled at each other.

Mary huddled by the fire, which did little to lessen the coolness of the evening. Naturally, the best thing to do would be to retire to the tent and the warmth of the skins there, as Joanna had already done.

But Mary knew she couldn't go yet. *Just a bit longer,* she kept thinking. *Then he'll come.* She glanced over at Matthew, who was deep in discussion with Simon. Both men seemed totally oblivious to the rest of the figures around the glowing embers. Their voices were too low for her to hear what was being said, but surely it could not be so important as a marriage proposal. And that was what she still expected the evening would bring.

Soon after Susanna had anointed Mary's clean, damp hair, Jesus had informed them that they were to begin the walk south to Capernaum within the hour.

"What is He thinking about?" Joanna grumbled. "We will be traveling during the hottest part of the afternoon, and we won't reach our destination until long after dark. Why couldn't we just stay here until morning?"

Mary wondered herself about the wisdom of the Master's decision, but as usual, no one protested to Him. They packed the supplies and left as scheduled.

By the time the darkness surrounded them, the group was still several hours from Capernaum, and Jesus motioned them to stop and spend the night where they were.

"I'm getting too old for this," Joanna sighed as she unpacked the fruit and bread they had to eat for the evening meal. It was all that remained of the food they had obtained in Caesarea Philippi.

"What I would give to be home, with a pot of lentil stew boiling on the fire," Susanna said wishfully. She pulled out the cups from the bag in which they were carried.

"Ah, yes," Joanna said. "With a regular house and clean robes

to put on . . . and Chuza's embrace . . ." Suddenly remembering
that both women listening to her were widows, she stopped
quickly and busied herself with dividing the dates into piles for
each disciple.

Mary didn't mind the reference; soon Matthew's arms would
always be around her. "Joanna, why don't you go home to your
husband?" she asked gently.

Without answering, Joanna turned from them to call the men
to eat.

"She will not be with us much longer," Susanna had whispered.

Now that the meal was long over, Mary remembered the comment and hoped her friend was right. Nevertheless, keeping her
thoughts on Joanna was impossible. She looked over again at
Matthew. Why didn't he hurry? But the former tax collector
seemed just as involved in speaking with Simon as he had been
for the past hour.

*I doubt if the fragrance of Susanna's perfume even lingers on
my hair anymore,* Mary thought, a bit crossly.

Just then, Matthew rose to his feet and peered around the circle gathered around the fire. As his eyes met hers, she too rose
and stepped outside of the area illuminated by the coals.

As if they had planned it, he joined her on the other side of a
large rock a short distance from the sprawled figures still by the
source of heat. Heart pounding, Mary stood beside him, delight-
ing in Matthew's height, his masculine odor, and in the seriousness which she could see impressed on his face, even in the
darkness.

"We must talk," he said, motioning her to sit.

One would think I am a young never-married girl, Mary told
herself. Why else would I be so thrilled by Matthew's presence? I
must not show him how eager I am for this match.

17

"Mary, I'm not sure how to tell you this," Matthew began solemnly. "You know I care for you. You have been a blessing to me, in spite of your being a woman."

"You have also been a blessing to me," Mary replied, "in spite of your being a man!"

"I did not mean . . ." Matthew began awkwardly, ignoring her attempt at humor as he realized his words were not coming out the way he planned. "Hasn't the Master often taught us that women are not the inferior creatures the rabbis have said they are? Forgive me."

Mary boldly took his hands in hers. After all, wasn't this the moment of their betrothal? "I understand what you mean, dear Matthew. Please continue."

"Yes, . . . well, ah, it regards your safety and well-being. I have thought very seriously about this, and I beg you to carefully consider what I suggest."

"Of course," she said, trying not to smile. Why didn't Matthew just come out and ask her to be his wife?

"As you know, the Master has informed us that He is going to die. He mentioned it again tonight. I told you before that many of us didn't think He really meant a physical death. But, Mary, I'm beginning to wonder. He talks of betrayal. He could actually mean what He says."

What was Matthew doing? Mary thought. It was difficult for her to keep her mind on his words, when so far they had nothing to do with her.

As if sensing her question, Matthew stopped. "I tell you this because I feel that following Jesus is not going to always be what it is now. The crowds, the miracles, and all that, are exciting, but if He is going to His death, it will change. Already we hear rumors that the Sanhedrin is increasingly irritated by the Master. Who knows what they may plan? I don't want you to be a part of things if they get dangerous."

"What are you saying?" Mary asked, her throat constricting. When was he going to get to marriage?

"Why, merely that I want you to go back to your home, to safety, while you still can," Matthew said.

Mary jerked her hands away from his. "I cannot go to Magdala. If I do, I face prison, as surely as I would if I were arrested by the Master's enemies."

"I expected you to say that, and I have an alternate plan."

Mary felt her tense body relax a little. Now he would ask her the question for which she waited.

"Why not go to Joanna's? If you mentioned it to her, I'm certain she would go home to her husband. He would welcome you, for he desperately wants his wife back. It would solve both of your problems."

Mary could not believe what she was hearing. Matthew had no intention of marrying her. He was only showing concern for a friend. She swung away from him.

Realizing his suggestion had not pleased her, the former tax collector tried again. "Or . . . or how about going to Simon's mother-in-law's? You know Leah; she would be glad to have you. Or there's Susanna's parents. They are also followers of Jesus."

"I am not leaving the Master!"

"But, you don't understand. Being with Him could cost you your life!"

Mary turned back to face Matthew. "I have made my decision. Don't bring it up again. Is there anything else you wish to say to me?"

Puzzled and a little embarrassed by her firmness, he shrugged. "I can't think of anything."

"So, your fine words about having to talk with me were just to tell me to desert the one I serve? You had nothing more personal to say to me?"

Matthew took a step back. "What?"

The tears were fogging Mary's eyes, and she was tempted to run away, anywhere, just to be rid of him. But she could not. She had to let him know how she felt. Besides, she knew she had not misread his eyes during the past months. Perhaps if she confessed her feelings, he would admit his. It was not how she had planned for this evening to go, but it might still end the same way.

"What do you mean, Mary? Why are you crying?"

"Are men so stupid?" she answered. "You spend the last few weeks seeking me out to talk, coming to my aid, longing to touch me . . ."

"I have never acted improperly toward you," Matthew interrupted stiffly.

"Acted? No, never acted upon! But you have thought it, thought it often. I have seen it in your eyes; you have wanted to caress me, just as I have wanted to be in your arms," Mary added bravely.

"I have not thought of you in . . ."

"Admit the truth, Matthew! Your days of dishonesty ended with your tax collecting, didn't they?" Mary was surprised at the barbs in her voice.

Matthew leaned weakly against the hugh rock, his head drooping. "Mary, why are you doing this to me?" he said brokenly. He had sunk to the ground. "I'm sorry," he was muttering. "I am attracted to you, yet . . ."

Mary knelt beside him, her anger gone. "Our Master doesn't teach against marriage."

"I know," Matthew told her quickly. "It's just that I, myself, have felt called not to marry. I . . . I would take you in marriage at once, if I were free to. But I am certain the Everlasting One does not want me to take this step." Seeing the expression on Mary's face, he continued more gently. "At least not at this time. Can you understand?"

Studying her hands, Mary nodded slowly.

"Perhaps it would be, ah, easier for both of us if we did not talk regularly as we have been," Matthew suggested.

Mary nodded again.

They reached Capernaum before noon, and being back in a familiar place seemed to lift nearly everyone's spirits. Within a short time after the travelers had stepped inside the coolness of Simon's house, to be greeted with water for foot washing and refreshment, a number of the followers who had not made the trip north to Caesarea Philippi filled the courtyard.

As usual, Mary smiled at the men and embraced the other women who were now reunited with them. But she wondered how any of them could fail to be aware of the pain that filled her heart.

Why had she counted so much on Matthew? How had she let herself get so convinced he would marry her? The sense of loss she felt was overwhelming.

Yet no one seemed to notice, not even Susanna, who had asked no questions when the women had awakened that morning and packed for the trip. She still had none as the two of them began preparing to cook the evening meal that Joanna felt should be started right away. There would be a hungry crowd by nightfall.

"Master, a story, a story!" clamored a number of the ones who had stayed in Capernaum.

The people took up the chant, and, smiling, Jesus took a seat in the middle of the courtyard. Immediately, all the room around Him was filled with listeners.

"What shall I talk about?" the Rabbi asked.

"Who is the greatest in the kingdom of heaven?" a man called out.

As if He had not heard the request, Jesus began peering around the courtyard. Mary thought that perhaps His eyes rested on her with more compassion than usual, but she couldn't be sure.

"Master, who is the greatest?" Judas repeated.

"I will tell you," Jesus replied, and motioned with His finger for someone to approach.

I wager it's a man, Mary thought, pricking her finger with the knife she was using to cut up leeks for the stew Joanna planned to serve that evening. *And it's probably one who has given up the most for Him.* She wiped the blood from her fingertip. *Yes, maybe one who had been wealthy or blessed with a high position.*

The Master was still motioning for a person to join Him, but no one was coming. Curious heads turned to find out who the reluctant one was.

"Come on, I won't hurt you," Jesus coaxed. "Walk up here to Me."

Mary glanced at the open courtyard gate where He was look-ing, just in time to see the small head of a child peek in and out. It happened so quickly that if one wasn't watching right at that instant, it would have been missed.

"Yes, you, small one," the Nazarene called again. "Please come up here to Me."

Slowly the little boy, perhaps four winters old, walked toward Him. His dark curls hung down over his lowered face so that his features were partially hidden, but Mary could see enough to know she did not recognize the child, though he did look vaguely familiar. Of course! He resembled Joshua at that age. The memory brought an ache to Mary's chest.

The boy had reached Jesus who gently swung the child up on His lap. Instinctively, the boy nestled his head against the man's chest and looked up at Him with such complete trust that it brought smiles to most faces who were watching.

"Unless you become like little children, you shall not enter the kingdom of heaven," Jesus told the hushed crowd. "Whoever humbles himself like this one is the greatest in the kingdom."

Mary stopped her chopping. A child, a mere toddler—the most important in the kingdom? She could hardly believe she had heard right. Why, that meant the attitude of the heart was what Jesus thought the most of, not how much a person left to follow Him.

Mary remembered overhearing Simon once say that he had left his profitable business, his family, his position in the synagogue, and everything to be one of the disciples. Simon's words had stung because Mary knew that she had left little. All that remained in Magdala for her was imprisonment.

"I say to you, if two of you agree about anything you ask the Father, it will be done for them." Jesus was saying, still holding the child.

Mary hardly heard Him. She did not have to be an inferior member of the Kingdom! If her attitude was right, she was as important as Simon or any of the other men. The Master Himself had said so.

Susanna was staring at the motionless knife in Mary's hand, and Mary quickly began slicing leeks again before she had to explain the reason for the delay. But the realization of her place among the disciples was as cooling water during the heat of the afternoon. It was the first thing she had felt good about since Matthew and she had talked.

"Lord, how often should I forgive my brother when he sins against me?" asked a voice Mary recognized as Simon's. "As many as seven times?"

Several heads nodded. Simon was being extremely generous to suggest that much mercy; the Law taught clearly an eye for an eye.

But instead of approving, as Mary expected the Master to do, Jesus said, "I tell you, not seven times, but seventy times seven."

A few people gasped. *Why, He was as good as saying one should forgive forever,* Mary thought. *Even if a person keeps hurting you over and over again* . . . Suddenly Eli and Ruth's faces came to Mary's mind.

Forgive them? But she couldn't. They had separated her from Joshua and Kezia, they had locked her up, and they had forced her to flee. Even now, Jedidiah said they were sending servants to bring her back.

Jesus lifted the child down off His lap, tickling him in the process. As the child scampered off, his high giggle rang through the courtyard.

The Master smiled after him. "Now I have a story to tell you," He said, turning His attention to the crowd. "Once there was a king . . ."

"Wait, Lord," John called. "Can't You move out of the courtyard? Already many have found out that You are back, and they are gathering outside to listen."

Jesus nodded and stood up. "We will go to the water's edge, and everyone will be able to hear."

"I will find a boat from which you can speak," John told Him, darting out of the gate. The rest of the people also rose and began filing out more slowly.

"Now we won't find out what happens to the king in the story," Susanna said forlornly. "With this many people to feed, Joanna will never let us go listen. We'll be cooking all afternoon."

"I'll let you know . . ." Mary started to say, but she stopped. Matthew was no longer sharing with her Jesus' teaching. She hadn't realized how much she depended on him.

As the people from inside the courtyard merged with those waiting outside to hear the Master, Joanna began in earnest her preparations for the evening meal.

"Here, Susanna," she instructed, pushing a water pitcher and a small leather bucket into her hands. "We'll need lots of water."

Susanna started out the gate toward the well. But the sight of two men leaning against the outside wall made her stop. Dirty and unkempt, they immediately struck her as not the usual types of people to be around Jesus. Yet neither did they look like the Master's enemies, usually well dressed Pharisees.

"May I help you?" she asked them courteously, and regretted it at once. She was so used to the informality between the men and women who followed the Master that she often forgot that to others, it was still highly improper for a woman to speak boldly to one of the opposite sex.

"Help us? No, ah . . ." the shorter one answered, and Susanna immediately thought he reminded her of slippery oil. "We have come to listen to the great Teacher. That's Him, isn't it?" He pointed a dirty finger toward Jesus' retreating back.

"Yes, that's Jesus," she answered, unexplainably suspicious of the two. She didn't like the way the taller man was eyeing her.

After the two men had joined the crowd walking to the beach, Susanna began again her trip to the well. But she stopped when she saw Andrew. "Do you know those two?" she asked him, pointing them out to him.

He shook his head. "I have never seen them before. And the

way they're acting, I don't think they're from around here. Maybe they are here to harm the Master. I'll keep an eye on them."

Susanna nodded gratefully.

As Azor and Sadoc moved with the rest of the people toward the water, the bigger man spat on the ground. "Why did you say we wanted to hear this Nazarene?" he growled. "I'm not going to sit and endure some dry old doctrine!"

"Oh, yes, you are, my friend," Azor answered. "You're going to act interested too. Do you want people to be suspicious of us? It's bad enough that we are so filthy. At least, we must appear to have come out of desire to hear this man Jesus."

Sadoc snorted. "Anyone who does has the mind of a donkey." He eyed a young woman who was hurrying past him. "Are you certain the one who spoke to us wasn't the Mary we seek?"

"Yes, of course," Azor answered impatiently. "That girl was far too young. The Magdalene is older, remember? She had children ten years ago. But surely the woman is here, among all these devoted followers. We'll find her."

"Yes, but when?" Sadoc muttered. "That fool Micah could be behind us any day. I say we find the woman today and get away quickly while we still can."

"This Micah who sends such fear into your heart is probably back at his master's by now, begging for more money to seek the woman. He would never try to follow us himself with an empty purse. Relax, my friend. We have plenty of time to find her." Azor smiled patronizingly at a woman with a baby who passed him.

18

As the sun dipped behind the hills that encircled the Sea of Galilee, Sadoc swore under his breath and stretched his cramped legs. For the past few hours, he had sat with the crowds surrounding Jesus, as Azor had insisted. Sadoc had never spent so much time in a stationary position except in sleep.

At first, Sadoc had tried to convince Azor that they should go back to the house where Jesus had been and look for Mary there. His arguments had been halfhearted; even Sadoc realized that the chances of finding her and then getting away with her were slim.

Later, Sadoc had turned his attention to the women around him. It was useless since they were all intent on what the Nazarene was saying. Besides, most of them were too old or too young for his tastes.

Disgusted, he had finally fallen asleep on the grass. It had never occurred to Sadoc to try to listen to Jesus.

But now, he was awake and his belly quite empty. The worst part was that the Rabbi in the boat in front of him was still speaking. Yet the people around him did not seem restless; they strained to hear each word.

Sadoc nudged Azor. "You may be content to stay here all night, but I've had it. I'm going back to the house."

"Not so fast, my friend," Azor replied. "While you were snoring, I had conversations with several of the ladies near us." He smiled benignly at a grandmother on the other side of him. "I have discovered where she is," he whispered.

Just then, the elderly woman leaned over toward them. "See? There she is, the woman you seek." She pointed to a figure coming up to the crowd from behind them. "She's in the blue robe."

Azor smiled his thanks at her and with Sadoc, he rose. "This will be even easier than I thought," he muttered. "We will be on the road to Magdala by nightfall."

Brushing a stray strand of hair out of her sweaty face, Mary hurried down the path. How could she ever find Simon in this mob? Even in the few hours since the Master had begun teaching, the number of people listening had increased. It seemed that all of Capernaum must surely be gathered on the beach to hear Him.

While it was irritating to have to search through the whole crowd, Mary found that a part of her was relieved to see that Jesus had lost none of His appeal. Perhaps it was even growing. There must be no basis to Matthew's talk about how the Master might really be going to die, and how it could be dangerous to be one of His followers.

She stepped over a sleeping child. It had been a long afternoon bending over the cooking fire, trying to prepare enough food for the masses that Joanna expected. The people who listened to the Rabbi were always invited to eat with Him and His disciples afterward. Of course, it was supposed to be just those who had traveled from a distance and had no way to buy their own food or the poor from the area. But Mary knew that many times others came too.

When Joanna had mentioned it to Jesus one time, he had only patted her shoulder. "Feed any who wish to eat," He had told her.

"They may come away with more than what they expected."

Mary wasn't quite sure what that meant, but she didn't question it. Whatever the Master said . . .

Now as she wove her way along the edge of the people, Mary wondered if the women's efforts would prove to be enough this time. Well, if not, perhaps Jesus would multiply the stew as He had done to the loaves and fishes several times now when there had been need.

Finally, as she was reaching the front of the crowd, Mary spied Simon. He was sitting on the sand, his feet in the shallow water, looking more like a boy than one of the disciples to whom Jesus was closest. *Maybe the teaching on being humble as a child earlier in the afternoon has spoken to him,* she thought.

She sunk down next to him. "Simon, Joanna sends word that the meal is ready, whenever the Master wants it. We've prepared quite a bit."

The former fisherman nodded, "I think He is almost done speaking. And I for one am starving. We will be there soon."

Mary rose and started back down through the people. She wanted to get back to the house before the crowd began to arrive. As she passed the last row of listeners, she did not notice that two men had risen from among them and fallen into step behind her.

Before she had gone a dozen steps, Azor and Sadoc were on either side of her. "Mary? Mary of Magdala?" Azor said. At her nod, he continued. "Forgive the interruption, but we bring greetings from your children."

Suspiciously Mary eyed them. "Who are you?" They did not look like the kind of men with whom anyone she knew would have anything to do. Could this be what Jedidiah had warned her about?

Azor gave her his warmest smile, revealing yellow teeth. "I

beg your pardon again, fair lady. I am Azor, and my distinguished friend here is Sadoc." He gestured at the huge man on
Mary's other side. "We have recently come from Magdala, sent
by request of Joshua and Kezia. Well, of course, not them personally, but on their behalf by the maidservant who cares for
them."

"Why? What's wrong with my children?"

"It's nothing, really. I mean, nothing you should concern yourself over. That is, you don't need to be extremely concerned
about it."

Mary stopped walking. "Tell me at once what you mean. Are
my son and daughter ill or hurt? I have no patience for this kind
of talk."

Azor smiled at her again. "Of course. I understand completely. I have no children of my own, but if I did, I would want to
find out right away how they were. Wouldn't you, Sadoc? Of
course, you would. And she has every right to know, doesn't she,
Sadoc?" As he spoke, Azor began gradually moving over to the
right, down the beach, hoping that Mary would not notice. Just
to hear him she had resumed walking.

"You have told me nothing," Mary said between stiff lips.

"Yes, well, the truth of the matter is this: Joshua has a wound.
Merely a scratch, of course, but he is crying for his mother.
Sometimes no one else will do, you know."

How stupid does he think I am? Mary wondered. *I would
hardly come back to Magdala just to comfort my son from such a
small problem. He has probably already forgotten it.*

Seeing her unconvinced face, Azor continued. The hours on
the beach had not been wasted; he had the story well in mind. "I
called it a scratch, didn't I? Well, perhaps it would be more hon-
est to say an *injury*. It was a fishhook that went through his
hand, wasn't it, Sadoc?"

The other man nodded, and Mary felt a tremor of fear dart through her. A fishhook injury was extremely painful, and sometimes it never healed right. She remembered one of Eli's servants who had died after such a wound, his leg swollen and red and oozing pus.

The effect of his words on Mary was not lost to Azor. "Your father-in-law does not know we're here, of course. Surely it's no secret to you that he wants you back. But Tabitha paid us out of her own meager funds to come find you, without Eli's consent, naturally."

Mary turned back to look at the crowd. Jesus had just finished speaking, and everyone was getting up. A number were already heading toward Simon's house. She was needed to help with the food. But what if these men were telling the truth?

Azor sensed her dilemma. "Mary, I don't want to scare you because the hook has been removed from his hand. But the poor boy! The site of the entry is rather red and swollen. That is, it was when we saw it four days ago. Of course, in that amount of time, it could be greatly improved." He glanced at her out of the corner of his eye. "Then again, it could be much worse . . ."

Why doesn't he just grab her and be done with it? Sadoc wondered. It could take hours to convince her to go with them.

But in spite of his friend's nervous eyes and frown, Azor was not to be rushed. "I'm sure the maidservant would not have risked sending us for you if she hadn't thought it to be a matter of importance. We have instructions to help smuggle you back into Magdala, see the boy—your daughter too, of course—and get away before Eli hears of it."

The more he spoke, the more convinced Mary was becoming. Tabitha could have done just as this Azor was saying. She would know to come up with such a plan. And as for choosing these two unlikely messengers, perhaps the servant thought that would be the safest way to handle it. She looked again at the people behind her, growing smaller with each step the three of them took down the beach.

"Then there's Kezia," Azor began. "Dear little thing! Such a shame to have it happen to her!"

Mary's head jerked back to face him. "You mean something's wrong with her too?"

"If she just would have done as her grandmother told her, that boiling water would have never splashed in her eyes . . ."

For an instant, Mary considered bolting away from the men. Really, now, both of her children hurt? It couldn't be! He had to be making it up. But as Azor described the accident with great detail, once again Mary could not help but believe him. It was so like Kezia to disobey. He must be telling the truth.

"Her face wasn't burned too badly, but they are concerned about her vision." Azor was saying.

The thought of her child laying helplessly on a mat, blinded by the water, was more than Mary could hear. Even if they had expanded on what actually had happened to the children, she had to go to them, if nothing else, to make sure they were all right.

Mary turned abruptly and started toward Simon's house.

"What are you doing?" Azor called to her.

"I knew she'd never believe all that," Sadoc muttered.

Both of them swung around to follow her. "Wait!" Azor shouted.

"I'll come with you, but I must get my things for the trip. It won't take long," she said over her shoulder.

"No, no, Mary," Azor panted, catching up with her. "You don't need them. We have everything you will want with our donkeys. In fact, Tabitha sent another of the servant girls with us to help you on the journey."

"Merab?" Mary asked, thinking of how she would like to see the girl who had lived with Ara and her.

"Yes, that is her name, isn't it, Sadoc? But please, come now. I didn't want to alarm you, but it is important we get back as soon as we can."

"But I must at least leave a message for the Master."

"We'll take care of that. We must leave at once." Both men moved closer to her and took her arms. "There is no time to lose," Azor told her. The sudden harshness in his voice shocked and frightened Mary, but she did not resist.

Early the next morning, Susanna was surprised to hear a knock on the courtyard gate. Usually at this time, most of the disciples were still on their mats asleep, but an hour ago, Jesus had taken the men out to the hills. Especially when the crowds got large, He liked to have time alone with his most devoted followers before dealing with everyone else.

So the knock was heard only by the women who had remained behind.

"Who could it be?" Joanna grumbled from her place beside the grinding stone where she and Leah were already to work. "They seek out the Master earlier each day."

Leah rose and brushed the barley flour off her hands. "Who?" she called, walking toward the gate.

"It is I, Micah ben Reuben, of Magdala." The man outside sounded frantic. "I seek one Mary, also of Magdala."

Leah swung open the gate, and Susanna moved closer to it. Did the appearance of this man have anything to do with the fact that Mary had not returned to the house the previous evening?

"This is the home of Simon bar Jonah, isn't it? Where the Nazarene called Jesus stays? I was told I might find Mary at this place." Micah nervously licked his lips. "It is a matter of great importance that I locate her."

"The woman you are looking for is not here. She was yester-

day, but we have not seen her since early evening," Leah told
him calmly. "But perhaps if you asked the Master Himself, He
would know."

Picking up the leather bucket and the water pitcher, Susanna
walked toward the gate. The man wore the simple garments of a
servant. She wondered why he seemed so tired and travel worn.
Was he a friend of Mary's?

"Where is the Rabbi?" Micah asked anxiously.

Leah shrugged. "He took the men out into the hills somewhere. You can wait here for His return if you wish, or You
might want to try to find them. It may be a while before they
come back."

"I'll look for Him. I must speak to Him."

The desperation in Micah's voice tore at Susanna's heart. Surprising even herself, she stepped closer to him. "Would you care
for a drink of water before you leave?" she offered timidly.

Micah looked at her as if he was just noticing her for the first
time. "I'm grateful for your concern," he said, and she realized
he was older than she had thought. But he seemed kind and
thanked her graciously when she left the bucket and pitcher to
go get a drink from the remaining water in the courtyard. Then
he was off.

"I hope everything is all right with Mary," Leah was saying.
"It certainly isn't like her to not come back here to sleep."

"Perhaps there is a problem at her home," Joanna suggested,
motioning Leah back to the grindstone.

Susanna suddenly remembered the two men who had stood by
the courtyard when the people had gone to the beach to hear
Jesus. "You know, I saw some strangers around here yesterday.
They didn't seem like the type to want to listen to the Master."

Joanna nodded. "Was one tall and the other of medium
height? Both unkempt looking? I saw them too. I thought I saw
Mary talking to them when I stepped outside the courtyard

briefly, just as we were getting ready to serve the food. I wondered then why she wasn't with us, where she was needed."

"We must pray for Mary," Susanna said. "She does have enemies, you know—even in her own family."

The other women nodded.

19

Panting, Micah ran up to the top of the hill. Ignoring the view behind him of the Sea of Galilee, stretched out like a huge pool of blue dye, he scanned the nearby slopes: no one. He could see absolutely no one. But the Rabbi and His followers had to be around somewhere.

Turning slowly to the left, Micah continued peering off into the distance. If Eli could see him now, it would surely result in a severe beating at the least. Again Micah cursed himself and his stupidity in letting Azor and Sadoc get him drunk. Why hadn't he known better than to do business with the likes of them?

There was nothing to the south of him, save more hilltops like the one on which he stood. And beyond them, Magdala, where Micah's master waited for him to return with Mary. He shivered to think of Eli's rage, if he were to return empty-handed.

But I won't, Micah vowed silently. *I'll get her.* Yet his words seemed void. How could he find and subdue her by himself? Now with the money Eli had given him gone, he could not even hire someone to help him. And what if Azor and Sadoc hadn't just run off with his coins? If they were also looking for Mary, perhaps hoping for a larger reward from her father-in-law upon her return, Micah would have no chance. What was he to do?

Turning his head to the north, Micah studied distant Mount Hermon, its pinnacles already again white topped, after the brief summer reprise it experienced each year from the snow. Stretching out between where he stood and the huge mountain were brown hillsides, waiting the winter rainfall to bring their deadness back to life. No men there either.

But wait. As Micah watched, suddenly there appeared a small moving group. It was coming toward him. Breaking into a run, Micah started toward them. It had to be the men he was seeking. Surely Mary was with them, or at least the Teacher would know where she was. He would find her first and be the one to bring the crazed woman back where she was supposed to be, where he too belonged. In spite of Eli's temper, Micah's life was a good one, and he had no wish to change it.

As he approached the group, Micah was disappointed to see no women were with them. It would not be as easy as he had hoped to find Mary. But there was still the rabbi.

"You are followers of the Nazarene teacher, aren't you?" Micah choked out to the first man he reached. At the man's nod, Micah went on. "Where is your master?" The disciple pointed to Jesus, and Micah bowed respectfully before Him, nearly speechless from the running.

"What is it you desire?" the Rabbi asked, motioning for one of the men to give Micah some water from the skin he carried.

Nearly collapsing on the ground, Micah drank deeply before answering. "I seek Mary, the Magdalene. Where is she, my Lord?" he finally got out.

"She's at the house," Simon told him, obviously irritated by the presence of the servant at what was supposed to be a private time between the Master and His men, "certainly not here with us."

"I've just been there," Micah said quickly, ignoring Simon's annoyance. "She did not return to the house last night, and the others have not seen her today." He turned again to Jesus. "My Lord, where is she? I must find her."

"The woman is in great demand, it seems," Judas muttered. "How many have there been searching for her now?"

The Master hushed him with a look. Turning back to Micah, He shook His head. "She is not here."

"But . . . but where shall I look for her? I must go . . ."

"It would do you more good to stay with us a while," Jesus told him. He gestured for the others to sit. "I have a story to tell you."

Micah knew he had to be on his way at once. But where would he start looking for Mary? He had no idea which direction to go. Yet, strangely, the urgency he felt did not bring him to his feet. Instead, he found himself settling back in the grass, feeling the warmth of the early autumn sun on his face, really wanting to hear what the unusual man in front of him was saying. He didn't notice the scowl on Simon's face.

As Jesus began speaking, Micah found himself thinking, *I don't have time for this. What if Azor and Sadoc find Mary first?* Yet as he was drawn into what the Master was saying, Micah forgot about them, about her, and about Eli. All of his attention was focused on the remarkable man before him.

The rope around Mary's wrists burned as it worked its way into her flesh. "Oh Merciful One," she prayed silently. "Send me help."

In front of her, Azor plodded along the dusty path, holding onto the other end of the rope, only rarely looking back over his shoulder. Behind her Sadoc walked, his eyes intent on her. It was he who she really feared. The previous night he had started toward her, and only Azor's curt, "Leave her alone," had kept him away from her.

Coughing as dust stirred up by their steps gagged her, Mary wondered again how she could have believed their lies. As soon as they had walked out of sight of the crowd listening to the Master, she had become suspicious. There was no sight of the promised donkey or servant. And when Mary had turned around, contemplating if she should get out of the men's company, they had bound her with the rope. Then she realized what she should have known from the start. They were actually bringing her back to Eli. But by then, it was pointless to resist.

They had walked for an hour that night, and Mary had wept silently along the way. Why hadn't she known they could not be who they said they were? If she had only consulted Matthew or one of the others, perhaps even now she would be with Jesus, safe from these evil men. She had barely noticed that at least the nighttime travel was easier, out of the heat of the sun, and that Sadoc had to keep his distance from her while they were on the road.

Finally, just when she thought she could walk no further, they stopped to sleep in a deserted shepherds' cave. Miraculously, Sadoc left her alone. Perhaps he was as exhausted as she was, Mary thought as she fell into a deep sleep, in spite of her fears for what the next day might bring.

At daybreak, they were on the road again, with only a cup of water and a crust of dried-out bread to sustain them.

The men had kept the rope around Mary's arms throughout the night, and now that it was early morning, her wrists were rubbed sore and her joints stiff.

"Please, my arms," Mary begged, speaking to the silent form in front of her. "I promise you I won't try to run from you."

Azor turned around, and they all stopped walking. "I would be glad to untie you under those conditions. Besides, soon we will be meeting other travelers on the road, and they can't see you bound, now can they?" Pulling out a dagger, he roughly cut through the rope which had connected her to him. "But listen well, woman! If you do try to escape from us, you have my personal promise that both Sadoc and I will hurt you as brutally as possible. Keep that in mind at all times. Do you understand?"

She nodded and looked away as Azor reached out to touch her face. "Neither of us will hesitate to do anything if you try to escape, will we Sadoc?"

Without answering, the taller man grabbed her shoulder and roughly spun her around to face him, ripping the shoulder of her tunic in the process.

Mary squirmed out of his grip. She struggled to keep her voice calm and free from the terror she felt. "Jesus knows by now that I'm gone. They'll be after me, I know they will. Some of them saw me talking with you. Some of the men will come looking for me."

Before she even saw it coming, Sadoc had reached out and struck her full force on the cheek. Pain exploded across her face, and with a shriek, she fell to her knees, hands rising to her injury.

Curses filled the air above her. At first, Mary thought they were aimed at her, but slowly, as the initial wave of pain waned, she realized it was Azor addressing Sadoc. He had not wanted her hurt, not yet anyway.

Already Mary's cheek was puffy. Even her eye ached, and she could feel it starting to swell shut. The pain filled every part of her, so much so that she was unaware of the men who still argued above her.

At last rough hands pulled her to her feet and half dragged, half carried her over to the side of the road. A wet cloth was applied to her face, by Azor, she assumed.

"Look at her!" the smaller man raved at Sadoc. "How can we travel with her now? Anyone seeing her will suspect what we've done. And how can we take her back to her father-in-law? Micah said very plainly that Eli had insisted she not be hurt. You have ruined everything!"

"No woman talks to me like she did," Sadoc muttered. "I could have done worse. Like maybe broken her nose . . ."

Mary cringed at the thought, and even that slight action sent more pain across her face. She groaned.

Azor dipped the rag back into the water skin and reapplied it to her cheek. "I did not plan for this to happen," he said softly to her. "But we must keep going. Do you think you can walk?"

Mary nodded slightly.

"Good. And remember, you are still under your promise not to try to get away from us. The same threat remains over your head." Almost gently, he helped her to her feet. "Here, pull your head covering down over your face. Perhaps your injury won't be so noticeable."

Mary didn't understand how anyone passing them could fail to be aware of the huge bruise on her cheek, which even then must be turning purple. She could barely see out of her left eye, as swollen as it was.

As they reached the town of Gennesaret, the halfway point to Magdala, they did encounter more people. Most merely looked curiously at the lone woman with the lowered head and her unkempt companions. A few questioned Azor when they glimpsed Mary's face.

"A terrible accident at daybreak today," Azor would answer, his voice artificially sorrowful. "A donkey kicked her as she bent to retrieve a coin she had dropped. It happened as we were leaving home. But now, it only looks bad. She feels little pain, do you, wife?" He would pat her arm.

At first, Mary tried to somehow tell the questioner that she did not want to be with these men. Perhaps if they saw the tear in her robe . . . She would fling back her head covering to make it plain. Then she would roll her eyes or silently mouth the word *help*.

But nobody noticed, or if they did, they did not come to her aid.

Finally, Mary gave up. Each step made her face throb, and just to keep putting one foot in front of the other took all her energy. Maybe being back in Magdala wouldn't be so bad, Mary thought. Yes, she would be confined to the little house by the sea, but how good it would feel to rest. She would be separated from Matthew, and possibly that would enable her to forget him. And once in a while, the children could slip in to see her. The memory of them suddenly overwhelmed her. To see Joshua's smile, to feel Kezia in her arms—being home would not be so bad.

Remembering again Azor's description of her children's injuries, Mary wondered if they could be true. Of course they were lies to convince her to come with them. Or were they? She had to know.

"Tell me, are my son and daughter in good health?" Mary called softly to Azor, hoping that Sadoc would not hear. "You did make up those things about the hook in his hand and her injured eyes, didn't you?"

Azor only laughed, a harsh sound that hurt Mary's ears. It was small reassurance, but, apparently, it was all she was going to get.

Micah stood up to stretch and took another drink from a waterskin someone held out to him. The Master was finished speaking for the time being, and the men began heading back to Capernaum.

But in the hour or so that he had listened to Jesus, Micah had sensed something very different was being said, even in the manner in which it was delivered. The Rabbi had a way about Him, a way of sending words right to one's heart, words that the servant instinctively knew were truth. They challenged Micah, alerted every part of his being, like he had never experienced before.

Without hearing more, Micah made a decision. He, too, would follow this unusual man, if Jesus would have him. He hungered to learn more about the kingdom of Heaven that the Master described, a place where there was peace and love.

"Wonder where Mary could have gone. You don't suppose . . ." As the words from one of the disciples behind him drifted up to him, Micah suddenly remembered the woman he had been sent to retrieve. He had completely forgotten about her. *What shall I do?* he thought. *I want to stay here. But if Azor and Sadoc find her first . . . Yet I don't know where to begin to look for her.*

Jesus had walked up to him. "Micah, have you discovered what you were seeking?" He asked, laying a hand on the servant's shoulder.

"Yes, Lord," Micah answered quickly. "And I . . . I wondered if I might . . . I mean, if You would have me . . ."

The Nazarene smiled at Micah. "You are welcome to join us, friend. But first, finish what you have begun."

Micah nodded and opened his mouth to ask Jesus if He meant he should go after Mary. If so, where should he start? But Jesus had already moved away from him to talk to another of the men.

I don't know what to do, Micah fretted silently. Yet as he walked, he found himself drawn to the main route which went south back to Magdala. *She's on that path,* he thought. *I know she is. Somehow I'm certain of it.* Purposefully, Micah speeded up his walking, leaving the others to take a more leisurely pace back to Simon's house.

20

Adjusting his head covering so that the glare from the morning sun did not directly hit his eyes, Micah stared at the road in front of him. He could see several families walking, a man on a donkey laden with pottery, and two women, their bundles of clothing on their heads. But so far, he had not found Mary.

Gennesaret was behind him, and though Micah had carefully looked over each person behind or ahead of him, he had come up with neither the woman he sought or the two scoundrels who were also after her.

Wearily, Micah wiped the sweat off his forehead with his sleeve. Why had he been so certain he should be on this road? It was impossible to find Mary, like looking for a mite on the beach. One could hunt for such a coin all day and come home with nothing.

But regardless of how hopeless the situation seemed, Micah kept on walking. Though his confidence in following his instinct had dimmed, there was no denying that he had felt something, something he had never experienced before, that surely must be the result of the time he had spent at Jesus' feet. Besides, Micah had no where else to go, no other ideas of where the woman might be. And he could not return to the Rabbi, not yet. Hadn't he been told to finish what needed to be done? At the very least, he must go tell Eli that he wished to leave his employ. Knowing his master's feelings toward the Nazarene, Micah had no intention of letting the old man find out his plans. Why have Eli think that his servant had also gone mad?

Passing an elderly woman carrying a basket of fish, Micah quickened his pace again. He wasn't sure why, but he was feeling an increasing urgency to get to Magdala as quickly as possible. Perhaps it was the same thing which had first propelled him down the road south. For whatever the reason, he was soon almost running, totally unappropriate for a man of his age, especially in the late morning heat.

But what will I do if I do find Mary? Micah thought suddenly, as the Sea of Galilee to his left blurred in the corner of his eye. *Do I bring her back to Eli? What if she is with Azor and Sadoc? Should I confront them about the theft of my money?*

Micah had no answers, and he could only pray that the men would not be with her. Ahead of him an almond tree stood, its branches extending out over the road. Nothing unusual about that, or about the small group of travelers who rested beneath it. But Micah's eyes were drawn back to the tree.

"Come on, no more rest," a masculine voice was saying angrily. "This is the fourth time we've stopped. We must keep moving."

"It's your fault. If you hadn't hit her, she would be able to keep going," another responded, and Micah tensed. He knew those voices. Azor and Sadoc were by that tree!

"Woman, get up," Sadoc growled again at the figure huddled by the trunk. "Perhaps a blow to your other cheek will hasten you."

What had they done to Mary? Micah wondered guiltily. For the one hundredth time, he cursed himself for ever talking to them. Why hadn't he seen what kind of men they were?

Mary had risen, and the men moved to each side of her as they started back down the road. Though they could not have missed seeing Micah on the road behind them, they ignored him. Micah was thankful he was not close enough for them to recognize him.

What should I do? the servant asked himself. *With one fist, Sadoc could kill me, unless I can somehow convince them I am not an enemy.*

An idea forming, Micah broke into a run to catch up with them. "Azor! Azor!" he called.

The men turned around abruptly and drew out their daggers. Mary was pushed to the side of the road.

"What kind of reception is this for your partner?" Micah asked, trying to smile as he came up to them. "I have been looking everywhere for you. Ah, I see you found the woman. My master is prepared to pay a handsome reward for her return." He tried not to look at Mary's injured face.

Azor was eyeing him suspiciously, and Sadoc took a step toward him, the knife blade gleaming in the sunshine.

It's not going to work, Micah thought fearfully. *They don't believe me.* He cleared his throat nervously. "You know, we must have had a misunderstanding back at the wine shop. I have rather fuzzy memories of that day—I'm not used to drinking so much—but, somehow I must have neglected to tell you that I was to come with you in looking for her."

Azor laid a restraining hand on Sadoc's arm. "Really? I thought you had instructions from your master to return to him, so we started off ourselves."

"I thought maybe, as soon as I had regained my senses, that must be what had happened," Micah continued, moving closer to them. "Perhaps I didn't make it clear to you that I was to go too. And when the wine seller suggested to me we had drunk away the rest of the money my master gave me, I was horrified to think you probably had to go off on your search with only part of your money. But I see all has ended well."

"I'll get rid of him," Sadoc said softly, raising his dagger.

"No," Azor told him quietly, and he smiled at the servant. "Well, it certainly is fortunate that you found us," he said. "We can approach the old man together and get our just reward."

As Sadoc reluctantly put his dagger back in his sash, Micah returned Azor's smile and nodded. *I know just what's in your mind,* he thought. *You think that if I am fool enough to believe a "misunderstanding" caused all this, then you will go along with it. But I am not as stupid as I look.*

After walking a short while with the men and Mary, Micah understood why he had been able to catch up with them. The woman was weak and often had to rest. Whether her weariness was due completely to her bruised face or not, he did not know, but whatever the reason, they moved very slowly toward Magdala.

For his part, Micah was glad the journey took so long. Though the plan to join the men—pretending to be on their side— appeared to have worked, he had absolutely no idea of how he was going to get Mary away from these ruffians without getting himself or her stabbed in the process. Only the firm conviction that somehow he must succeed kept him going. And for a reason he could not explain, he knew that he would be able to do it.

The worst part, Micah decided, was watching Mary and not being able to tell her what he was actually doing. Her face, purple and swollen to the extent that she surely could hardly see out of her left eye, expressed such discouragement that he could not bear to look at it. Each time she stumbled, Micah longed to reach out a hand to help her, but he forced himself to ignore her distress. If he showed anything but aloftness toward her, Azor and Sadoc would notice.

Micah could not afford to take that risk; Sadoc still seemed suspicious of him. The taller man insisted on walking behind the rest of them, and his hand was never far from the dagger hilt. *As if a humble servant would single-handedly try to attack the other two men.* Micah almost grinned at the thought.

No, in order to rescue Mary, Micah would have to figure out a way to trick them. Or at least get rid of one man.

"Only a short way to Magdala," Azor told him, moving over next to Micah, "if we can keep her moving."

"Eli will not be happy to see her injury. He specifically said she was not to be hurt," Micah said, immediately regretting it. Angering Azor was not going to help him.

But the other man merely muttered a curse. "I told that fool Sadoc not to touch her, but he didn't listen. It has been difficult enough to keep him from hurting her. Now, me, I don't like hurting women," Azor glanced over at Mary to see if she was listening, but her head was bent. "I might have told her I would hurt her if she tried to escape, but it was just to scare her. I prefer not to harm women. To Sadoc, it makes no difference. In fact," Azor lowered his voice, "he seems to take pleasure in slapping women around a little. But then, he's a violent man."

Horrified, Micah studied the road in front of him and tried to act nonchalant.

Azor shook his head. "I'm not like that. I partake in a little trickery, perhaps. I do some things others might frown on, like convincing a man to give me his money." He cleared his throat as he remembered his past association with Micah. "Not often, of course. Just to give me enough to live on. I don't use a dagger unless I have to. It gives me no satisfaction, like it does Sadoc. Why, he'd as soon twist a knife into your gut as he would to greet you."

Micah turned his head to glance at the big man behind them. Sadoc glared back at him.

If ever Micah had felt unequal to his task, it was then. How could he possibly help Mary? It was just too difficult for any one man, let alone a servant, short of statue, and with no weapon.

A low moan escaping from Mary's lips focused all their attention on her just as she fell again into the dirt.

"She's passed out," Azor said, leaning over her. "Now we'll have to carry her or wait until she comes to. Sadoc, this is your doing. If you had kept your hands to yourself . . ."

Sadoc cut him off with a growl. "So what are we going to do now?"

"Look!" Micah pointed behind them. "Here comes a man with a donkey. Why not buy it from him and let her ride on it?"

Azor looked at the servant with almost an air of respect. "A good idea. I will go talk to him. You two, take her out of the sun. There's some mustard trees over there."

Micah looked doubtfully at the thin branches of the scrawny trees. They would provide little shade, and besides, he wanted Mary to be shielded more from the view of people on the road. Then with Azor gone, he could perhaps take care of Sadoc.

The larger man had picked up Mary's limp form and was heading for the trees.

"Ah, Sadoc," Micah called. "Why not here under these acacia trees? It would be more shelter from the sun for her."

At first Sadoc seemed ready to refuse, but, suddenly, he turned toward the more bushy forms of the acacias at which Micah had gestured. "Perhaps you're right," he muttered.

When Mary had been placed under the trees, the larger man pulled out his waterskin and let the liquid inside it pour down over her face. She sputtered and opened her eyes.

"Now while Azor is occupied, I can have some fun," Sadoc said. He raised his hand as if to strike her again.

Looking at the woman's terrified eyes, Micah could barely shake his head. *I don't want to put you through this,* he silently told her. *But his eyes may not be on me, and I can strike his head with a rock.*

Sadoc turned to Micah and eyed him suspiciously. "You have

no objections to this woman being roughed up a little, do you?" he asked Micah. Then grinning he asked, "Have you ever hit a woman? Why don't you try it? You go first."

"We both may not have time before Azor returns with the donkey," Micah told him casually. "In fact, he may be starting back here now. You go ahead. I'll watch for your friend. I can always hit her later."

The servant could feel Sadoc's eyes boring through him. Would he believe the excuses? It wouldn't be much longer before Azor would return. Micah studied the ground near him for a rock small enough to hold but large enough to injure.

Finally Sadoc grunted his approval. He grabbed Mary, who screamed feebly and tried to struggle.

He's going to kill me, she thought wildly. *How can Micah just stand there and let this happen?*

With a laugh, Sadoc doubled his hand into a fist and swung it at Mary. But he did no more; the man's body suddenly went limp on top of her. Then before Mary could determine what had happened, Micah had shoved Sadoc off her and was helping her up.

"What . . ." Mary began, but Micah hushed her.

"I hit the back of his head with a rock. He may be dead or perhaps just hurt. Either way, we must escape before Azor comes back. Can you walk?"

Mary nodded. "I think so."

"Pray to the Mighty One that you can, for it is your only chance!" Micah took her arm and hurried her over the browned grass toward the beach. "There's a lone fisherman over there. If we can reach him, maybe he'll help us. If not, we will probably both die this day."

"Micah, . . ." Gratitude swelled up inside of her.

"Save your words for later. You must have enough strength to walk," he interrupted, glancing behind him. "Azor is coming."

Panting from the effort, Mary stumbled along with him.

Though she had felt exhausted from the morning, she found that she had a mysterious new sensation of strength. The walk was difficult, but somehow Mary was able to keep going, which she had not thought she could manage to do.

They were not far away from the circle of acacia trees where Sadoc lay when they heard curses coming from there. Azor had found his friend.

"Hurry!" Micah urged, giving Mary a little shove toward the water. "He probably already sees us."

Pain from her bruised cheek mingled with the aching in her chest from the running, but she kept going. They were nearing the fisherman, who had noticed them and had risen from his squatting position next to a small fire. He was cooking his noon meal, and even in the midst of the terror she felt, Mary found her stomach twisting in hunger at the aroma of the fresh fish on the hot stones near the flames.

"They're coming!" Micah told her. "Faster!" He had seen the two figures running after them, and while he had been a bit relieved that he had not killed Sadoc, he feared what would happen when they caught up with him and Mary. For it was only a matter of time until that happened. She would not be able to run much further; her face was white, except for the purple bruise on her cheek, her breath coming in short gasps. If only the fisherman would take them out on the boat . . .

But as they approached him, Mary slowed down, even turned from the man in front of them.

"This way," Micah gestured frantically. "What are you doing?"

"I cannot go to him for help."

Micah jerked on her arm. "We have no choice! Come on!"

Still Mary resisted. "You don't understand! I know him; the last time I saw him, I struck him. He won't assist me, not now."

But as they spoke, Jedidiah ran up to them. "What is it?" Concern covered his face. "Are they after you?"

Micah nodded. "No time to explain. Take us out to sea, at once!"

With no further explanation, the fisherman scooped up Mary and darted for the boat, Micah just behind him. With her safely on board, the two men pushed the craft into the deeper water and climbed into it.

By then, Azor and Sadoc had almost reached the shoreline. They shouted curses after the escaping boat. Though his hair was bloody, Sadoc was obviously alive and well enough to kill. Mary could see the hatred in his eyes even from where she lay panting in the boat.

"Let the wind blow," Jedidiah mumbled, quickly unrolling the sail. "Without it, we have no chance."

The pursuers had come to the water and splashed out into it. Jedidiah's craft was still in shallow enough water that the men could reach it.

"The wind, oh Mighty One, the wind!" Micah prayed out loud. The sail gave a halfhearted flap in the breeze, but it was not sufficient to blow the boat out to sea.

Mary squeezed her eyes shut. Jedidiah probably had no weapon, and even if he did, she doubted that he and Micah could defeat the two men who had nearly reached the boat. *I must prepare to die,* she thought. *But Great One, I am not ready for that.*

21

"Fisherman, we do not desire to hurt you," Azor called. "Simply toss the woman and the servant overboard, and we will trouble you no more." His voice was as sweet as honey, but Mary knew that he and his friend would have no qualms about killing Jedidiah too.

Awaiting his reaction to Azor's suggestion, she fearfully turned toward Jedidiah. He might very well believe Azor was sincere, and she could not blame him if he accepted the offer. Why should he endanger his life for a servant he did not know and a woman who had treated him shamefully the last time they had met?

But without answering, Jedidiah shifted the mast, trying to find another breath of air to fill the sail. Mary sighed with relief. Though she did not understand why, apparently the fisherman was not going to take Azor's advice. Yet maybe it made little difference.

The water up to their thighs, Sadoc and Azor were within an arm's length of the boat. Mary cowered from their angry eyes that were even closer each time she looked.

"If you do not turn them over to us, you will regret it," Azor continued, his voice turning hard. "We will kill you all!"

"Can't you do anything?" Micah shouted at the fisherman.

"My breath won't fill the sail!" Jedidiah snapped back at him. "We must have wind!"

Just as Sadoc's hairy fingers clutched the boat, and Mary's scream echoed around them, the prayed-for gust of wind swept over the sail. With a lunge, the craft slid over the waves, the force knocking off Sadoc's grip.

Caught off balance, Sadoc fell with a splash into the water. He was quickly back on his feet, cursing, and waving his arms. Azor was just behind him. But it was no use; they could no longer reach the boat.

Micah stood triumphantly on the deck on the small fishing vessel. "We did it!" he announced. "We . . ." Before he could say more, he gave a gasp and half fell, half stumbled down into a crumpled position on the deck.

"Micah!" Mary called, not comprehending. Only when she reached him did she see Sadoc's dagger protruding from his chest. A pool of blood, rapidly growing, surrounded the entry site.

Before she could think about how to help him, Jedidiah had joined her kneeling next to Micah's limp form.

"May the Just One punish for a thousand years the scoundrel who did this!" Jedidiah muttered, glancing toward the shoreline to which Azor and Sadoc were returning. Satisfied they had accepted the fact that the boat was beyond their reach, the fisherman reached down to grip the hilt of the knife.

"What are you going to do?" Mary cried, horrified to see him touch it.

"Pull it out, of course." Jedidiah gave a quick yank, and the bloody blade was free. Micah moaned.

"Oh, Micah, you saved my life and now you may lose yours," Mary whispered, trying to blink away the sudden tears that had filled her eyes. She moved behind him and slipped his head into her lap.

Purposefully, Jedidiah ripped the servant's robe away from the injury. Using his own head covering, he dabbed at the blood so as to get a better look at how severe the wound was. "It doesn't appear to be that deep. I don't think you need to be mourning his loss yet," Jedidiah said drily. "I was under the impression that I was the one who saved your life!"

"Oh, you did, and . . . and I am most grateful!" Mary said, keeping her eyes on Micah. "But he rescued me before that, when that evil man was . . ." The memory of Sadoc's face before her was so repulsive that she could say no more.

"Is that what happened to your cheek?"

She only nodded, not wanting to talk anymore about her ordeal. In all that had occurred in the past hour, Mary had almost forgotten about her own injury, which still was painful, but in a dull aching sort of way that could be ignored.

Jedidiah had pulled out a small bottle of wine and was pouring it in Micah's wound. "I'm sorry I have nothing to offer you to eat," he told her. "It's back on the beach."

Mary's hands flew to her lips. "I forgot! You had to leave everything."

Shrugging, Jedidiah carefully wrapped a clean piece of the head covering over the wound. "It has not been the first time. There, now if your friend here can sleep, the healing will begin." He stood up and together they gently half carried, half slid the injured man inside the small tent pitched in the center of the deck.

"At least I left my coat on board," Jedidiah said, pulling his sheepskin over Micah. Then he came and sat down next to Mary. "Now, where do you want to go? I assume not to your father-in-law's."

Mary shook her head, trying to get comfortable on the rough wooden planks of the deck. "Back to Jesus, of course. Although . . . perhaps it isn't possible, but if I could see my children first, just briefly . . ."

Jedidiah scanned the beach. "Your captors seem to have left, for the time being, anyway. But as angry as they are about losing you, they will surely be looking for you. We will have to avoid them."

"I know. Maybe it is too much to ask. It's just that it's been so long since I've seen the children, and Azor said . . ."

"Azor?"

"You know, the shorter man who was chasing us. He told me that Joshua had a fishhook through his hand."

The fisherman threw back his head and laughed, a deep, hearty laugh that reminded Mary of Matthew's. "A fishhook? Through Joshua's hand? How often do you remember that boy of yours having any interest in fishing? Where would he, of all people, have such an accident? No, Mary, your son's hand—and the rest of him—is just fine. To my knowledge, Joshua has never been closer than this boat's length to a hook."

Mary nodded. "Of course. He never did like fishing." Why had she ever believed Azor's lies? "And Kezia? She is all right too?"

"What did he tell you about her?"

She was embarrassed to say. "Something about hot water splashing in her eyes."

"Well, now, at least that sounds more like your girl. She would do something like that. But she hasn't. No, no, both of them are perfectly all right."

Relief washing over her, Mary leaned back against the boat and closed her eyes. Although she hadn't really believed what Azor told her, wondering about the children's health had been a heavier burden than she would admit, even to herself.

"If you like, we could stay out here on the sea until daybreak," Jedidiah said gently. "Just to make sure your assailants are gone. Then we could slip into Magdala to see the children, leave

Micah with Eli, and still be back on the water by the time most people started the morning. You could be up in Capernaum with the Rabbi by evening."

"You mean you would sail me there?" Mary asked, opening her eyes. "Help me visit Joshua and Kezia? Do all this for me, after the way I treated you?"

"I would do the same for any woman," Jedidiah said gruffly, hoping she believed him. For though he'd sworn he was done caring for her after she slapped him, the feelings of love were back, full force.

"Jedidiah, I . . . I'm sorry about what happened the last time we met."

He shrugged. "You and I both have tempers. We say and do things we do not mean." He cleared his throat. "As for what I said about you and the children . . ."

"I understand," she said quickly.

Awkwardly they sat next to each other, avoiding looking in one another's eyes.

Finally Jedidiah spoke. "Tell me, how did those two ruffians ever capture you?"

"You warned me, didn't you? But I fell into their trap anyway." Slowly Mary told him about the past day.

"Where was your betrothed when this was happening?" Jedidiah could not keep a trace of bitterness out of his voice.

"I have none," she said stiffly.

"I thought . . ."

"I am not betrothed."

"He did not feel the same toward you as you thought? I know what it is to experience that!" Jedidiah gave a short laugh.

"I don't wish to discuss it with you. Besides, the only thing that concerns you is my current feelings toward you. And they have not changed, as grateful as I am for what you've done for me today," Mary said.

"All right. We will leave it at that, for now."

Mary had the uncomfortable feeling that Jedidiah knew something she did not, but she was too weary to think about it. Her body was finally reacting to the day's events, and it was all she could do to keep her eyes open. "I thought Micah was on their side. He acted like he was, but it must have been to fool them, for he was the one who got me away from them. I don't remember him being a man capable of either compassion or wisdom, yet he demonstrated both today. If only he lives for me to thank him . . ."

Noticing her drooping eyelids, Jedidiah pulled himself to his feet. "Speaking of Micah, I better see how he's doing. Why don't you get a little rest yourself?"

Without protesting, Mary stretched out on the deck.

"I wish I had another coat or robe to put over you," Jedidiah began, but her eyes were closed, and he realized she was not listening.

After checking the injured man, Jedidiah settled back down on the deck. Micah was sleeping peacefully, and his wound seemed to have stopped bleeding. Some water to drink would probably be good for him, but the waterskins had been left on the beach. Oh well, when they went to see the children, he could get some more. And food too. Jedidiah regretfully remembered the fish left cooking and tried to ignore his empty stomach. The sea was calm, and since he had left his nets on the beach, there was no work to do. All that remained for him was to keep watch, in case Mary's assailants had found a boat and were out looking for them.

The gentle lapping of the water against the stern, the night breezes, and Mary's soft deep breathing—all worked together to give Jedidiah a sense of peace that he rarely experienced. Gradually his muscles relaxed, and he found it more and more difficult to keep alert.

Shaking himself, Jedidiah tried to wake up. But why bother? No one would come for them tonight.

Some time later, the fisherman awoke with a start. A figure was lying next to him, almost touching him. He quickly realized it was Mary. She must have rolled over toward him in her sleep. It was chilly on the deck.

Suddenly she reached for him. "I'm cold, my love," Mary whispered sleepily. "Hold me . . ."

Hope stirred in Jedidiah. Could her feelings toward him have changed already? Willingly, he enveloped her in his arms. Mary snuggled against his chest.

Guilt filtered through Jedidiah's mind. *I have no right to hold a woman I am not married to,* he thought. *If someone should see, her reputation would be ruined.*

But there was no one to watch, and now wide awake, Jedidiah gently touched her hair. *Nothing could be more right than this,* he told himself, feeling the warmth of her body against his. Caring for her is all I need.

"Hold me, Ara," Mary whispered again.

Jedidiah stiffened. She was dreaming, dreaming of her late husband. She did not know she was in his arms. For an instant, he considered releasing her. But then his body relaxed. She might not be aware of what was happening, but he was. And he would treasure these moments. Why shouldn't he? They might never be his again.

At daybreak, Jedidiah landed the boat. He had chosen a deserted spot to the south of Magdala, in hopes of avoiding Azor and Sadoc. From there, he would go to Eli's home, get the children, and bring them to their mother.

"Micah and you will have to stay here alone on the beach until I get back," he pointed out to Mary. "But I must anchor the craft this far south, out of sight."

"I understand."

"I'll bring some food and water when I come, if Tabitha can help me. Then when I take Joshua and Kezia back, I can drop off Micah. You realize it will be a short visit?"

She nodded. At least she would see them again.

The fisherman surveyed the beach stretching in either direction. "I don't like this. If they were to find you, you would be defenseless. No one would even hear your screams."

"But you yourself said that only you could get the children. Please go. We'll be all right."

Jedidiah reached into his sash and pulled out a small fishing knife. "Here. Take this. Do you think you could use it?"

She reached for it. "On them, I could," Mary said boldly, but he noticed the trembling of her hands.

"Good! Stay down on the deck, so that the boat looks deserted. Don't talk to anyone who comes by."

She nodded impatiently. "Please go."

Jedidiah opened his mouth to speak but thought better of it. With a casual wave of his hand, he started off across the sand.

Jedidiah is a brave man, Mary thought, and a little of the coldness she had felt for him melted. Of course, she could never feel for him as she had towards Ara, or even Matthew. But perhaps they could at least be sort of friends. Jesus actually seemed to encourage that among His disciples, as unheard of as it was for anyone else.

For what seemed like a long time, Mary sat on the deck, low enough so she would not be noticed but high enough so that she could see the beach. It remained deserted.

Then a moan startled her, and Mary moved over into the small tent to check on Micah. His eyes were open, and she was encouraged to see that he looked at her with recognition.

"How do you feel?" she asked him.

"Hurts. Water!"

"I know. But I have nothing to give you to drink. If you can just wait a bit longer, Jedidiah will be back with some. Then soon, you'll be at Eli's where you can get proper care."

The man shook his head weakly.

"You will recover," she assured him. "You can rest and get back your strength."

Micah continued to disagree. "No, . . ."

She shook her head in confusion. "You don't want to get better?"

"Not at Eli's. With Jesus," Micah murmured.

"You? You want to follow the Master?"

This time he nodded.

Surprised, Mary wondered what had happened to bring him to such a decision. "But . . . but you can't just leave Eli's service. You have to at least tell him." Yet if her father-in-law knew, he would be able to find Mary. "You must stay here in Magdala, until you're better."

Mary had to bend close to Micah's lips to hear what he was saying. "Told me, 'don't return without Mary,'" he got out. "Take me with you."

"Eli said that?" Again Mary was surprised at the efforts being made to bring her back. "Well, I don't know if Jedidiah will take you."

"Will if you ask. Loves you." Exhausted from the talking, Micah shut his eyes.

Mary turned away. Were Jedidiah's feelings toward her so obvious, even to an injured servant?

Then she heard people approaching the boat. Gently touching Micah so he would look at her, she raised a finger to her lips. No one must know there was anyone on this boat.

The footsteps were heavy; she knew they could only be a man's. Could Azor and Sadoc have found them? Mary fingered Jedidiah's knife gingerly. Perhaps whoever was coming would glance on board and not bother to check the inside of the tent.

The ones nearing the boat did not speak, but she could tell there were several of them. And Jedidiah should not be back yet. Fear rose within her.

"Oh, Mighty One, protect us," Mary prayed silently.

The footsteps were getting closer. There was nowhere else they could be going but the boat. Mary studied the dagger in her hand. Could she actually use it on a man? She had never cut anything more than a fish or chicken.

Then she remembered the sight of Sadoc's face, his hand as he slapped her. The thought brought the taste of venom to her mouth. If he was even now about to reach her, she would plunge the knife into him. He would not touch her again.

22

The people approaching Jedidiah's boat were so close that Mary could hear their breathing. There were at least two of them and an animal, probably a donkey. She knew it could not be Jedidiah, since he would have no beast.

What was she going to do when they reached her? She tried to think, but the fear pounding in her head made it almost impossible. Even if it were not Azor and Sadoc, she still had reason to be frightened. Most of Magdala would know Eli was looking for her and that she was considered insane. Anyone who recognized her might feel he was doing her father-in-law a favor to bring her back. If only Jedidiah would return.

Mary drew back the knife, prepared to use it. Breathlessly, she peered out of a small hole in the tent canvas. Then Joshua's head poked over the side of the boat.

"Mother?" he called tentatively.

The dagger dropped with a clatter onto the deck. Her fear transformed into joy, Mary pushed her way out from the tent and over the side of the boat to him. "Oh, my darling!" she cried, reaching for him. Her tears made it difficult to see, but immediately Mary noticed how much taller and older her son was.

Jedidiah was lifting Kezia off of a donkey. She would not look at her mother but clung to the fisherman.

Giving her son another kiss, Mary started toward her. "Kezia, . . ."

"Tabitha helped us get away with Eli's donkey, to bring Micah back on," Jedidiah explained to Mary, putting the child down. "I knew it would get us here more quickly too." He gave the little girl a gentle push in her mother's direction. But she would not go.

It's been so long since she's seen me, Mary told herself, but there was no denying the pain she felt, to see her daughter more comfortable with Jedidiah than with her.

Turning her attention to her son, Mary gave him another hug. "I have missed you so!" she said. "Tell me all about what you're doing." They settled side by side on the sand, and Joshua was soon sharing about his school and life with Eli and Ruth.

At least, he is happy there, Mary thought, *and well cared for. I could not ask for more, except to be with them myself.*

As they talked, she watched Kezia out of the corner of her eye. The girl would not make eye contact with Mary, but she did move closer and closer. Jedidiah had climbed on board the boat with the food and water Tabitha had sent.

"Are you well, Mother?" Joshua was asking. "Do you still serve the Nazarene?"

She nodded. "Yes, and it has been wonderful. I have learned so much."

"I hear terrible things about Him," Joshua told her, "that He will be killed. If He is, they won't hurt you, too, will they?"

"Of course not. Anyway, Jesus is not in that great a danger." She tried to smile at Joshua. "Where do you hear such things?"

The boy stared at his hands. "Grandfather."

"Does he continue to be angry with me?" Mary asked, not sure she wanted to know.

"Yes. I cannot mention you to him."

Mary reached for one of Joshua's hands. "You must listen to him. He is doing what he thinks is right."

Kezia had crept up behind her. "Are you coming home with us, Mother?" she asked softly, placing her fingertips lightly on her mother's shoulder, as if to see if she was really there.

Resisting the urge to swing around and pull her daughter to her, Mary laid a gentle hand on top of Kezia's fingers. "Well, I . . . I don't know." Suddenly the desire to be with these children of hers seemed overwhelming. Maybe it was time to go back.

Jedidiah joined them. "I've got to return them," he said, and Mary could tell he hated separating her from them.

"Come with us, Mother," Kezia begged.

"She cannot. You know that," the fisherman answered before Mary could say anything. "If she did, your grandfather would imprison her." He leaned down to speak to Mary. "Micah says he will not go back to Eli."

"I know. He wants to follow Jesus."

Jedidiah shook his head. "He's wounded! He needs to recover first."

Mary could only shrug. "You must do as he wants. He is of age. Tell Tabitha to give my father-in-law the message that Micah has left his service."

Finally Jedidiah agreed they could do nothing else, and Micah remained on the boat when the fisherman loaded the children on to the donkey and began leading it across the sand to Eli's house. With tear-filled eyes, Mary watched them go. *Oh, Powerful One, when will we again be a family?* she prayed. *I cannot bear this separation much longer.*

The sun was high over the hills encompassing Capernaum when Jedidiah's small boat slid across the gleaming waves that washed up on the black sand beside the fishing village. Jumping out of the craft into the shallow water, he hoisted onto his shoulder the thick rope attached to the stern. Then with mighty heaves, the fisherman pulled his vessel up on the beach.

Mary watched him silently, a barrage of emotions running through her head. Of course, there was joy at the prospect of soon being reunited with the Master and His followers. Relief, too, at the end of what had been almost three days of nightmare-turned-reality. But then there was the memory of Kezia's soft query, "Are you coming home, Mother?" as well as Joshua's arms around her neck.

Mary had had plenty of time to think during the sail north from Magdala, and more than once she had determined to go back to her hometown, accepting whatever consequences awaited her. Yet each time she was ready to tell Jedidiah to turn back, something stopped her. She could not be certain what, or whom, it was, but it was strong enough that now, she was back in Capernaum.

"Where shall I carry Micah?" Jedidiah asked, helping her out of the boat.

"To Simon's. Even if Jesus has left, at least some of the women will be there," she told him. Though only a finger length deep, the water on her sandaled feet was chilly enough to make her hurry the rest of the way out of it.

"Didn't Azor and Sadoc find you there? I doubt that it's very safe for you to go back now." Jedidiah climbed back on board to get Micah.

"Thank you for your concern," Mary said stiffly, "but I'm no longer your problem."

"This is what you say to me after I risk my life to save yours?" Jedidiah snorted, carrying the servant's limp form through the water.

"I am grateful for all you've done," she snapped. "But I don't owe you any more than my thanks. I'm not yours."

"Thank the Mighty One for that!" he retorted. "Never has anyone succeeded in angering me as often or as deeply as you have!"

"I might say the same of you!" Mary felt the same fury rising within her which had resulted in her slapping him the last time they had argued. She bit her tongue, so she would not say any more.

Jedidiah strode past her, his every footstep speaking anger, and they did not acknowledge each other the rest of the way to the house of Simon.

That night the fire in the courtyard burned late as Mary told of her experiences over the past few days. And at the conclusion, as she stretched out on her mat, Joanna on one side and Susanna on the other, Mary knew that she had made the right decision in returning to Jesus.

The women arose earlier than usual the next morning, for the Master and His followers were leaving that day for Jerusalem. The Passover Feast would soon be upon them, and He had decided to celebrate it in the Holy City, as should all faithful Jewish men who could possibly arrange it.

As Mary packed dried dates and raisins into a leather bag, she thanked Yahweh again that she had arrived back in Capernaum in time to make this trip with Jesus. In spite of her words to Jedidiah, she had to admit she was a little worried about the possibility of Azor and Sadoc finding her. Traveling, especially to a city like Jerusalem, which already would be fairly crowded for the festival, would lessen the chances of their discovering her whereabouts.

"Ready to leave, Mary?" Joanna asked, coming over to her with her arms full of wineskins. "The Master wants to go as soon as possible."

She nodded. "I have all this fruit, and Leah gave me some

fresh melons to take too." She pointed to the small pile of green melons waiting to be put in a bag. "By the way, have you heard from Chuza lately? I didn't get to ask you yesterday."

The older woman shook her head, and Mary was surprised to see tears fill her eyes. "He will not contact me anymore—until I come home. Oh, Mary, I'm so confused! I love Chuza, and I can understand that he wants a wife again. But how can I leave the Master? Something is going to happen to Him, I'm sure of it. I need to be with Him."

"Have you spoken to Jesus about it?" Mary asked gently.

"No. I suppose I am afraid to."

"Afraid of what He might say to do?" Rising, Mary gathered up the leather bags of food which surrounded her.

Joanna nodded. "I know what He will say."

"Then you must do it, no matter how hard it is. Don't the writings of the prophet Samuel say that obedience is better than sacrifice?"

Trying to smile, Joanna nodded again. "Then perhaps this will be my last trip with Him." She wiped away a tear. "I cannot imagine how I will be able to endure life back with Chuza. Oh, not that he's unkind. He is the most patient of men. Who else would permit his wife to travel with a rabbi for this long? But after hearing the Master, seeing the miracles, all else will seem useless."

"But it doesn't have to, Joanna!" Mary told her. "Think what an opportunity you will have. You can share with others the new life that Jesus has given you, a life of purpose. You are not just returning to your cooking and washing and weaving. You have a mission, to tell others the stories you have learned, to show them life can be more than what they currently are experiencing."

"Yes, why, yes. I guess you're right. I never thought of it like that," Joanna said, looking more hopeful.

"What the Master teaches cannot be just for those of us who are on the road with Him," Mary continued as the women carried the food and wineskins to the waiting donkey and loaded it. "If it were, He would tell no one the stories He knows. But He does speak so that everyone who would hear, can. His lessons must apply to people in all walks of life. That means it can be carried to wherever we go."

Joanna nodded slowly, "I suppose I will not miss sleeping outside and always being on the road." She squeezed Mary's hand. "Thank you, for helping me know what to do."

As the small group of men and women left Simon's courtyard for the trip south, Mary felt pleased that at last, Joanna would be at peace again. She knew her friend had been struggling for a long time. Yet she had to admit a sense of sadness; she would miss Joanna.

"You never cease to surprise me," a masculine voice behind her said, and Mary looked over her shoulder to see Matthew walking up beside her. "I overheard some of what you told Joanna," he told her. "That was quite impressive. I had never thought of what we have learned here as something to take with us when we leave."

Mary smiled at him, hope rising within her. This sounded like the old Matthew with whom she had spent so many hours talking. "Yet of what use for us would it be, if it were not so? We may not always be with the Master, and I find comfort in the fact that, nevertheless, I can take a part of this new life with me, wherever I am. It's almost like He will go with me."

Matthew bent his head close to hers. "You mean you think that He is actually going to die?"

"No, oh, no, I meant if I should have to leave Him . . ."

"Oh!" The disappointment in Matthew's voice was clear. "You know, since the Master told us about His death, each of us has been trying to figure out what He meant. Some feel it will be a symbolic experience, like if He were to withdraw to the desert for a period of time, long enough to make people forget Him. Then when He reappeared, it would almost be as if He had died."

"Joanna thinks He meant He really will die."

"I know. Some—a few—believe that way. I suspect that maybe He means He'll be imprisoned for a while. That could be a deathlike experience. You know that the Sanhedrin is increasingly irritated by His teaching. They could influence the Romans to arrest Him on some made-up charge."

"Perhaps," Mary said. "But remember, if He is the Messiah, as Simon said, He surely would not let even Antipas harm Him."

"Or someone said it could be that He will be quite sick and have to stop His ministry for a while to recover. He might even die from it, like that little girl in Capernaum, and be brought back to life."

Remembering the twelve-year-old daughter of Jairus who had succumbed to her illness until Jesus had gone to her house and brought her back to life, Mary shook her head. "He has such power over all kind of disease. He would not let such a thing happen."

"Perhaps you're right," Matthew admitted. "I suppose we'll find out soon enough. Still, it doesn't give one great confidence in the Master when He keeps talking about dying."

"I know. It frightens me."

"I wish you would go somewhere, away from Him, just in case it does get dangerous to be seen with Jesus."

She turned from Matthew. "You have already told me how you feel about that. Please don't start again."

"As you wish," he answered stiffly. "What's happened to your fisherman friend?"

Mary shrugged. "I have no way of knowing, but I suppose he went back to Magdala." She remembered again Jedidiah's stormy face as she had reached Simon's courtyard. Well, it wasn't her fault that he was so hot tempered. Of course, she had been angry too. Why did they seem to trigger that emotion in each other?

Even as Jedidiah had gently placed Micah on a mat in one of the small, enclosed rooms off of the courtyard, where Leah would tend him until the wound healed, the fisherman had not spoken to Mary. She had meant to at least say good-bye before he left, but somehow Jedidiah had been out of the courtyard before she had finished greeting the women, the disciples, and, of course, the Master Himself.

She was sorry, for, after all, Jedidiah had done a great deal for her. *Yet I did thank him once,* she thought. *And perhaps when I see him again, he will be in a better mood.* Not that she expected that to take place very soon. Who knew when she would be back in Magdala?

Matthew had moved on to talk to Judas in front of them, and Mary was left to her musings. Yes, she had to admit that in spite of his temper, Jedidiah was in many ways a good man. He would make a decent husband and certainly an excellent father. He had already proved that in the relationship he had built with Kezia and Joshua. She could do much worse than marry him.

But I don't love him, she told herself rebelliously, even though she realized that most women could say that about their spouses. Mary let out a sigh. If she had not known love with Ara, perhaps she would be willing to settle for less than that now.

Glancing up ahead of her, Mary watched Matthew gesturing to Judas. Her heart stirred at the sight of him. It did not matter that he had rejected her, that he gave her no indication that he would ever care for her as more than a friend. She could not change how she felt about him. No, as long as there was the former tax collector in her life, Mary could not marry Jedidiah, no matter how much he said he loved her.

23

"I do not like it, not one bit," grumbled Andrew, his feet making tiny angry puffs of dust on the road which had taken them out of Capernaum. "Jerusalem is no place for Him, even if it is Passover."

Matthew nodded. "He has enemies across the country, and almost all of them will be in the Holy City next week. Doesn't He realize that?"

"I am not certain He does. I tried to warn Him when He first said we were going. 'Master, surely you do not plan to be at the temple this Passover,' I said. 'You will be arrested within an hour of arriving.' Simon told him the same thing." The former fisherman shook his head in frustration. "But He was determined. You know how He gets. Nothing you can say does any good."

From her position behind them, Mary overheard his words. She smiled a little as the two men continued their conversation. Andrew was right. Sometimes Jesus still did things that none of them could figure out, and asking the rest of them to meet Him, Simon, James, and John in Jerusalem was certainly one of them.

Shifting her bundle to her other shoulder, Mary remembered again when the Master had sent word that He was leaving Jericho and wanted them to rejoin Him and the three others.

Everyone had been shocked; they had expected Him to come back to them in Galilee. Objections had filled the air like hailstones: the danger of imprisonment or worse, not just for Him, but for all of them, the risk to those who would come to hear Him speak, and the work He had been doing that would be abandoned.

Of course, it had not made any difference, and they had left as scheduled. From what Mary had heard during the past hour, many of the disciples were confused and even angry about the trip, which she could understand. But what else could they do except obey the Lord? As Thomas had said, they would go and die with Him.

The thought was frightening, and Mary tried to push it from her mind, concentrating instead on the beauty around her. Spring had come once more, sprinkling splotches of color across the plateaus that ascended from the southwest to the northeast, where they overlooked the Sea of Galilee. On the rugged hillsides, known to be havens for those who needed to hide from others, there were hyacinths. Their deep blue blossoms gave off a perfume so heady that she could detect it from the road. There were narcissus, their yellow or white flowers in the shape of miniature trumpets. Beside the occasional streams which snaked their way down to the lake grew abundant patches of yellow iris. And everywhere there was the brilliant green of the grass, lush after the rains of winter. To her left, the sea was calm and of a deep blue hue. Though it was probably a Sabbath day's journey of two thousand cubits or a half a mile away, Mary could make out several fishing boats.

"Mary, what did you want to serve for the evening meal tonight?" Susanna asked, joining her.

"It depends on how far we get," Mary replied thoughtfully. "If we keep going until we reach Ginaea, it will be too late to cook anything."

Susanna frowned at the mention of the Samaritan town. "Do you think we'll travel that far?"

"Who knows? The men probably won't decide until late this afternoon. Anyway, if we do end up there, we'll have to stick to cheese, fruit, and bread."

"Well, we have plenty. But just the same, I hope we stop before then. A hot meal would taste good," Susanna said without her usual enthusiasm.

"Though not right now," Mary answered lightly, wiping the perspiration off her face with the end of her head covering. Already in the morning, the heat was getting oppressive. "However, if we do have a chance to cook, I think a lentil stew would be fitting."

Susanna nodded.

For a while, the two of them walked together in silence, Mary again marveling that she was the one asked to make the decisions in matters concerning the women since Joanna had left.

In the six months that had passed, after the older woman had reluctantly returned to her husband, Mary had often thought about Joanna. Was she satisfied, back with Chuza? Could she share the new life she had? Mary hoped to know someday, just as she wanted to tell Joanna all that had happened to the band who followed Jesus.

Mary had been surprised when the other women asked her to take Joanna's place. "I? But I have been with the Master a shorter time than most of you. I have so little experience in handling the details of our life on the road. And I don't have the wisdom of years . . ."

"You may have joined us totally unprepared," one of the older women said, "but you have learned quickly. As for your age, it is of no concern. We are confident you will do as well as Joanna did."

"Yes, Mary, it makes no difference how long you have been a

part of our group," Susanna had added. "What matters is your commitment to the Rabbi."

A bit apprehensively, Mary had accepted. To her amazement, she had soon felt comfortable in her new responsibilities. Stepping around some broken pottery in the middle of the road, she almost laughed out loud to think of what Eli and Ruth would say if they knew what their "insane" daughter-in-law was doing.

"What amuses you?" Susanna asked glumly, and Mary turned quickly to her. It was not like the younger woman to sound so discouraged.

"Nothing. I was just thinking about . . . never mind. Why are you upset?" Embarrassed that she had been so involved in her own thoughts as to miss her friend's troubled mood, Mary reached over to squeeze her hand. "Please tell me."

Susanna sighed. "Micah is leaving."

"Really? We will all miss him." In the time that Micah had been a follower of Jesus, Mary had come to appreciate him not only as a man of bravery who had helped save her life, but as one of sensitivity and loyalty.

"Mary, you don't understand. He is more than just a friend to me." Susanna's cheeks reddened.

Suddenly Mary realized what Susanna was saying. "You mean you and he are planning to . . ."

"Well, there's nothing that's been said, not for certain, but I have hopes that perhaps things will work out." The color on her face deepened.

"What about the Master?" Mary asked gently. "Have your feelings for Him changed?"

"Oh, yes. I still love Him, of course, and would give my life for Him. But it is no longer the love of a woman for a man." Susanna thought briefly. "I suppose it is more that of a child for her father. I feel like He will take care of me and I can trust Him to know what's best for me."

Mary released Susanna's hand to hug her. "Then I am truly pleased for you. You have wanted to remarry for so long." She forced out the unbidden thoughts of Matthew. Six months before, she could have been saying the same thing her friend was. But it had not happened as she had thought it would.

"He feels he must go back to Eli, that it wasn't right to just send a message that he was leaving Eli's employment. He wants to speak to him about the Master," Susanna said.

Mary rolled her eyes. "Eli will not appreciate hearing it. He may even have Micah imprisoned."

"That's what I fear. But he's as stubborn as the Rabbi. He says he must do this thing."

"Surely you admire him for his courage in doing right."

"Oh, I do! He is truly a man of strength and wisdom. But I am afraid I may not see him again, and that I could not bear." Susanna's love for Micah shone in her eyes.

"Couldn't you go with him?"

"No, no. We are not betrothed; it would be unseemly. I must remain here."

"Then I will pray for you and for him," Mary told her, "that you both will be protected until you can be together."

Susanna smiled a little. "Thank you. Perhaps he will not be away too long. The Mighty One will give me the strength to endure the separation."

"Susanna!" a voice called, and the women turned to see Micah coming up to them. Mary discreetly moved ahead of them, so they could speak privately, but not before she saw them exchange smiles. And the balding short man and the plain-featured young woman no longer looked unattractive; their love for each other made them appear comely.

Mary turned her face from them, only to catch a glimpse of Matthew, still talking with Andrew ahead of her. Why couldn't things have turned out differently for her? A tear fogged her vision, and she angrily blinked it away. There was no time for self-pity. Her responsibilities of providing necessities for Jesus and the men kept her too busy to dwell on her own sorrow. Nevertheless, Mary's eyes remained blurry.

By midmorning, the travelers had reached the outskirts of Magdala. Here Micah was to leave them, and the warmth of his farewells spoke of the closeness he had developed with those who followed Jesus. As was appropriate, Susanna remained well behind the men, but Mary could tell her friend was struggling to keep from weeping. Going over to her, Mary patted her back. "It's in the Powerful One's hands now."

"I know, and I do trust Him." She swallowed and straightened her shoulders. "Aren't you nervous about being here? If your father-in-law sees you . . ."

"I, too, must depend on Someone to protect me." In spite of her words, Mary was relieved to see Matthew moving closer to her. He would do all he could to keep her safe, even though he had only recently made it clear that he still did not feel free to have a closer relationship with her.

The twenty-some followers of the Nazarene moved on down the dusty road, and Mary positioned herself in the midst of the men. One never knew who might be walking toward them.

She could think of a number of people she did not want to see. Of course, Eli and Ruth were among them, as were the hired men Azor and Sadoc. The memory of them sent shivers down her spine. She still had occasional nightmares of her abduction by them, and she was certain that they would recognize her and not hesitate to carry her off again, if the opportunity arose.

"Mary, whatever are you thinking about?" Susanna asked. "Your face looks so . . . hard."

"Oh, it is nothing," Mary said, trying to relax. Even to her close companion, Mary could not admit the hate and fear she had for the men who had hurt her. And what would Jesus think of her if He found out? Mary did not want to know.

Yet perhaps He already was aware of how she felt. In some way, He seemed to always know things which there was no way of discovering. But if He did, He had never rebuked her for her feelings. She trembled a little at the thought of hearing Jesus bring it up. More than anything else, she wanted to please Him, and the thought of His disappointment was more than she could bear.

Willing herself to think of something else, Mary pictured her children. Being back in Magdala also brought back some pleasant memories—from the days when Ara was alive. She again saw her husband tossing a young Kezia into the air and chasing a little Joshua down the sandy beach.

"Mary!" a voice called, interrupting her remembrances.

She looked up to see Jedidiah carrying a bundle and coming toward her. It was then that she noticed a boat pulled up on the beach. His, obviously. Had he landed at this spot just to speak with her? But no, he could not have recognized her or her companions from such a distance. They must have chanced upon him.

"Shalom, Jedidiah," she said politely. Behind her, she noticed a suspicious-looking Matthew moving closer to her. *He still doesn't trust the fisherman,* she thought, a trifle pleased.

Greeting the others, Jedidiah held out the bundle. "Freshly caught fish, for your pleasure. I, too, wish to serve the Rabbi."

"Your thoughtfulness is appreciated," Andrew told him kindly. "But the Master is not with us."

Jedidiah put the bundle into Andrew's arms. "No matter. You are his followers. It is enough that you are fed."

"Again, our thanks." Andrew told him. "We must continue our journey. May the Just One bless you." He turned to go, and the others joined him.

"Mary, wait. I must speak with you," Jedidiah said, looking more like a small boy begging a favor than the grown man he was.

Reluctantly Mary let the rest of the group pass her as Jedidiah came to her side. Matthew moved on too but continued to keep his eyes on Mary.

"You look beautiful," the fisherman told her, his muscular tan frame towering above her. Before she could answer, he spoke again. "I know, you don't wish to hear that kind of talk. What I really wanted to discuss with you is your children."

"Yes?" she said tensely. What had happened now?

He recoiled slightly at the tone of her voice. "They are well, quite well. It's just that I thought you would want to hear about what they are doing."

"Of course. I'm sorry," she told him quickly. "Please tell me."

As he informed her of the details he was familiar with concerning Joshua and Kezia's lives, Mary absorbed it into her being. Who knew how long it might be before she heard more about them?

The rest of the disciples were far beyond her, Susanna casting anxious glances in back of her to make certain Mary was still behind them. Even though Mary reassured her several times with a wave that nothing was wrong, she continued. Matthew had also turned around twice to see where Mary was.

She knew she should catch up with the others, but she could not make herself say farewell to Jedidiah. Each thing he could remember, no matter how minute, drew her as a thirsty camel to a well. From the length of Kezia's hair to the newest riddle Joshua was telling, she had to find out.

The more Mary heard, the more she realized she could not bear to be parted from her children any longer, in spite of the excellent care they were receiving under Eli, Ruth, and Tabitha.

Jedidiah could see it in her eyes, for he surprised even himself in the number of particulars he was able to share with her. He felt a little guilty, knowing he was contributing to her craving to stay in Magdala. But his love for her burned like the glowing embers in the bottom of his cooking stove, steady and continuously. And the Powerful One knew how long he had waited for her. When other women smiled at him, he could only think of Mary. Thoughts of Mary left no room for thoughts of others.

The troublesome part, Jedidiah decided, as she walked beside him, was that what made her eyes glow so was not being with him but hearing about her children. In fact, as far as he could tell, her attitude toward him had not changed since the last time they met. Once again, Jedidiah silently cursed himself for his quick temper.

"My father-in-law—how is he?" Mary was asking.

"Eli? Well and pleased, for the most part, with the children's progress. But if you want to know his feelings toward you, they are just as before. Should the opportunity arise, he would imprison you."

Mary sighed, and Jedidiah resisted the urge to wrap his arms protectively around her. "Are you certain? I thought that perhaps by now . . ."

The fisherman shook his head sadly. It would be simple to let her think that perhaps Eli was softening. Then she might be convinced to leave the Rabbi's followers, and anything could happen with her back in Magdala. She might even grow to love him as he had her. Or at least, she might consent to marry him.

He pictured himself defending her from the wrath of Ara's father.

But no, that would not be right. Only his selfishness could cause him to deceive her in such a way. Besides, what he really wanted was for her to come willingly to him, not just for the sake of her children. He would have to wait—some more.

He glanced at the woman beside him. She was worth it, he told himself, and tried not to think about his lonely existence.

"You will give my love to Kezia and Joshua? And, here, this is for my little one," she said, quickly untying a brightly colored piece of ribbon from her hair. "But I have nothing for a boy."

"I happen to have a small, carved toy boat," Jedidiah offered. "I could give it to him from you."

She smiled at him. "Oh, would you? Thank you." She peered ahead of her at the small group of travelers. "Then I must go. I cannot leave the Master now."

"I hear He has enemies everywhere and that many who once followed Him have deserted."

"That is true. I admit, I don't understand why He wants to go to the Holy City for Passover. It will be very dangerous. But the Everlasting One will protect us." She pushed from her memory the times Jesus had talked about His death.

"Mary, be careful," Jedidiah told her gently.

She nodded. "My thanks again for the boat. Joshua will be pleased." Without looking back, she hurried off to catch up with the others.

She would never know the hours Jedidiah spent carving a small wooden boat, a toy that he did not begin until the evening after he saw her.

24

The men's conversation blended into a low murmur that reached Mary back in the cooking area. Listening carefully, she strained to pick out Jesus' voice as she hurriedly finished piling the tray with olives, figs, and dates. Yes, it was there, strong and in control, as always. Once again, she breathed a prayer of thanksgiving that the Rabbi's followers were safely reunited.

Even Joanna had returned with permission from her husband to be with them until after Passover. The older woman had already joyfully related to Mary her success in sharing her new life with those in her locality, as well as the growth of a stronger relationship with Chuza.

Laughter was filling the room when Mary entered with the laden tray and placed it close to where the Master was reclining on a coach beside the low table. Although she had not heard what was amusing, she smiled too. It was good to be near Jesus, to see the familiar twinkle in His eyes, to hear His chuckle, and to watch Him enjoying being with His friends.

"What is it, Mary?" Jesus asked, looking up at her and noticing her expression.

"Nothing, my Lord," she assured Him, offering Him a platter of parched corn. "I am just pleased to be with You again."

"And I, to be with all of you." Scooping some of the corn into

His bowl, He gave her a grin and turned toward Simon, who was leaning over to speak with Him.

Mary walked around the table to leave. She had not been expected to help with the meal; this household had several servants. The other women from Galilee were eating in another room. But she had insisted, and in spite of the extra work, she knew she had made the right decision. After the time away from the Master, it was precious just to be near Him, even if it was only to place the food next to Him.

Especially because this evening, the mood was light. Perhaps it was being in Bethany, where He was comfortable, surrounded by friends. Or maybe it was the upcoming Passover feast, a time of joy to devout Jews. Whatever the reason, Mary was glad that there was no heaviness in their midst this night.

In fact, Jesus had not made any mention of His death since the group had been back together. She tried not to think of the grim warnings of His approaching suffering which He had given them, and when she did, Mary quickly forced herself to push them out of her mind.

As the jesting and lighthearted conversation continued around the table, that was not difficult to do. Mary could even convince herself that things had changed, that somehow the Master was no longer in danger. Or at least that His enemies would be powerless against Him.

At last, the men were finished, and Mary helped clear away the empty dishes. Yet Jesus made no move to go, and the disciples seemed content to stay with Him, perhaps savoring the mood as much as Mary. They moved closer to the rabbi, their eyes fixed upon Him, waiting for what He had to tell them.

Lingering in the doorway, Mary had the sensation that something important was going to happen. Would there be a new teaching? Or could it be another miracle?

But the Master continued talking individually with His followers, teasing Simon about his appetite, describing how the first wooden table He had built as a child had fallen apart, and inquiring about the well-being of James and John's family.

Finally, deciding that her feelings had been wrong, Mary was about ready to leave when she noticed Mary of Bethany behind her. Along with her sister Martha and brother Lazarus, this Mary was a close friend of the Rabbi's. They had only recently experienced a spectacular miracle at the hand of Jesus. Even in Jerusalem, talk was still circulating about the Master bringing the dead Lazarus back to life.

Just thinking about it gave Mary such a feeling of awe that she hesitated speaking to the woman, but Mary did greet her with a friendly nod. Perhaps this other Mary also wanted to assist with the meal to be near their Lord, although her sister Martha was usually the one who did most of the household work. Tall and slim, the woman smiled back at her and slipped around her into the room. Her tunic was of a soft blue, finely woven, speaking of her family's wealth, and embroidered with the traditional pattern of Bethany. Beneath her head covering, her thick hair hung in a gleaming cascade reaching her waist.

It was then that Mary noticed a small vial in her hand. What could she be doing? It looked like a perfume jar.

The men paid her little attention as she approached Jesus, but when she dropped to her knees in front of Him, the conversation ceased. The questions in Mary's mind were mirrored on their faces.

Yet the Master seemed to understand. He sat silently while the woman removed the stopper on the jar, releasing the unmistakable fragrance of oil of nard.

Mary gasped as the costly perfume was poured over Jesus' feet. The woman's fingers deftly massaged it into the calloused soles and heels, around the toes, and down the arches.

Across the room, there was silence, although behind her, Mary could hear footsteps. Undoubtedly the strong scent had drawn the others in the house, who must be just as confused as she was by what was happening.

As she watched, Mary suddenly realized how similar the scene before her was to that of a body being anointed for burial. Of course, she had not seen Ara's anointing; being too numb with grief to help as she should have, she had remained in the courtyard. But she had been around enough other deaths to know exactly how it was done. And for some reason, the scene before her reminded her of such an anointing.

Again, fear as cold as mountaintop snow slid down Mary's back. But there is no reason to be frightened, she told herself sternly. It is not the same. Nevertheless, the mood of the room had changed, and Mary could feel the heaviness.

The massage completed, the woman went to reach for a cloth to wipe off the excess oil of nard. She frowned a little, apparently realizing she had forgotten to bring one. Refusing to let that deter her, she quickly pulled off her head covering and began to use her hair.

"Why wasn't this perfume sold, and the money given to the poor?" Judas suddenly asked, invading the silence which had enveloped the room. "Why, it could have brought in probably three hundred denarii."

Everyone turned to stare at the disciple, but no one answered him.

Why is he asking such a question? Mary thought, a little irritably, though she knew the perfume was worth nearly a year's wages as Judas had said. But then, lately Judas had been acting rather strangely. There was nothing specific she could think of, just a comment here, a facial expression there. Yet she could not help wondering exactly was going on in his mind.

Ignoring the remark, the other Mary finished her task. Retrieving the empty vial and her head covering, she slipped away toward the door. Her once beautiful hair was streaked with the perfume.

The Master smiled at her, then looked directly at Judas. "Don't bother her," He said gently. "You will always have the poor, but I won't be here forever. She was preparing for my burial."

Again, Mary felt a tremor of fear. She had not been the only one to link the anointing with death. The Master Himself had said it. Suddenly Mary would have given anything to be able to take Jesus far north to Caesarea Philippi, away from the Holy City where so many sought to kill Him. For the first time, she began to think that they might actually succeed.

Cupping her hand over her brow, Mary surveyed the scene in front of her. Down from where she stood on the Mount of Olives, beckoned Jerusalem, most of which was less than fifty years old. In the foreground, dominating everything, the massive gold-embellished Temple on its huge platform of white blocks seemed to have never gleamed so brightly in the sun. Black smoke from the sacrifices hovered over it.

To the south of the temple site was the so-called lower city, with its rows of buff-colored, limestone small homes. The hippodrome, the long oval building in which were held chariot races and other entertainment deemed forbidden by the pious, rose behind the houses. Behind it, the ground sloped down into the Tyropoeon Valley, which divided the Holy City into two parts.

Mary could make out the theater, another attraction ignored by the devout, on the other side of the valley where the land rose again, this time to form Mount Zion. Here was the upper city, where the rich lived. Their luxurious white marble palaces and villas, surrounded by gardens, sparkled in the daylight.

Beyond them, on the far western side of Jerusalem, just inside the city wall, her eyes made out the usually unoccupied palace of Herod, called the Great by some. The half-Jewish monarch had died some thirty years earlier, but his lavish yet heavily fortified residence still evoked the hatred of those who remembered his deeds.

Mary smiled, remembering Ara's comment that it was better to be Herod's pig than his son. The king had murdered several of his children, yet he kept the Jewish law that forbade eating pork, especially when it suited his purposes.

Scattered across the walled city were pools, which shone like the bronze mirror Mary had had in Eli's home. They not only collected rainwater but also adorned the homes of the wealthy.

Between where she was and the thick grey walls of the city, Mary could see the brilliant white of burial caves, freshly whitewashed for the festival. It would never do to have unknowing travelers mistake a tomb for a cave in which they might find shelter, thus making themselves ceremonially unclean.

"It's stunning, isn't it?" a voice said, and Mary turned to see Matthew. "No matter how evil the deeds that take place there, the Holy City always appears beautiful."

"Yes, it does," she told him, pleased to have him join her. "What is going to happen now?"

Stepping back to avoid a small boy chasing another, Matthew shrugged. "I have no idea. The Master sent James and John to get a donkey. Until they return, we wait."

"I thought we were going into the city." Mary smiled at two women walking past them with full water pitchers.

"You know our Lord. We'll find out what He has in mind when He wants us to."

Mary looked around at the groups of disciples near her. Some were talking, several had lain down on the grass, and a few were examining the view. Jesus was conversing with Simon, and

Judas stood off by himself, kicking up dust with the tip of his sandal. She could not see James and John returning yet.

"Might as well sit down," Matthew offered, spreading his cloak on the ground for her. "We could be here for a while."

Mary quickly accepted. Since he had made it clear he could not marry, he had only spoken to her privately on a few occasions.

"Where were they to find this donkey?" Mary asked, tossing her hair back over her shoulder.

Again Matthew shrugged. "I only heard Him tell them that when they came into that village, they would see one. They were to bring it here. If anyone questioned them, they were to say that the Lord has need of it."

The smoke from one of the many cooking fires nearby blew into Mary's eyes, and she turned her head to avoid it. The Mount of Olives was usually a quiet place, but this close to Passover, it was swarming with pilgrims. The law said that all must stay in Jerusalem during the feast, but, of course, the city was nowhere near large enough to take in the devout from across the country. So, conveniently, the borders of the city were expanded for a week to include the nearby hills, thus accommodating the two million people who stayed in Jerusalem.

Unless they were blessed enough to have family who resided in the city proper or to have arrived several weeks early so that they could obtain the choicest location, the temple site, most Galileans camped here among the olive groves to the west of Jerusalem. The place where the Rabbi had chosen to stop was in the midst of children playing games, women trying to prepare meals in front of tents, and tethered donkeys weary from the long trip from the northern province. *Why hadn't the Master asked to borrow one of them instead of sending to the village?* Mary thought. The noise was unending, and Mary hoped that they would not have long to remain in it. At least the people around them did not seem to recognize Jesus, for no one was crowding around Him as they usually did when He appeared in public.

Mary was just about to remark to Matthew about how strange it was when he motioned behind her. "Here they come."

They stood up and joined the other disciples as James and John approached with the donkey, its colt close behind. Unlike the Galilean animals, this donkey looked plump and almost frisky, as if it were pleased to serve the Rabbi. A red rag hung down between its eyes, in keeping with the superstitious tradition that it would prevent the animal from falling.

"Why, the Master is going to mount it," Matthew said as they watched Jesus prepare to climb on the beast. "Wait, my Lord," he called, shaking off the cloak on which he and Mary had been sitting. "Let me put this on first."

The Nazarene waited patiently by the donkey until Matthew and several others had draped their cloaks over the broad brown back of the animal. Then he climbed on and pointed toward Jerusalem.

"He wants to ride into the city!" Matthew called to Mary, as he ran back to her.

Laughing, Mary nodded. "I can see that." All around her, the people were suddenly noticing what was happening. They began hurrying toward the man on the donkey, shouting and waving.

"It's a king!" someone yelled, and the commotion around them grew as the cry was picked up and carried into the crowd.

"A king must not ride on dirt," a man called out. He raced in front of Jesus, laid his cloak in the dusty road in front of the donkey, and stepped out of the way.

Immediately others followed the pilgrim's example, and the path into the city was strewn with garments of every color and size.

"Who is this King?" Mary could hear the people asking as the donkey slowly made its way down the road. "Who is He?"

"Jesus, the prophet from Nazareth in Galilee," came the answer from somewhere.

The crowd became even more excited at the news that this man was the miracle worker who had touched so many lives.

"He healed my sister's child. The boy was seven summers old but had never walked until the Rabbi touched him," a man told those near him.

"Well, I saw Him cure a leper in Capernaum," another put in.

"Did you know He fed over five thousand with one youngster's lunch? I was one of them."

The talk went on around Mary, and she hurried to catch up with the other disciples, not an easy task in the midst of so many enthusiastic people. Where had they all come from?

Then she noticed that someone had cut a branch from a nearby palm tree and was waving it toward the Master, who was smiling. Once again, others jumped to imitate him, and soon a sea of palm leaves swirled about her.

"Blessed is He who comes in the name of the Mighty One!" a man called, and others answered with cries of "Hosanna! Hosanna!"

"Do you believe this?" Matthew shouted when Mary finally reached him. "I have never seen such excitement!"

She shook her head in amazement. As they continued down the road, more and more joined the joyful procession descending into the Kidron Valley. They waved the branches and tossed down their clothing in the path of the donkey.

"It seems as if all of the city is here!" Mary told Matthew, but the noise was so great that she had to repeat it three times before he heard her.

"I think this crowd will make Him king today!" Matthew predicted. "They will follow Him anywhere!"

Mary nodded joyfully. And to think, they had been so fearful of what the Holy City would hold for Jesus. Instead of enemies waiting to arrest Him, they had found jubilant supporters. Perhaps she had worried needlessly. These people had no desire to hurt the Master. They were grateful for what He had done; they wanted Him here. Even the Sanhedrin would not risk angering this crowd by openly opposing Jesus. Perhaps this would be a time of new power for Him, with His enemies unable to act, due to the widespread devotion of the people to Him.

Glancing over at the Rabbi, Matthew grabbed Mary's arm. "Look!"

The surprise in his voice was reflected in her own when she saw the Nazarene's face. "Why, He's weeping! What's happened?" she cried.

Matthew shook his head in confusion but did not move any closer to the donkey to find out the problem. Impatiently, Mary pushed her way past Matthew, through the mob, until she reached Simon, who gripped the harness and was leading the donkey.

"What has hurt Him?" she queried, pulling on Simon's arm like a persistent child.

The big fisherman looked down at her with puzzled eyes. "I don't understand myself, Mary. The last time I turned around, He was grinning, waving at the crowd. Now, He weeps. I only heard something about the city being destroyed because it did not recognize the day of its visitation." Simon shook his head. "I'm not certain, but I think He may be grieving over Jerusalem herself."

Moved, Mary slipped back behind the donkey and let everyone pass by her. Somehow much of the joy of the afternoon had dissolved like the morning dew, and the doubts and fears that had seemed so far away to her as she had joined the excited people had returned full force. As the procession reached the bottom of the valley and started the ascent to the Golden Gate which led into the huge Temple courtyard, Mary turned and started back to Bethany.

25

"Over here, John," Mary said, gesturing to the work space beside her.

The disciple placed the full wineskin next to the water jug and bowl she had set out. "Shall I mix the wine, or will you?"

She shrugged. "Whatever you prefer. Do you know yet how many will be with us for Passover?" The Law said that at least ten but no more than twenty could share a lamb, yet Mary wanted to know the exact number of places to set in the large room upstairs which Simon had engaged for their seder or service.

"Apparently, it will be just our Lord and us twelve. Everyone else has joined family or close friends here in the Holy City. But when I told the Master, it did not seem to bother Him. In fact, He acted like He expected this to happen and even preferred it."

Mary looked away. There was no one here who would welcome her.

Always sensitive to others' feelings, John quickly reassured her. "Naturally, you are to serve us. You are also one of His closest followers, and, besides, a woman must light the lamps to begin the service."

Pleased, Mary nodded. How could she have thought that the Rabbi, who knew everything, would leave her by herself on this of all evenings, when they would celebrate one of the most joyful and meaningful feasts of the year?

"I have already taken the goblets upstairs," Mary told John as he began pouring the warm water from the jug into the bowl. Adding the red wine, he gently stirred the liquid.

"Is the preparation complete?" asked Simon, entering the cooking area of the house. Located in the lower city, it belonged to distant relatives of his, who had allowed the Master to use it since they had moved in with other family members for the feast.

"Yes, I think so," Mary said, pointing to the unleavened bread she had baked, the raw vegetables ready to serve as bitter herbs in the seder, and the charoseth, the sweetened apple-nut mixture.

Simon glanced behind them at the cooking fire. Over it on a pomegranate-wood spit hung the paschal or Passover lamb, roasted whole, without breaking any of the bones, in accordance to tradition. Simon and John had purchased it in the Temple courtyard and had it slain by the priests; it had to be totally consumed by midnight.

Satisfied, Simon nodded. "I will check upstairs to make sure all is in readiness. The Master will be here soon." Walking outside, Simon headed around to the side of the house where smooth stone steps led up to the room they would use.

Quickly Mary slipped into one of the sleeping rooms to change into her best tunic, a red one of fine linen, which Ara had purchased for her the last year of his life. Although it was not new, it was beautiful, and she had kept it for special occasions. She could not help missing her husband again, but she whispered a prayer of thanksgiving that the pain was not overwhelming, as it had been.

No, this pain was bearable, though uncomfortable, and Mary had accepted that it would be a permanent part of her life. Whenever she thought of Ara, it would hurt; she would wish he was beside her. But she could go on without him.

After tying around her waist a white sash embroidered with red pomegranate flowers, which exactly matched the hue of her robe, Mary combed her hair, applied perfume, and washed her face and hands.

Mary was just about to put on her head covering, a filmy white veil interwoven with fine strands of gold thread, which she had also saved from Ara's home, when she noticed a small bronze looking glass on the table in the room.

Ignoring her thoughts—that she had no time to waste in admiring herself, that it did not matter how she appeared anyway—Mary went over to it. What did she look like? Since she had left Eli's house, she had not known or even cared. But somehow, seeing the mirror made her want to find out.

Slowly she reached for it. The woman who stared back at Mary in the looking glass was beautiful. Hair the color of ripe barley though streaked with gray, thick and flowing; eyes bright and large, fringed with dark lashes; skin smooth and healthy—Mary could hardly believe it was her. Yes, following the Master had been good for her in many ways.

"Mary! The men are going upstairs!" John called outside the doorway. "Are you ready?"

Guiltily, Mary put back the mirror. "Yes, I am coming," she answered, draping the head covering over her hair. She tried to control the excitement rising within her. It was time to celebrate the Passover, she felt pretty, and the Master was safe. She could want no more, besides, of course, her children.

Entering the dimly lit upper room, where the men had already assembled, Mary went about her tasks, pouring the diluted wine into each man's goblet and placing the various bowls in position.

"You look lovely," Simon told her as she handed him his filled goblet, and, next to him, Matthew nodded approvingly. Mary smiled her thanks to both of them.

Finally, as the sun's last rays disappeared, the men took their places on the couches around the low table. Though the custom had originally been to partake of the meal while standing, walking staff in hand, as their forefathers had done when they left Egypt, it was now acceptable to recline in comfort.

Jesus motioned to Mary, and she lit the oil lamps. Then when he began the kiddush, or opening prayer of consecration, Mary took her position by the door, holding a basin, towel, and small jar of water.

As she watched, Mary could not help but think how families and groups all over the city were doing the same at this very time, just as they had ever since anyone could remember. Yes, across the country and in every land in which people of her race lived, loyal Jews were celebrating the deliverance of their ancestors out of the hands of the Egyptians in the exact way that the followers of the Nazarene were. *There was something comforting in knowing that,* Mary thought, something that linked each one of them to every other Jew and to the Mighty One Himself.

After the prayer and the first cup of wine, the Master nodded at her, and Mary gave Him the basin, jar, and towel. But what was going on? Instead of washing His own hands, setting apart Himself as the most important person there—as was supposed to happen—Jesus removed His outer garment. Wrapping the towel around Him, He knelt in front of Judas.

"What are you doing, my Lord?" the startled disciple asked.

Silently the rabbi slipped off Judas' sandals, and pouring the water into the basin, He proceeded to wash the man's feet.

Mary could see that the disciples were as shocked as she was. Why, their Master was taking the role of a servant, not the position of host of the feast which was rightfully His! Whatever would make Him do such a thing?

After Judas' feet were dried, Jesus moved down the row of men, doing each one in turn. Several tried to protest or question

Him about it, but their words died on their lips when He merely looked at them.

When the rabbi reached Simon, the disciple stubbornly pulled back his long legs. "Never shall you wash my feet!" Simon declared.

"If I don't, you have no part with Me," Jesus answered, smiling a little. He must have expected the former fisherman's reaction, as did Mary. Simon was not one to simply follow everyone else.

As the implication of what the Master had said hit, Simon stretched out his legs and arms in a rapid motion. "Then Lord, do my feet as well as my hands and my head!"

At this, Jesus laughed out loud. "If one has bathed, he needs only to wash his feet to be clean." Then His voice became serious. "And you are clean but not all of you."

Mary was still trying to understand what He might have meant by that when the rabbi finished the last disciple. Then He put his robe back on and took His place again at the table.

Usually at this point of the seder, the small table of food was carried in from outside the doorway, to be placed beside where the men reclined. But Jesus made no gesture to Mary to do so, and she waited anxiously by the door, wondering what would happen next. Never had Passover been different from all the other times it was celebrated; she could not comprehend why He was doing it this way.

"You call me Teacher and Lord," Jesus was saying to the men, "and you should do so. Nevertheless, I am serving you; therefore, you should also serve each other."

At last, the gesture Mary awaited came, and she carefully carried the portable table in and placed it next to Him. Not knowing what to expect, she resumed her position by the door. Would He change anything else about the Passover service?

But the seder proceeded as customary; the bitter herbs were

dipped in salt water and passed out to each participant, and the ritual questions were asked and dutifully answered with the history of their people. After explaining what each food represented, the Master led the group in the traditional singing of the Hallel, and the second cup of wine was drained.

As the service continued, Mary began to relax. Perhaps nothing else would be changed.

Jesus broke one of the unleavened loaves of bread, gave thanks, and began dipping a piece for each one of them into the bitter herbs as well as the sweet charoseth, symbolic of the red clay used by their ancestors to build bricks for the Egyptians.

"One of you will betray Me," He told them as He worked.

Startled, Mary thought she had not heard the Master correctly. One of these men, turn his back on the one who he followed? Impossible!

But some of the men were asking, "Is it I, my Lord?"

Not answering, Jesus continued dipping the bread.

Mary saw Simon nudge John, who was next to the rabbi. Then John whispered something to Jesus. She could not hear the Master's reply; He only began passing out the dipped bread by giving the first one to Judas.

Slipping out to retrieve another wineskin, left in the cooking area to keep warm, Mary wondered again about who could possibly betray Jesus. She was so intent on her thoughts that she was surprised when a figure pushed past her on the stairs.

"Forgive me," she said quickly, seeing it was Judas. "You must hurry; you know the lamb will be served next."

He gave her such a harsh look that she scarcely recognized him. "I will not be back."

"What do you mean?" she asked, shocked. Not partaking of the lamb was unheard of; it was the same as missing the entire seder. Was he ill? But Judas appeared more angry than anything else.

She could ask him no more, for Judas had descended and was walking rapidly across the courtyard. She heard the gate slam as she reached the bottom of the stairs.

The men were ready for the meal, so she had no more time to think about the reason for Judas' absence. Only when they had finished eating did she lean over to ask Matthew if he knew. He shrugged as she reached over to fill his cup for the third time.

"Wait, Mary," he said suddenly, pointing at Jesus.

She looked up, surprised again. The Master had picked up another loaf of bread, and after praying over it, broke it into pieces. "Here, all of you, eat this. It is My body, broken for you."

Mary gasped. The lamb had to be the last food in the mouth during the seder; it was more of a certainty than perhaps any other part. Jesus knew that as well as any of them. How could He ask them to actually consume more bread?

Shock was registering on the faces of most of the men around the table, but like obedient children, they took what the Master offered. Only when the bread had disappeared did Jesus motion for Mary to pour more wine.

"This cup is the new testament of My blood," He told them solemnly. "Do this, too, in remembrance of Me."

After they had finished it, Mary refilled the goblets one last time. When this fourth cup was emptied, and they had sung a hymn, the Passover was completed.

Quietly the men rose from the table and started down the stairs. As Mary began to clear the remains of the seder, she overheard one of them say something about the garden of Gethsemane, one of Jesus' favorite places. Apparently, they were all going there.

Mary was not disappointed that she had not been invited to join them. By the time she had finished cleaning up the room and the cooking area, it would be late. She would see the Master and the men in the morning. For now, as she worked, Mary had much to think about. It was a Passover seder she would never forget.

The pounding penetrated Mary's consciousness again, and resentfully, she rolled over on the mat. Why was anyone driving in nails at this hour? It could not be much past dawn.

Persistently, the noise continued, and as Mary became more awake, she realized it was not nails being hammered in; it was knocking at the door. Expecting one of the men to respond, she remained where she was.

Then, as the pounding did not cease, Mary arose and sleepily stumbled through the open courtyard to the gate leading to the street. Just as she had thought, it was only beginning to get light, with pink and gold fingers stretching across the early morning sky.

Passing the entrances to the other sleeping rooms, Mary was surprised that they seemed unoccupied. The family who lived in this home was still at a relative's home on the other side of town for the feast, and the Rabbi and His followers were to spend the night here. Hadn't they returned from the garden?

Suddenly Mary felt chilled. Could something have happened to Jesus?

When she opened the gate and saw Joanna, her hair tangled, her face wet with weeping, Mary knew the answer to her question. "What is it?" she asked, the words sticking in her throat.

Tears followed one another in rapid descent across Joanna's cheeks. "They have arrested the Master."

Clutching the gate, Mary tried to keep from falling. It had finally taken place. The nightmare that had been at the back of all their minds, pushed away from contemplation because it was inconceivable that such a thing could actually happen to their Lord, was no longer just a distant possibility. Mary felt dizzy from the blow.

Shaking her head to clear it, Mary attempted to think. "Where is He now?"

Joanna tried to stop crying. "He has already been before the high priest, and He is being sent to Pilate next."

"That will be at the Antonia," Mary said. They could go to the massive Roman fortress that was dwarfed by the Temple it stood beside. And do what? She struggled to control the fear rising within her. There was only one reason she knew of for the Rabbi to be taken before the Roman governor. The Sanhedrin, seventy members strong, with the high priest at its helm, could not impose the death sentence. Pilate could. How many times had Jesus himself warned them that He would die?

"I think we should go find the rest of the women," Joanna said, working to keep her voice steady. "His mother is here somewhere—we must tell her. There is nothing we can do for Him at the fortress."

Though her greatest desire was to be with the Master, Mary realized her friend was right. They must go and inform the others. She ran back into her sleeping room for her head covering and a cloak, and the two went out the gate.

In their haste, they forgot to kiss their fingers, then touch the mezuzah, in the tradition of faithful Jews entering or leaving a house. Hanging on the doorpost, the small ornate case contained the prayer which began, "Hear, O Israel, the Lord our God is One," and only the gravity of the situation at hand would have caused such neglect.

This early, the many shops which lined the streets were closed, their awnings rolled up, and the constant enticing voices of the merchants offering their wares were silent. The exotic smells and sights that drew one into purchasing—copper from Cyprus, pottery from Greece, or white linen from Egypt—were absent. People were just beginning to come out of their homes to begin the day's activities.

"Where are the men?" Mary asked suddenly, ignoring a sleeping beggar who had curled up in front of a fish shop. "Have they also been arrested?"

"No, but I don't know where they might be," Joanna told her. "We are staying with my husband's family in the upper city for the feast, you know, and the residence of the high priest is across the road. Voices outside awakened me in the middle of the night. When I looked out to find the source of the commotion, I saw a number of the Temple police escorting a prisoner into the home of the high priest." She paused to wipe her eyes. "I would have just gone back to sleep if I hadn't seen John going in with them. Fearing the worst, I hurried over to speak with him. But when I arrived, I could not find him."

"John is acquainted with the high priest; perhaps he went in with the Master." She stepped around a puddle of spilled wine in the paved street.

Joanna nodded. "Anyway, I asked the gatekeeper who the prisoner was. And, Mary, she said it was our Lord!" Emotion again overwhelmed Joanna, and the two of them stopped in a doorway to hug each other and weep. When no more tears would come, they resumed their sorrowful journey, whispering prayers for the safety of the Master.

Finding Mary of Nazareth and the rest of the women who had followed Jesus was no easy task in a city swollen to four times its normal size for Passover. But at last Mary felt satisfied; the Master's mother had joined them, as did several of the others. Susanna and another woman agreed to try to locate the remaining Galileans while Joanna, Mary, and their party went to the Antonia, the fortress built by the late king, Herod called the Great. Connected to the adjoining Temple by a passageway which enabled soldiers to fill the outer Court of the Gentiles at the first sign of trouble, it was a bitter reminder of Roman authority.

When they arrived, panting, they found only a bored soldier at the gate. Clean shaven, he wore a bronze helmet that completely covered his hair and extended down over his cheeks. Under his sleeveless armor cuirass of hardened leather was a dirty red tunic.

"Go away, woman," he told Mary when she approached him.

"Where is Jesus the Nazarene?" Mary asked boldly. At his blank look, she tried again. "The . . . the prisoner from Galilee being tried this morning."

"Oh, Him! The governor pronounced sentence on Him, and it's being carried out right now." The soldier picked at his teeth.

"Where? What sentence?"

He pointed a boney finger to the west. "Over there, outside the city wall. I think they call the hill Golgotha. It's where they crucify the criminals," the soldier sneered.

Once again, Mary felt dizzy. This could not be happening.

As they hurried across Jerusalem, the women did not speak, each trying to control her emotions. But when they went out the city gate and neared the small hill called the Place of a Skull, due to its rocky indentations that resembled the bones of a human head, they could not help weeping again at the sight of three crosses, complete with writhing figures.

Several of the women fell to their knees, moaning, but Mary rushed on. The Master could not be one of those nailed to the harsh instruments of death. Perhaps sentence had been pronounced and He had been brought here to die, but the Mighty One would not let His own son suffer in such pain and humiliation.

She approached the crosses, weaving between the onlookers, ignoring her revulsion at the blood and agony. Scanning each one, she breathed a sigh of relief. She had been right! The Rabbi was not here, only some criminals receiving the punishment they deserved. Where could the Nazarene be?

"Mary!" a voice called, and she turned to see John. He appeared exhausted, and none of the other men were with him.

"Show me our Lord," she begged him, dashing over to John and gripping his arm. "What have they done with Him?"

Silently, he gestured to the middle cross.

"No!" she shrieked. "That is not Him! I looked. I would know Him if I saw Him, the Rabbi I have followed for so long . . ."

John enveloped her in his strong arms, and over his shoulder, she once again raised her eyes to the cross he had indicated. The Man who hung there was unrecognizable. Dried blood plastered His cheeks; portions of His beard had been ripped out. A twisted wreath of thorns had been pressed into His forehead, and fresh droplets of scarlet blood made their way down from the wounds created by them, only to merge with the darker blood from the scourging he had received.

His once-strong arms were useless, fastened to the crossbar. Even His feet had been rendered inactive by the nails which held them to the wood of the upright post.

In horror, Mary turned away. As in a nightmare, she heard the people mock Him, watched Him speak to His mother, saw the life ebbing out of Him. By midday, the sky had darkened as if it were night. Many of the onlookers left, but Mary would not—could not—go. At last, in the middle of the afternoon, it was over. Jesus died.

Later Mary, numbly, watched the body being removed from the cross. As it was carried away to be entombed in a nearby garden, in keeping with the custom of burial soon after death, she followed. It was the last thing she could do this day for the Master she had loved.

26

The sleeping room was still dark, its latticed window boarded shut for the night, when Mary wearily rose from the mat and slipped out into the open courtyard. She was immediately aware of the overwhelming pain which, by its ache, had kept her awake for almost the entire night. *Jesus is dead, Jesus is dead,* it repeated relentlessly.

Trying once again to cast away the unwelcome refrain, Mary peered at the starry sky for a glimmer of light. *Certainly dawn has come by now,* she thought.

Sure enough, the faintest touches of lavender were appearing behind the hills. Relieved, Mary hurried back into the room she had occupied for the night and began to prepare herself to leave. The distinct moment of sunrise, in which the stars rapidly vanished and the lilac sky became streaked with gold and pink, would occur imminently.

At last, Mary could go do what she needed to do. Never had the Sabbath passed so slowly, nor the night taken so long to end. For the first time, she had actually resented the law that kept her bound to the house as securely as any chain.

After slipping on her sandals, Mary crept quietly back towards the courtyard, hoping that the other women would not wake up. The past few days since Jesus' death had been so difficult for all of them that she knew they needed the rest.

"Mary!" A whisper came from across the room, and a shadowy figure sat up on her mat. "What are you doing?"

Recognizing Joanna, who had moved in after the crucifixion to mourn with them, she made her way around the other sleepers and the wooden pillar in the center of the room to her friend's side. "It's morning, and I'm going to the tomb."

"Why?"

"His body was never anointed. I may not have been able to do Ara's, but I will do this last thing for the Master." Mary's voice was soft but determined.

"Oh, Mary, it won't do any good. You told me yourself that they rolled a big stone in front of the tomb. How could you even get to our Lord? And besides, weren't there guards at the place?"

"I know, I know. But I have to at least try. I must. He didn't even have a proper funeral," she said, remembering all of the hired mourners and flutists at Ara's.

Joanna sighed. "Well, then, if you're going to be so stubborn, wait a little, and I will come too. Maybe the two of us can convince the soldiers to push the stone away."

"Three would have even more of a chance of success," a third voice put in, and the other two looked over to see Mary, the mother of James, also sitting up.

"I'm sorry we awakened you," Joanna began, but the other woman stopped her with a wave of her hand.

"No, no, I slept little anyway. But may I accompany you?"

"Of course," Mary told her, stifling her disappointment. She had wanted to go alone to Jesus, to have the chance to mourn His passing in her own way. Yet these others also shared her grief; how could she deny them what she herself craved?

Without speaking further, the two women began to dress in the dim light of the ever-burning oil lamp sitting on its shelf on the pillar. Mary returned to the courtyard to wait for them.

Leaning against the cold lime-coated plaster wall, Mary still could hardly believe this trip was necessary. Why, even now the gate should swing open, and the Master enter.

"My Lord, you were up all night praying again," she would say, the slightest rebuke in her voice.

He would grin. "Oh, Mary, the sweetness of sleep is nothing compared to that which I find in my Father's presence. But I admit to being hungry now. Would you prepare Me something?"

Rising quickly, she would return His smile. "You know that I will, gladly." Then she would hasten to find His favorite melons, talking with Him as He ate, eagerly awaiting to hear His plans for the day.

But never again would He partake of the food she offered. No, now his body lay lifeless and battered in the tomb, and she could no longer tend to even His simplest need. *Jesus is dead, Jesus is dead.* The harsh cadence of the words echoed in her ears.

Though she had cried the day before until she was convinced she could weep no more, the tears worked their way out from under her eyelids. Why had the Master died? How could she bear this, the greatest of sorrows?

"Mary, we are ready," Joanna said, gently touching her shoulder.

Standing up, Mary silently handed each of them some of the anointing oils—nard, myrrh, and aloes—and cloths she had collected. As they walked through the narrow winding streets that led to their destination, Mary could hear the sad rhythm which was haunting her for the third day: *Jesus is dead, Jesus is dead.*

As they passed through the low stone walls which surrounded the dark quiet garden where the tomb was located, Mary was again thankful that the Master at least had a proper place to rest. How degrading it would have been to find that His body had been dumped in the trench reserved for criminals in the Kidron Valley to the east of the city! But due to the courage of one Joseph of Arimathea, the Rabbi had not suffered that final humiliation; the man had approached Pilate and received permission for the remains to be buried in Joseph's own never-used tomb.

"The soldiers must be sleeping. We are almost at the place where our Lord lies, and there is only silence," Joanna whispered as they followed the well-kept path between the olive trees, now covered with white flowers. Since they did not bear fruit until about their fifteenth year, this garden had been planted a number of years earlier.

Mary nodded. "Perhaps we can do our work without their knowledge."

"But how can we move the rock with no one helping us?" the other Mary asked softly as they passed a large stone olive press.

"There must be a way," Mary told her in a low voice. "I'm not leaving until I have done that for which I have come, one way or another." She pulled out a small coin bag from her waist sash and jingled it.

Half expecting the other women to object to such obvious bribery, Mary quickly tucked the bag away, but they said nothing.

Reaching the end of the path, they braced themselves for the task ahead of them. Mary tried not to remember the disfigured body she had seen Joseph respectfully place in the cave, but the dreadful rhythm that had been with her since then blared in her ears. *Jesus is dead. Jesus is . . .*

It was abruptly interrupted by Joanna's gasp as they stepped beyond the trees into full view of the tomb.

"The stone—it's rolled aside!" the other Mary exclaimed, pointing to the gaping entrance which beckoned them. She started toward it, then suddenly stopped. "Look! The soldiers! I've awakened them!"

But the soldiers appeared oblivious to her voice; they continued lying motionlessly a short distance from where the women stood.

"There's something about them that is not right," Joanna said, peering at the still figures. "Are they . . . dead?"

Mary walked over toward them. It was possible that during the night, they had been attacked by some of the Master's more radical followers. Could any of the twelve, enraged by grief, have resorted to such a thing? Well, Simon did have a sword.

But as she leaned over one of the soldiers, Mary could see no wounds. Instead, his belly gently rose and fell. "He's breathing," she announced to the others. "But he doesn't seem to be merely sleeping. I don't understand." The rest of the guards were in the same condition.

"Come on, Mary," Joanna called. "We must see if the body is here."

The women hesitantly started toward the tomb. What would they find within? Had someone moved the stone to steal the body or to desecrate it? As if it was not bad enough for the beloved Rabbi to undergo crucifixion, now it appeared that even His body could not be left undisturbed.

"Wait," Joanna whispered. "Maybe we should get some of the men."

"You can go if you want," Mary told her grimly. "I'm not leaving until I've seen myself what's in that tomb."

Joanna nodded reluctantly, and the three of them linked hands and stooped to enter the blackness of the cave. Once inside, they could resume standing upright, and they stopped to let their eyes adjust to the dimness.

The other Mary was the first to notice the figure before them. "Look!" she gasped. "Who is it?"

As the women watched, pale light seemed to radiate from the form, and they could see a big man sitting on the stone ledge where the deceased should have been. There was no sign of the Master's body; it being a new grave, even the shelves above the slab, used for the bones of those less recently departed, were empty.

Mary stared at the man. Dressed in a white robe, he was young and beardless. He did not appear surprised at the presence of the visitors. "Don't be amazed," he said in an unnatural singsong voice. "You are seeking Jesus the Nazarene, who was crucified."

At the sound of his words, they all took a step back toward the opening of the cave. Who could he be?

Smiling at them, the stranger continued. "Jesus is not here; He has risen." Perhaps because of the unconvinced expressions on their faces, he gestured at the stone slab on which he sat. "See? This is the place where He was laid."

Mary clutched her friends' hands. What was this stranger trying to say?

"Go and tell Simon and the others," the man instructed.

Wordlessly, the three backed away from the man, then turned and hurried out of the cave, ducking so as not to bump their heads on the low lintel of the opening.

Before she knew it, Mary was running, running as she had not run since she was a child, with wild abandon, past the still sleeping soldiers, through the clearing for the whitewashed tomb, and onto the path. Joanna and the other Mary joined her, but soon the older women had to slow down.

"Mary, wait!" Joanna called, exhaustion in her voice.

Willing herself to stop, Mary faced them. Her body was trembling uncontrollably, her breath coming in short gasps, and there was a tingling sensation in her ears. Could the man in the tomb be speaking the truth? Was it possible that their Lord was not dead, as they had supposed? She was not sure anymore, not sure of anything. Nothing seemed to be as it appeared. The soldiers, the stone rolled away, and the man with his news—what did it all mean?

Joanna and the other Mary were as confused as she, but they agreed they must find the disciples. Maybe they could make sense out of such unusual circumstances.

As the women turned onto the road leading to the house in which they were staying, they met Simon and John.

Eagerly, Mary hurried up to them. But as she looked at their grief-stricken faces, some of her excitement that just maybe the Master could indeed have risen, as they had been told, dissolved. *They will never accept it,* she decided.

"What is it, Mary?" Simon asked, puzzled by her silence. He appeared exhausted, with huge circles under his eyes and a wrinkled robe.

"We've been to the tomb, and . . . and . . ." Somehow she was unable to say the words. After the nightmare of the past few days, it was too much to believe that Jesus was risen. And if Mary could not have the faith to be certain herself, how could she convince them? The refrain which had been muted since they had talked with the man at the cave returned full force: *Jesus is dead. Jesus is dead.*

"Yes?" Simon asked, his voice strained.

"The body has been taken, and we don't know where it is," There! It was out. Not the way the man at the cave had worded it, but at least the disciples knew about the empty tomb.

The two men exchanged distressed looks, and without speaking, both spun around and darted toward the garden from which Mary and the others had come.

"We must find the rest of the disciples," Joanna said, not mentioning how Mary had shared the news, though she must have clearly heard.

"Perhaps some of them are back at the house," the other Mary suggested.

"You go," Mary told them. "I must return to the tomb."

"But . . ."

For once, Mary did not wait to hear the older woman's objections. Abruptly, she turned and ran back down the road, much as she had done when they left the garden.

Joanna and the other Mary shook their heads and started toward the house.

As before, the garden was silent as Mary walked along the path to the tomb. But it was no longer as dark; even in the time she had been gone, the early morning sunshine had begun to penetrate the branches. Panting from the wild dash most of the way there, Mary peered through the olive trees for a glimpse of Simon and John. But she could see no one.

Had the men also spoken to the strange man in the cave? Could they believe the incredible tale he told? How was it possible that one whom they had seen die actually returned to life? Oh, she remembered well enough the little daughter of Jarius and the youth from Nain, both lifeless until the Nazarene rabbi came. And who could forget their friend Lazarus, in his grave four days before the Master simply called his name to draw Lazarus away from death?

No one would deny that Jesus had great power to do such things. But this, this was different. He could not restore Himself as easily as He had brought back the others.

When she approached the clearing which led into the tomb, she tried to stop the questions which tormented her. But that only let the melancholy chorus crescendo in her ears. *Jesus is dead. Jesus is dead* . . .

Just as it was during her earlier visit, the huge stone which had blocked the cave's entrance was rolled off to one side. Nervously, Mary moved toward it. The soldiers were gone, and she still could see nothing of the two disciples who had preceded her.

The thought of entering the tomb by herself was terrifying, but she had to know what—or who—was inside. Snatching up a pomegranate-sized rock from the ground, she cradled it in her palm. At least it would offer a small amount of protection if she needed it.

When she finally worked up the courage to tip-toe in and let her eyes adjust to the dimness, she was surprised and even a little disappointed to find emptiness. The shelf for the body was bare, and no soldiers or men in white awaited her. Only the anointing oils and cloths left next to the entrance by the women on their first visit remained.

Dropping the rock, she did not linger in the cool darkness. Back out in the morning sunshine, diluted somewhat by the numerous trees which surrounded the clearing, she decided to return to the house. There was no need to stay by the tomb. *Jesus is dead. Jesus is dead:* the chorus had never been louder.

But before she had reached the pathway out, grief overtook Mary in such waves that she slumped to the ground. The tears coursed down her face. What difference had it made, following the Master for so long? He had died a criminal's death, and as for what had happened to His body, she did not know.

And she could not explain the man in white or the stone rolled out of the way or the condition of the soldiers. Nothing made sense anymore.

The sobs which came from deep within Mary would not cease, and it no longer mattered that someone might hear her. She wept for what seemed like a long time, oblivious to the large damp splotches the tears made on her robe, unaware that the sound of her distress traveled out of the garden. Her mind could only focus on what she did know: *Jesus was dead.*

At last, Mary rose, spent. If she could just find the body, perhaps she would not hurt so much. The anointing had still not been done. But where could she look? She had no idea.

A sudden urge to once more visit the tomb compelled Mary to walk toward it. *This is foolishness,* she chided herself. Her feet paid no attention.

Inside again, Mary gasped as her eyes focused on the two men sitting on the stone ledge which had held the Master's body. She could not tell if either of them was the one she had seen earlier, but they were dressed in similar white garments which appeared to reflect light.

"Why are you crying?" they asked.

"Because my Lord has been taken away, and I don't know where He is," she answered quickly, embarrassed they had heard her weeping but unwilling to tell them the true cause: the death of the Master. Before they could question her any more, Mary backed away. There was something unreal about the men.

When Mary reentered the small clearing, she immediately noticed a man walking among the slow-growing olive trees, most of which were nevertheless five times the height of a person. He was stooped over and seemed to be examining the blossoming branches that surrounded Him.

Relieved, Mary started toward Him. Perhaps it was Joseph, the owner of the garden. He might even have been the one to move the body.

As she got closer, Mary realized the man checking the trees was too tall to be Joseph. Ah, but the Arimathean was wealthy. He would not bother tending this garden himself. The figure in front of her must be his hired gardener. At least it was good to find someone besides the strange white-clad men in the tomb. She tried to wipe the tearstains from her cheeks.

"Woman, why are you weeping?" He asked suddenly, looking over at her. He continued to be semihidden by the branches around Him. "Who are you seeking?"

"If you have moved the body, let me know where He is," Mary answered boldly. "We'll carry Him away." Not wanting Him to see her eyes, swollen from her sobbing, she was careful to keep her face averted from Him.

Pushing the branches aside, the man took a step towards her. "Mary!"

At the sound of His voice, she jerked up her head to look straight at Him. Only one spoke her name like that—the Master.

"Rabboni!" she cried, flinging herself at His feet, still marked with the wounds from the nails which had bound Him to the cross. Her tears flowed unchecked as she grasped that He had indeed risen as the man in white had said.

Jesus laughed and gently touched her hair. "Don't cling to me," He told her, yet the rebuke was anything but harsh. "I haven't yet returned to my Father. But go and tell the others . . ."

His laughter lingering in her ears like the sweetness that remains in the mouth after a honey cake, Mary obediently rose and hurried down the path for the second time that day. But this time, the melody which played inside her was one of joy. *Jesus is alive! Jesus is alive!*

And nothing would ever stop that chorus from filling her heart.

27

The heavy millstones rumbled in Mary's ears as she sat grinding grain with Joanna. It was strenuous work, alternately pushing and pulling the wooden handle that rose from the horizontal stone on top. A funnel-like opening received the grain, that filtered down through the first stone, made of porous lava stone so that its surface would not get polished by the constant fiction. Then it went through the second, which was of heavier limestone, finally reaching the sheepskin below the mill as flour.

Mary remembered that when she had first started following Jesus, she had dreaded her turn to grind. But now her arms were no longer the weak limbs of a pampered woman. The time she had been with the Master had toughened her, and she was pleased with her lean and strong body.

Because of the noise of the stones, the hours spent there were not good for lengthy conversations, even though the two women sat opposite each other, the mill between them. Mary had learned to use such time to think, and she found herself almost looking forward to the uninterrupted chance to reflect upon what was happening in her world.

Truly, life had been brimming with new challenges since that day when the Master had appeared to her in the garden. Smiling a little, Mary gently chided herself for not believing the man in white. Only viewing Jesus Himself had convinced her of the resurrection. But then, at first none of them had thought it could be true. And the Lord had not rebuked her for her lack of faith.

If anyone should have been chastised, Thomas would be the one. He had not been present when the Master had first appeared to the disciples, and he had been adamant that they were dreaming.

"Won't you at least consider the possibility that our Lord has risen?" Mary had asked him. "He did tell us this would happen."

The doubter had stubbornly shaken his head.

"But, Thomas, I saw him! We all did. You can't ignore the facts," Simon told him, a bit impatiently.

"Unless I put my finger in the wounds in His hands and side, I won't believe," Thomas swore, turning away.

Mary had felt sorry for the man. Perhaps, because he was not present when Jesus appeared to the other disciples, he wondered if the Master loved him as much as He did them. It could be that he was not as unbelieving as he said. But maybe he was. Thomas had never been gullible; she had heard him query Lazarus extensively about his death before he accepted what the rest of them had just by watching the man walk out of his tomb.

But happily, the next time Mary was with Thomas, all his doubts had vanished.

"Did you hear, Mary? The Lord came back again, just to show me His wounds, as I'd requested. How could I not believe?" His face glowed with joy, and Mary was pleased that Jesus, always so responsive to each one of them, had reached out to Thomas in just the dramatic way the disciple needed.

Her memories were interrupted by Joanna.

"Why are you smiling, Mary?" she asked loudly, tossing another handful of barley into the mill.

"Oh, I'm remembering Thomas's excitement after he saw our

Lord," she answered, leaning towards her friend to make certain her voice carried over the rumbling millstones.

The older woman nodded and smiled too.

As she continued working, Mary looked up to find Matthew and several of the other disciples entering the courtyard. The men settled in a shady corner, and as Susanna served them cups of cool water, they talked, laughing and gesturing enthusiastically.

Though Mary could not hear their exact words, she could guess what they were discussing. Now that the Master had returned to heaven, and the Holy Spirit had been given to His followers, each one had big plans about how he was going to proclaim the coming of the Messiah.

Some were focusing on a particular synagogue in the city; with over 350 of them in Jerusalem, it was not difficult to find one with people of similar background or interest. Others frequented the marketplaces, explaining to passersby the good news about Jesus. The rest of them thought of different places, as unique as they were, in which to share the vital message.

It had not been long before everywhere one went, the talk seemed to be about the Man who had died and come back to life as the Son of God. And many who heard, believed. They joined the followers of the Nazarene for prayer, teaching, and fellowship.

But somehow, Mary felt strangely uncomfortable in the midst of it all. There was really no reason for it, she reflected as she and Joanna picked up the ends of the laden sheepskin and poured the flour into a basket. She was doing the same things she had for the past year; even with Joanna back, Mary had continued to direct the women in their duties.

"You know what to do now, while I have not taken care of such details for a long time. Besides, I will be returning to Chuza soon," Joanna had insisted. Mary reluctantly agreed.

Still, she had to admit she did not have the satisfaction she once had in tending to the men. At first she had thought it was just because she missed the Master. After all, the new relationship she had with Him was fulfilling, but it was not like having Him with her each day as He had been. Yet she soon realized it was more than that. But what, she was not sure.

When Joanna and she finally finished the grinding and began to make the flour into bread dough, Mary brought up the subject with her friend.

Joanna nodded thoughtfully. "That is just how I felt when the Mighty One was calling me to return to my husband. But as you know, I would not listen." She grimaced, remembering that unhappy time in her life. "It was a mistake."

"Perhaps I am discontent here because I am to be somewhere else," Mary proposed.

"Ask our Lord to show you," Joanna told her. "You will never be at rest until you know what you should be doing, and then obey it."

Mary shook her head in agreement but did not respond. As her friend had been talking, a distressing thought had entered her mind: *Magdala. Return to Magdala.*

Her immediate reaction was one of panic. Go back to Eli, who would probably imprison her at once? Exchange her life of freedom and purpose for one of confinement? Give up all she had here to be labeled as crazed? Out of the question!

Mixing the water and leaven into the flour, Mary tried to push out thoughts of Magdala.

"You will drown the leaven, stirring so hard," Joanna said, smiling at her.

Mary tried to laugh. "It is just that I am trying to hurry. I imagine the men are hungry by now."

Her friend nodded and walked over to check the fire in the

clay cooking stove. It must be exactly the right temperature when the dough was put on it.

After the ingredients had all been added, Mary began kneading. She could not go to her hometown. The Lord had something special for her to do. Even if it meant traveling to a faraway country, she was willing.

But you are unwilling to take the news to Magdala? a quiet inner voice seemed to say.

Quickly covering the bread and placing it on a shelf to rise, Mary pretended she did not hear. The Master knew what she faced at home; He would not ask this thing of her.

"Mary, come here!" Susanna called, and Mary was relieved to have her thoughts interrupted. She immediately knew that one thing alone could put such joy in her friend's voice. Micah was back.

Sure enough, there he stood next to Susanna. The smile he wore covered his face; it was obvious that the time apart from the young widow had only strengthened his feelings toward her.

"Shalom, Micah," Mary greeted him. "How are you?"

"Well, as always." The little man could hardly take his eyes away from Susanna, even while he spoke to Mary. "I have a message for you from your children."

"Yes?" She could not keep the eagerness from her voice as a powerful wave of longing for them rolled over her.

"They send you love and say to you that they are in good health. But they beg you to consider coming to see them. Especially, the girl seemed to need to know you are near."

Mary blinked back tears. Kezia, who had been so distant, wanted her? She must find a way to go back for a little bit, to reassure them both of her love.

Once more, the thought of staying in Magdala returned.

Annoyed at its persistence, Mary rejected it again. Living there was not an option.

"Did Eli try to have you arrested?" she asked anxiously.

"No, perhaps because he has been ill," Micah told her. "But he is recovering. Naturally, he was a bit pleased with the news of the Master's death."

"Did he hear about the resurrection?"

Micah grinned. "Oh yes, and so did the children and everyone else in the household. Most of them do not believe it, but that can change."

"Are you returning to Magdala soon?" she queried. Perhaps if he were, she could go back with him.

"No, I don't think so," he said. "Eli generously accepted the termination of my employment, probably because he was weary of hearing the Master's name. And I have felt our Lord's call to be in Jerusalem. I have work to do here." He glanced at Susanna, and Mary suspected the first job he tackled would be getting betrothed.

She smiled at the two of them. "I wish you every blessing," she said sincerely.

"Thank you," he replied, blushing. Then his voice became solemn. "Mary, you should also know that Eli has not forgiven you. In fact, the anger he feels toward you smolders. I know you want to see Joshua and Kezia, but it will be very difficult. Because of the child's longing for you, Eli is watching for you now. If he gets the chance, he will most certainly lock you up."

"I know, and I appreciate your concern."

"Those awful men who abducted you before could still be looking for you," Susanna added.

Micah shook his head. "No, she need not fear them anymore. I heard last month that with several soldiers they became involved in some gambling. When Azor and Sadoc were discovered cheating, the Romans were not amused." He could not resist smiling a little at the thought of Azor and Sadoc finally getting what they deserved.

Mary felt almost light-headed with relief. They would never hurt her or her loved ones again. She could release her hatred for them.

"Well, even though they are dead, it is too dangerous for you to go. You will not risk it, will you?" Susanna asked anxiously. "Besides, you are so needed here that you cannot seriously consider leaving."

"Of course not," she told them. But almost right away, Mary once more felt—rather than heard—a voice from deep within her: *Go to Magdala. Go.*

She ignored it.

Matthew found Mary weaving part of a robe at a small portable horizontal loom, its two beams held in place by ropes tied to pegs in the ground. "You are almost finished," he said, coming up from behind where she sat. "Who will wear it?"

"Yes, I have completed the other two pieces. It was for Judas, but now . . ." Working the shuttle with the woof threads over and under the lengthwise warf, Mary shook her head sadly. It was still difficult to accept the disciple's betrayal of the Master and his subsequent self-inflicted death. "Sometimes he irritated me, but nevertheless, I miss him. I keep expecting to see him walk in the gate," she said.

"I know. We all feel the void."

"Why do you suppose he did it?" She picked up another linen thread for the shuttle.

Matthew shrugged. "We will probably never find out. Even those who spent the most time with Judas are puzzled. Some think he might have become disgruntled that the Rabbi did not assume more of a kingly role. Others feel he could have believed he was helping protect our Lord from the crowds."

"By putting Him into the hands of our enemies?" Mary wrinkled her nose in disgust. "Hardly!"

"Well, the Mighty One alone knows what really happened. Nevertheless, it is sad to have lost one who had followed the Master for so long."

"A while ago, he seemed to be acting strangely," Mary said slowly. "But I did nothing. Perhaps if I would have talked with him about it or at least shared my concern with another person, he would be with us now. Our Lord would have never gone through all He did." She tried to shut out the memory of the horrible scene at Golgotha.

"Mary, you must not blame yourself," Matthew told her gently. "You weren't the only one to wonder what was going on with Judas. Yet none of us tried to intervene. Even if we had, he might have chosen to do what he did anyway."

She nodded reluctantly, realizing he was right but still wishing that, somehow, things might have gone differently for Judas.

"And you know it had to be that our Lord went to the cross. If not by Judas's hand, it would have been by someone else's."

"I think I will give this robe to Matthias," Mary said, ready to discuss something different. "He is about the same size as Judas, and perhaps it will help him to begin to feel a part of the twelve. If one did have to leave us, I am pleased that as fine a man as Matthias was chosen as a replacement."

"He will do an excellent job sharing the message we bring to Jerusalem, and I am certain he will appreciate your thoughtfulness." Matthew stroked the nearly complete piece of brown linen that would form the back of the new tunic. "I hear that Micah is back. Did he bring word of your children?"

"Yes, they are well." Mary did not look at Matthew so that he would not notice the pain in her eyes. "I must see them soon. It has been so long since we have been together."

"Maybe you should take some time to go to Magdala. We can manage here without you; Susanna and the others would have no difficulty."

"Susanna said just the opposite to me," Mary told him, "but I am sure she exaggerates. What I am really concerned about is Eli. Micah warned me that my father-in-law has not stopped wanting to put me away. It would be dangerous for me to return to Magdala; I might not be able to come back here."

"You have been in such situations before. Hasn't the Powerful One protected you? If your children need you, you should go," Matthew advised.

"Perhaps you are right." Once more, the desire to see Joshua and Kezia rose up within Mary, and she could hardly keep from packing for Magdala at that moment.

"If you want, I will check about caravans leaving for Galilee in the next few days," Matthew offered.

"Yes, I would like that," she heard herself saying. There, it was settled. She would journey to her hometown. But it was just for a short visit with the children, she assured herself quickly, before the inner voice could speak. She would not stay there any longer than necessary.

Matthew and she talked at length; Mary had time to finish the back of the robe and carefully remove it from the loom to prepare it to be sewn to the other pieces. When Matthew finally left, she felt again the familiar ache that there could not be any more than friendship between them. But there was something different; the determination to keep holding on to him, no matter what, had weakened.

Still in front of the loom, Mary lowered her head before her God. "I give him to You," she prayed silently. "I see now that he is not to be mine, but Yours only. If You have someone else for me, bring him into my life that we may serve You together. If not, then I will follow You myself, for as long as I live."

A tear made its way down Mary's cheek, but in her heart, she knew she had done the best thing for both Matthew and her. And, in time, the pain would lessen.

28

Matthew kept his word. Less than two weeks later, the day arrived when Mary was to leave with a caravan for Galilee.

Many of the disciples did not understand her decision. Even Susanna protested again as Mary put the last of her clothing into a cloth bag for the trip.

"Are you certain you are to go?" she asked, handing her a pair of sandals.

Mary nodded glumly from across the sleeping room they had shared. "I hate to say farewell to all of the Master's followers; they have been like a family to me. But you I will especially miss." She walked over to hug her friend. "Nevertheless, I must return to Magdala for a while."

"You will make every effort to be back to Jerusalem in the fall for my wedding?"

"Of course! I would have to be physically chained to keep me from attending." She grimaced, remembering that she could indeed be restrained in that way, if she were unsuccessful in avoiding Eli.

"I shall pray for you daily, that our Lord will use you mightily to advance His kingdom. Surely there are other believers in your town. Perhaps they already have some sort of meeting, as we do."

"Jedidiah would know," she thought out loud.

Susanna smiled a little. "So you will be seeing him?"

"Only briefly," Mary told her quickly. "You are aware that we seem to bring out the worst in each other."

"Sometimes that ends up working well."

"Not in this case." As far as the fisherman was concerned, Mary had no desire to even be around him, except to find out information about followers of the Master in Magdala.

"Mary, are you ready?" Matthew called.

"Yes, I will be right out." Giving Susanna a last embrace, she picked up her bundle and started out the door. At least she did not have to say good-bye to Joanna; the previous week, the older woman had returned to her husband.

Nevertheless, Mary could hardly keep from weeping as she told the other women and the disciples farewell.

"I will be back soon," she assured them, wondering if they believed it any more than she did. Did she have any real chance of visiting the children without her father-in-law finding out? Of course, Jedidiah would help her.

Disgustedly, Mary tucked her bundle under her arm and accepted a packet of cheese and bread from the other Mary. Why did she always have to think of the hot-tempered fisherman? This time she was not going to depend on him for anything.

The last shaloms said, Matthew and Mary left the courtyard. As they followed the narrow winding streets of Jerusalem, he a step ahead of her, as tradition dictated, Mary could not help but question if she would ever see the city again: the blind man on the corner, promising the Holy One's blessing on passersby who gave him alms; the camel loaded with baskets of grain; the half-wild dogs that roamed the streets seeking garbage to devour; the chanting of the synagogue school boys reciting their lessons that could be heard a block away from their classroom; a white-robed Temple priest, hurrying about his business; the booths lining the street, offering apples from Crete, sandals from Laodicea, and plates from Babylon. In spite of its weaknesses, this was the city Mary loved. How hard it was to depart!

Even Matthew seemed melancholy as he silently refused a street vendor who offered freshly baked raisin cakes. Little was said between the two of them as they walked, but Mary was not sure if it was because he also had mixed feelings about her leaving or if it was simply because custom frowned on men and women—even when married to each other—conversing in public. In the city, a man was not even to greet a married woman.

In spite of her mood, Mary was again thankful that tradition was not observed in Galilee like it was here. More than once, she had received glares from Jerusalemites when she—used to the comfortable relationship between the sexes of those who followed Jesus—had spoken to one of the disciples on the street or in the Temple.

When they neared the meeting place for those joining the caravan north, Matthew finally slowed down to be beside her.

"You know, it will seem very strange with you gone." He awkwardly cleared his throat as a donkey carrying building stones passed him. "I am fond of you, as I am of all of those who serve our Lord."

Mary could not help smiling. Poor Matthew! He always had a hard time communicating what he wanted to say.

"What I mean to tell you is . . . ah, well, you know . . ."

"Why, no, Matthew, I have no idea," she said innocently, although she knew perfectly well.

He stepped into an alley where they would be unobserved and motioned for her to join him. Then he faced her. "It is simply this: I will miss you. You are special to me, and I will always care a great deal about you."

"Thank you, Matthew," Mary told him sincerely, trying to ignore the pungent odor from the piles of refuse near her.

"I wish that it could have been different between us," Matthew admitted. "If I were free to marry . . ."

"I understand." Mary was touched by his honesty, and though she still regretted the way things had turned out, she was certain that their parting was what their Lord had intended.

Before Mary could move out of the alley, Matthew took a rapid step toward her and, contrary to all custom, silently embraced her. Then he strode purposefully out onto the road.

Mary followed.

"We are going back to Nazareth, and we can't get there soon enough, says I," the heavyset woman told Mary. Her yellow tunic was stained, and her mud-colored hair swung back and forth, nearly touching first one, than the other of her broad shoulders as she waddled down the road. "The Holy City is beautiful, no question about it. Everyone should go there for the festivals. But there's nothing like returning to one's hometown, don't you agree?"

"Ah, yes, . . ." Mary began.

" 'Benjamin,'—he's my husband—'Benjamin,' says I, 'we must get the young ones home to Galilee. I've had my fill of the big city life.'

"Why, one of those snobby innkeepers there served us lentils instead of sheep's feet, as we'd ordered, just because he said Benjamin mispronounced one syllable. Well, of course the two words sound similar, and we from the north do speak a little differently than people in Judea. But he knew what we wanted. Called us ignorant, he did." Wiping the sweat from her brow, the woman nodded emphatically. "Yes, we belong in the country. I could easily spend the rest of my life there."

Mary smiled halfheartedly at the woman, but inside, she wished she was anywhere else but on this road. She had tried to avoid socializing with the other women on the caravan in order that she could have time to plan for her arrival in Magdala. Until now, she had succeeded. Nevertheless, Mary still had not decided what to do once she reached her destination.

"I am called Dinah," the woman from Nazareth told Mary as she wiped the runny nose of a small child who clung to her robe. "Where are you going?"

"Magdala." If she did not encourage conversation, perhaps Mary would be left alone.

But Dinah moved nearer. "Are you visiting, or is it your home?"

"Ah . . . yes." How could she answer that question? It had been her residence, but now she considered Jerusalem where she lived.

Dinah looked a bit confused but did not ask for further clarification. Instead, she jabbered on about her house and family in Nazareth, stopping occasionally to wipe the child's nose or to settle a spat between two slightly older boys who walked behind her.

After some time, Mary began to hope that Benjamin, whoever he was, would soon need his wife. But there was no sign of him, and Dinah continued to talk.

"Have you children, dear?" she asked.

Mary answered quickly before the woman started speaking again. "A girl and a boy."

"How nice. There's nothing like them, is there?" She stopped suddenly and peered at the donkey following her family. A sharp wail penetrated the air.

Quickly, Dinah moved to the animal and scooped a small baby from his basket which was tied to the side. Then she was back beside Mary, talking again as she nursed the baby.

"Were you acquainted with a Jesus of Nazareth?" Mary asked carefully when the woman took her next breath.

"Acquainted with Him? Why, the Miracle Worker lived down

the street from us. We saw Him every day." From her tone, it was obvious that Dinah had achieved some status from the proximity of her home to that of the Master's family. "Did you hear that the Romans crucified Him at Passover?" she asked, leaning closer to Mary.

"So I understand," Mary said, amused. If anyone would be aware of such news, she would.

Dinah lowered her voice. "I'll wager you don't know the latest about Him. They say He has risen from the dead!"

"No!" Mary could not resist saying.

"Yes, it's true. The rumor that He's alive, that is. As far as Him being truly come back from the dead, well . . ." Dinah shrugged. "What do you think?"

For the next hour, Mary shared with Dinah the good news about the Master. The baby dozed in his mother's arms, and the other children, bored, ran off to find their father. When she had finished, her companion asked how she too might experience the new life of which Mary spoke.

"You must pray, asking forgiveness for your sins. Then you may invite our Lord into your life. That is what He called being born again." She gestured to the sleeping baby. "Just like him, you will have a new start, cleansed of the wrongs you have done and fit for the Master's service."

"Will you pray with me?" Dinah asked eagerly, and Mary nodded.

"Now you must find others in Nazareth who share faith in Jesus as the Messiah," Mary told her when they had finished. "They will have meetings which will help you. Take time to talk with the Merciful One every day; He is concerned about each thing in your life. Our Lord called Him Heavenly Father, and so may we. And tell others about what has happened here on the road."

"I will do all you say," Dinah assured her.

Later, Mary realized that Dinah was the first person with whom she had helped to experience new life. She thanked the Powerful One for putting her on this particular caravan where a woman needed to hear the words she had. Perhaps there *was* something special for Mary to do in Galilee.

Nothing had changed, Mary thought as she stood on the road just outside of Magdala. To her right, the Sea of Galilee lay, blue and sparkling in the sunshine. The brisk scent of the water, mixed with the ever-present odor of fish that always lingered in the villages which depended on that product as a major source of income, filled her nostrils.

On the other side, the familiar landscape greeted her. The small houses of mud bricks, the synagogue which by law had to be built taller than any other building, and the high watchtower from which Magdala took its name—they looked the same.

The caravan was long gone, but still Mary stood by the dusty road. Fear dripped down her back, refusing to permit her feet to move toward the village in front of her. What would Eli do if he discovered her?

Beyond the fear was something else, something she could not quite bear to identify, something that looked very much like the hate she had had for Azor and Sadoc.

Oh, no, Mary told herself quickly, I do not dislike anyone that much. But her father-in-law's face would not leave her mind as she sank down on the brown grass beside the road.

He was the one who kept her from Joshua and Kezia. He virtually imprisoned her. His money hired the abductors. He had made it so that she was unwelcome in her own hometown. He had completely rejected the Master and His teachings.

Yes, the truth was that Mary could not forgive Eli, and worse yet, no one would deny that she was justified in feeling that way.

The problem was Jesus had spoken much on the subject of

forgiveness. Mary remembered that He had stressed again and again how believers must forgive, even when they were wronged. And on the cross, He had done as He said, forgiving those who had put Him to death.

As many times as she had heard about forgiveness, had agreed with it, and had known that it was something she must do, Mary realized that until now, she had never been tested in this area. It seemed as if the Master Himself was waiting to see what she would do.

But I cannot forgive this man—part of my own family—who has done so much to me, she cried silently.

Immediately, Mary thought of the day when she had angrily slapped Jedidiah and gone to the Master, begging Him to forgive her. What had He said when they had spoken about her temper? Something about her not being able to do it herself, that the Holy Spirit alone could enable her to live the way she should.

Perhaps only through Him could she do this thing too. And do it, she must, not only to please and obey her Lord, but because He had also taught that if a person did not forgive others, the Mighty One could not forgive that one's sins either.

Mary rose and moved over to sit beneath the branches of a sycamore tree. Though the road had few people on it, it being late afternoon, she wanted the extra privacy.

"Help me, Heavenly Father, to forgive this man who has done so much to offend me," Mary prayed. "You know I wish to do so, but I am unable myself."

Her back against the rough trunk of the tree, Mary sat there waiting for something to happen. What would the Powerful One do? But all she could hear was the gentle waves washing up on the beach, the chirping of the sparrows, and the slight rustling of the leaves above her.

Mary was beginning to get irritated when the thought struck her that perhaps the Master was also waiting for her.

"All right, my Lord," she whispered. "I will do it. I forgive him, not because I feel like it, but because I want to do so."

She opened her eyes, and the brightness of the day made her dizzy. But it was at once apparent that the burden Mary had carried for so long had been lifted. The feelings she had toward her father-in-law had not all instantly been reversed, yet somehow she knew that they would go in time. The important thing was that Mary had been obedient. *Perhaps,* she reflected, *the biggest step in forgiveness is making a decision to do it.*

"Mary? Mary, is it you?" an easily recognizable voice called, and she looked up to find Jedidiah on the road. For some reason, she was not surprised to see him. However, it was unexpected for her to feel no displeasure at being with him again.

"Shalom, Jedidiah," she said, rising.

"You have returned!" he shouted, coming towards her.

"Yes, but only for a brief visit . . ." Before she could say more, the inner voice spoke again: *This is your home now,* it seemed to say. *You will not depart from it.*

"Does Eli know of your plans?" Jedidiah asked. "He is still anxious to find you, you know. I warned Micah."

"He told me. I had not intended to make this trip, but sometimes, things change. In fact, I had thought to try to see the children secretly and then leave. But . . ."

She thought again of the consequences of remaining in Magdala, of the work to be done in Jerusalem, and of the friends there who awaited her. But somehow, none of those things seemed important anymore.

"Yes?" He waited for her to continue.

"But I have decided to stay in Magdala."

"Where can you hide? Eli will hear of it from someone."

"He will not need to. I am going to him now." She stooped to retrieve her bundle of belongings.

"Mary, this is madness! He will lock you up!" Disbelief covered Jedidiah's face. "You cannot do it."

"I must obey my Lord."

"Then let me go with you. Perhaps I can convince him to be lenient with you."

His love for her was so evident that Mary could not help smiling at him. Fleetingly, she wondered if being around him was no longer distasteful because of her final release of Matthew.

"Mary, I am coming with you," Jedidiah told her firmly. "You cannot stop me."

For an instant, the old anger at him began to resurface. Who did he think he was, telling her what he would do? But before Mary spoke out at him, she could feel the Master's presence.

Taking a deep breath, she faced him. "Thank you for your concern, but if you care for me as you say you do, you will permit me to go myself. This is something I must handle."

She sensed he was beginning to feel frustrated with her, but he finally nodded. "If you are certain."

She shook her head up and down.

"Then may I come to see you sometime? If Eli permits, of course?" Hope replaced his irritation.

"Yes, Jedidiah."

The look of pure joy he gave her would always remain in her memory. Perhaps I am not to be alone the rest of my life after all, thought Mary as she left him. The idea was not repulsive. Of course, there was the matter of their tempers clashing so often. But surely the Master could help them.

Eli's residence had also changed little in the time in which she had been gone. Though the sturdy gate was closed as usual, Mary could see the top of the olive tree extending above the

mud-brick wall around the roofless courtyard. In the fall, it
would produce enough fruit to meet all the family's needs as far
as olives for food and oil to cook with and to light lamps. She
heard a child's laughter and the low mumble of conversation.

Taking a deep breath, she knocked on the gate. *Lord, I give to
You my future here,* Mary prayed silently.

"Who?" Eli sounded relaxed.

"Open," she said boldly, giving the traditional response of a
family member, instead of identifying herself, as outsiders
would do.

The voices stopped abruptly, and Mary could hear Eli gasp
from behind the gate. Then it quickly swung open, and she faced
the startled eyes of her father-in-law. He seemed older than the
last time she had seen him, but perhaps it was due to the illness
of which Micah had spoken.

"You are back!" he said.

"Yes, if you will have me."

"Come in." He gestured to the open courtyard, which was
empty of other people. She immediately noticed that the fishing
gear remained in the same place next to the cistern in which it
had been when she had last been at the house.

Together they seated themselves in the corner to which guests
were escorted, shaded from the sun by an awning of leaves and
brush. Watching him carefully, Mary tried to determine his
mood. Was he angry? Surprised she was still alive? Disappointed she had returned? She could not tell.

"Are you hungry? I will have Tabitha prepare something for
you," he offered.

She shook her head. "Thank you, but not now. I have come
back because the Just One has so ordained. As you know, the
Master I served, Jesus of Nazareth, was crucified."

Eli nodded almost triumphantly. "And you admit it was a
mistake and a sin to steal away in the night to follow Him."

"No," Mary answered, struggling to keep her voice calm. "I would do it again. I had no other choice at the time. But my Lord did not only die; He lives again. And He has given me a new life, one of wholeness and purpose. Yet I have felt that now I am to again submit myself to you."

"It appears you have regained your senses," Eli said coolly.

"I have been well for quite a while, functioning in a position of responsibility."

Eli stroked his beard. "Hm. Well, perhaps you are sane again. Naturally, we will want to have a physician examine you. As far as your staying here, I do not think it wise. That is, until we know that you will not take off and join the next miracle worker who passes through Magdala."

It was as Mary expected; he would put her back in the little house by the sea. "I am prepared for whatever you suggest," she said quietly.

"Good. Then it is settled. I will send a few things out to where you will be lodging. In a few days, I will come myself, and we will talk again." He motioned toward the doorway of the nearest sleeping room, and a male servant she did not know came out. Apparently, he was Micah's replacement. "Joseph, go with this woman," he instructed. "And stay with her at the house to which I direct you. At no time are you to have your eyes off of her." He gave Mary a piercing look. "Now that you are so much 'better,' I trust we will not have the problems with you which arose in the past."

"May I see my children before I leave?" Mary tried to keep the urgency out of her voice.

Eli hesitated, and Mary bit her lip. Even if she could just be with them for a short time . . .

"Perhaps later," he said. "It would not be in their best interests to let them think you were returning for good, when it may not be so." He gestured to Joseph that it was time to go. "Tabitha will bring over the things you need soon."

Wearily, Mary followed the young man through the court-yard. It was obvious there was much to do here, and it would not be an easy process convincing her father-in-law of her trust-worthiness. But the Master had not promised that there would be no difficulties, only that He would be there to help her.

As Mary reached the courtyard gate, she paused and looked back towards the sleeping rooms. From one of them, unseen by Eli, two small smiling faces were watching her.

In front of her father-in-law, Mary could not acknowledge she saw them. She turned back around, but the picture of Joshua and Kezia, obviously approving her return, remained in her mind, giving her the strength to continue walking.

Nevertheless, Mary did not know if she would ever leave the small house to which Eli was returning her. How could she do anything for the Master from within its walls?

Yet despair did not overwhelm her. She had the children, her old friend Tabitha, and Jedidiah to help her with this burden. Above all, she had her Lord, who had delivered her from the voices that had tormented her, called her into His service, and given her a new life, one which extended far beyond the months Mary had followed Him down the roads of Galilee and Judea. No matter what happened in the future, no one could take Him from her. With that knowledge, Mary held up her head and fol-lowed Joseph down the road.

People Making A Difference

Family Bookshelf offers the finest in good wholesome Christian literature, written by best-selling authors. All books are recommended by an Advisory Board of distinguished writers and editors.

We are also a vital part of a compassionate outreach called **Bowery Mission Ministries**. Our evangelical mission is devoted to helping the destitute of the inner city.

Our ministries date back more than a century and began by aiding homeless men lost in alcoholism. Now we also offer hope and Gospel strength to homeless, inner-city women and children. Our goal, in fact, is to end homelessness by teaching these deprived people how to be independent with the Lord by their side.

Downtrodden, homeless men are fed and clothed and may enter a discipleship program of one-on-one professional counseling, nutrition therapy and Bible study. This same Christian care is provided at our women and children's shelter.

We also welcome nearly 1,000 underprivileged children each summer at our Mont Lawn Camp located in Pennsylvania's beautiful Poconos. Here, impoverished youngsters enjoy the serenity of nature and an opportunity to receive the teachings of Jesus Christ. We also provide year-round assistance through teen activities, tutoring in reading and writing, Bible study, family counseling, college scholarships and vocational training.

During the spring, fall and winter months, our children's camp becomes a lovely retreat for religious gatherings of up to 200. Excellent accommodations include heated cabins, chapel, country-style meals and recreational facilities. Write to Paradise Lake Retreat Center, Box 252, Bushkill, PA 18324 or call: (717) 588-6067.

Still another vital part of our ministry is **Christian Herald magazine**. Our dynamic, bimonthly publication focuses on the true personal stories of men and women who, as "doers of the Word," are making a difference in their lives and the lives of others.

Bowery Mission Ministries are supported by voluntary contributions of individuals and bequests. Contributions are tax deductible. Checks should be made payable to Bowery Mission.

 Fully accredited Member
of the Evangelical Council
for Financial Accountability

Every Monday morning, our ministries staff joins together in prayer. If you have a prayer request for yourself or a loved one, simply write to us.

 Administrative Office:
40 Overlook Drive, Chappaqua,
New York 10514 Telephone: (914) 769-9000